SHARKS
NEVER SLEEP

William F. Nolan

SHARKS NEVER SLEEP

A Novel Featuring
The Black Mask Boys:

DASHIELL HAMMETT,

RAYMOND CHANDLER,

and

ERLE STANLEY GARDNER

ST. MARTIN'S PRESS ✖ NEW YORK

THOMAS DUNNE BOOKS.
An imprint of St. Martin's Press.

Library of Congress Cataloging-in-Publication Data

Nolan, William F.
    Sharks never sleep / by William F. Nolan. — 1st ed.
        p.   cm.
    "Thomas Dunne books."
    ISBN 0-312-19331-9
    1. Gardner, Erle Stanley, 1889–1970—Fiction.
    2. Hammett, Dashiell, 1894–1961—Fiction.   3. Chandler,
    Raymond, 1888–1959—Fiction.   I. Title.
    PS3564.O39S52   1998
    813'.54—dc21   98-19396
                                                                         CIP

First Edition: November 1998

10 9 8 7 6 5 4 3 2 1

For my dear friend,

NORMAN CORWIN

A role model
A continuing inspiration
An awesome talent

One thing you must remember: a shark never sleeps. It keeps circling endlessly in the water. You are never safe with sharks. They can attack you at any time. Day or night, it is all the same to a shark.

—Hans Paytr Mannheim, Ph.D.
Vienna, 1936

NARRATED BY ERLE STANLEY GARDNER

ONE

I'm a plainspoken man. When I feel like saying something, I just go right ahead and say it. Always have. Always will. Not that I set out to hurt people. Basically, I'm a nice guy. In fact, my friends call me "Uncle Erle." But I *do* have a temper, and I don't let anyone take advantage of me. When I'm upset, I let people know it.

I sure let those bozos at Warner Brothers know what I thought about the way they handled Perry Mason on the screen. Made him into a drunken playboy! I got so mad watching those pictures I choked up and my face went beet-red. They wanted to buy more Masons and I said, hell no!

Hollywood doesn't understand me. I don't kiss anyone's fanny.

I'm the same way as a writer. Joe Shaw, when he edited *Black Mask*, always talked about Hammett's style. Raved over it. Joe tried to make all the rest of the boys imitate Hammett. I wouldn't do that. I won't imitate anybody. And as for style, I guess I don't have one as a writer. I just lay out the words.

Chandler has a style. In fact, he can get pretty lush at times. When he came along in '33, four years ago, Hammett was out of the *Mask* and doing his *Thin Man* novel in New York. So Chandler and Hammett never competed, head-to-head.

1

Me, I'm still churning out stuff for the magazine under their new editor, but I don't compete with anybody. God knows, this writing game is tough, and it's no cinch being your own man. A lot easier just imitating another writer, but you'll never get anywhere that way.

I admit I've been *influenced* by Hammett. Hasn't everybody? I've even been accused of writing like him, but that's damn tommyrot. Dash can be harsh, overly cynical, and hard-boiled to a fault. I like the guy personally, but we don't approach writing the same way at all.

If I have a style—and I'm honestly not aware of one—it's that I'm as plainspoken on paper as I am in life. Plain and direct. Pick up any one of my Mason novels and you'll see what I mean. I don't linger over things that don't need to be lingered over.

The other day I tried to read a book by some English lady mystery writer and stopped cold in the first chapter. Bored me silly. She used five pages to describe this guy's flat in London—detailing the intricate stitching in his imported rugs and describing every flounce in his custom-designed draperies. Spent a whole *paragraph* on some dust motes floating in the sunlight near an open window.

That kind of nonsense is not for me. Absolute waste of time. A storyteller should get on with the story. Sure, I do a lot of sweating over my plots. Make a ton of notes. Wrestle with the characters. But when it comes to action and dialogue, I just let the words flow. Once I've got my plot straight, then I run with it all the way to the finish. Like a fast horse on a quarter-mile track.

Now, with regard to this hellish situation I just went through with Dash Hammett and Ray Chandler . . . well, I'll slow down a bit and tell you what happened with as many details as I can muster. The full story is worth the effort.

I have a house in the hills above Hollywood. I won't name the street, since I'm not partial to strangers dropping in. That's the price you pay for becoming a celebrity: you have to put up with strangers invading your privacy. Not that I'm much of a celebrity. I'm no Gable—or anything close. But with Mason taking off the way he has, enough people know me by now to make things a bit uncomfortable at times. Minor annoyance. Nothing to complain about, really.

Five months ago, in May, I was at home, finishing up a Terry Clane story for *Cosmopolitan*, "Murder Up My Sleeve," when Tomas, my Filipino houseboy, brought me the evening Los Angeles *Herald*. The front-page story hit me square in the gut.

THOMPSON SON DIES
Child of Famed Movie Idol
Victim of Tragic Accident

My heart was beating fast as I read the story:

> Three-year-old Lawrence Thompson, only child of international film and radio star Lloyd Hadley "Tink" Thompson and Mrs. Thompson, suffered fatal head and neck injuries yesterday, the result of an accidental stairway fall at his parents' Beverly Hills home. He was pronounced dead upon arrival at Good Samaritan Hospital.
>
> "This is a terrible tragedy for me and my wife," declared Thompson. "Larry was very precious to us both."
>
> Mrs. Thompson, the former Amy Latimer, is in seclusion and was unavailable for comment. Funeral services are pending.

"My God, poor Amy!" I blurted the words aloud, envisioning the pain she must be suffering. We hadn't been in contact since an exchange of Christmas cards the previous December. I remember precisely what she wrote on her card:

Can you believe that another year has passed? I think of you often. Hope we can get together soon and talk of all our yesterdays.

Happy 1937!

She had signed it:

> With much affection,
> Amy

I slumped into a chair, letting the newspaper slip from my hand.

"All our yesterdays." How long ago they seemed. Yet it had been just four and a half years since I'd lost her, when we said those final good-byes to each other with tears in our eyes. I was a fool to let her go, but back then I thought it was the right thing to do. I even felt heroic, giving her up to Tink Thompson.

"Are you absolutely *sure* this is what you want?" she had asked me, uncertainty clouding her beautiful eyes. Her shining blonde hair, framing that perfect, classically sculpted face, had been luminous under a full California moon. Her mouth had trembled. A small blue vein had pulsed in her neck, and she had held my right hand in a tight grip, as if she never wanted to let go. Of course, she *didn't* want to let go.

To my shame, I *could* have said: "Natalie will agree to a divorce. That will clear the way for us. Don't go, Amy. Stay with me. I love you."

I could have said that, but I didn't. I'm certain it's what she wanted to hear. Instead, I told her she should marry Tink Thompson. For all kinds of logical reasons: because her parents wanted her to become the wife of a famous film star; because I was just starting my career as a novelist and had no idea whether or not I'd ever be successful; and finally, because I felt guilty over asking Natalie for a divorce. We were two people who no longer had any reason left to maintain a marriage except for the love we shared for our daughter, Grace, but divorce had seemed too harsh a step then, too contrary to my sometimes conservative nature. With Tink Thompson out of the picture, I *would* have divorced Natalie, I know I would have, but Amy—my beautiful, wonderful Amy—deserved something better than the life I could have offered her.

In 1932, I had been a year away from giving up the law profession to write full-time. That was in January, when Amy Louise Latimer came to work in my Ventura, California, law office as my partner's secretary. Although I was struck by her blonde beauty from the day she was hired, it was strictly business for a while, with my growing appreciation concentrated on her exceptional secretarial skills.

Until the evening (following a grueling twelve-hour day we had spent preparing for an important court case) when I took her out for a well-deserved dinner at the Pierpont Inn, an establishment that had long functioned as our partnership's "outside office." Sitting across the table from her, getting lost within the depths of those deep blue eyes, I never wanted to come out.

We talked about books we'd read and films we'd seen, political views we shared, our mutual love for the outdoors and the rugged Southwest, and I discovered that she had a mind as beautiful as her body.

We fell in love. Deeply and completely.

After considerable internal debate, I was on the verge of telling Nat about my new romantic relationship when my law partner, Frank Orr, phoned me one Saturday morning to say that he'd just fired Amy. But *why?* Frank said that her mind was no longer on her work. He suspected that she'd fallen in love; in his opinion, Amy's love life was adversely affecting her office responsibilities. He mentioned some legal papers that had been misfiled and some dictated names (all in Chinese) that she had misspelled in English on a deposition she had transcribed.

I started to protest his action, to point out how unfair he was being to her. I was ready to demand that Amy be reinstated, and admit that she and I were emotionally involved, when he mentioned Tink Thompson. That she'd spent a weekend with Thompson in Hollywood, and that there was a "lovey-dovey" photo of the two of them together on Thompson's yacht on the "Features" page of the Los Angeles *Examiner*.

I couldn't believe it. I was stunned. Amy loved *me!* What was she doing with some rich movie star?

Which is when the word hit me: *rich.* Thompson was among the highest-paid talents in Hollywood. He had everything a young woman could ever want: a huge gated mansion in Beverly Hills, a fleet of sleek automobiles, a yacht fancy enough to entertain the President (Herbert Hoover and the First Lady had been guests on it the previous summer), a collection of art that rivaled the Metropolitan's, and enough money to buy a ton of jewelry and furs. (I'd heard that he had an ermine-covered toilet seat in his private bathroom.)

How could any thirty-five-dollar-a-week secretary resist him?

And Amy didn't. That night she told me all about him.

They'd met when she and her parents had visited Los Angeles three months before. Relatives had been celebrating a wedding anniversary, and a swanky French restaurant on Wilshire Boulevard was selected as the site of the anniversary dinner.

From the moment Amy walked into the restaurant, Thompson, who was already dining at the best table, began openly staring at her. Then, during the meal, he ostentatiously walked across the room, bowed to Amy like a Spanish cavalier, and presented her with his card.

Naturally, she was in shock. Here was one of the world's most famous film stars obviously attracted to "a nobody like me" (as she put it).

The next day he began a relentless campaign to win her favor. He had huge gilt-and-velvet-covered boxes of See's chocolates delivered each weekend. Sent expensive flowers several times a week to both

Amy and her mother. And had gourmet delicacies mailed to the family from all over the world.

She confessed that he'd been phoning her at work every day, pressing his case and pleading with her to accompany him to a variety of social events. Then, two weekends before, he'd sent his limo up to Ventura to drive her out to his yacht for a romantic interlude on the water. Dazed and flattered, she had finally accepted. A news photographer at the dock had recorded the moment for publication.

Thompson began taking her out every night, making a circuit of the most romantic restaurants in Ventura County.

That evening at the Pierpont Inn, as she told me about Tink Thompson, I knew that the situation was serious. Her parents were urging her to see him; they wanted her to take full advantage of this stunning opportunity. Here was Hollywood's most eligible bachelor pursuing *their* daughter. What a catch he'd make!

"But you love *me*," I said. "At least I thought—"

"Oh, I *do*, Erle. I *do* love you. But I'm all mixed-up. Tink gets me half dizzy. When I'm with him—"

"—you forget about me. Is that it?"

"Not always," she said, looking down at the tablecloth. Her eyes began to fill. "I feel terrible about this."

"Don't," I said, covering her hand with mine. "Seeing Tink Thompson is like dating God. I can understand."

"But can you understand that I want to go *on* seeing him? Despite the fact that I still love *you?*"

I tried to keep the pain out of my voice. "I don't own you, Amy. I'm a married man, and up to now, I've just never gotten around to asking my wife for a divorce. I can't dictate who you see or don't see."

"But you're worried, aren't you? You're afraid I'll fall under his spell."

"I'd say that's already happened."

She started crying softly, dabbing at her eyes with a hankie. "I've never met anyone like Tink," she confessed. "I mean—anyone so rich and famous. I keep asking myself, why is he interested in *me?*"

"Because you are a very beautiful woman," I answered. "Who's going to believe that Thompson is the great romantic lover they pay to see on the screen if he doesn't always have a gorgeous woman on his arm?"

She was hurt. "You make it sound so cheap, and it's not like that at all."

"Have you gone to bed with him?"

She was startled by my directness. "No. No, I haven't."

"But not because he hasn't been trying, right?"

"Well, he . . ."

"The situation is obvious, Amy. You're the current hot item on Tink Thompson's sexual hit parade."

She slapped me. A hard, stinging slap that rocked me back in my seat and caused everyone in the dining room to stare. Her eyes blazed with anger. "I thought that you—of all people—would at least try to understand."

She walked out, leaving me with my uneaten dinner.

Amy saw a lot of Thompson after that night, and I tried to erase her from my mind. With no luck. She meant everything to me. When I saw an article in *Photoplay* about "Tink's Torrid Tootsie," complete with photos of an adoring Amy cuddling up to him, I actually thought about murder.

I've written about murder many times in my pulp stories and novels, but I had never before considered the possibility that *I* was capable of such an act. I guess we all are, if driven to it.

I must admit it was a comforting thought. Thompson dies and I get Amy back. Clean and simple. But of course it was never a reality in my mind.

I never actually planned to murder Tink Thompson.

Three months later, in October of 1932, Amy came by the office and asked me to have lunch with her. Startled, I readily agreed; we left immediately for the Pierpont Inn. We ate in silence. I knew she had something to tell me and I was dreading it. She was planning to marry Thompson. That had to be what the lunch was all about.

But I was in for a surprise. She waited until we were having coffee before she told me that she still loved me, and would marry me if I would get a divorce and accept her. She said Tink was great fun, made her laugh, gave her (and her mother) fabulous gifts, dazzled her with his fame and riches. And, indeed, he *had* asked her to become his wife. Her parents told her it was the chance of a lifetime, and that she would be insane to pass it up.

But she was in conflict. She still loved me. The question in her mind was: did I still love her?

Yes. Oh God, yes. More than ever.

But I had not been prepared for her honesty. I had expected her to reject me for Thompson. Who was I, a small-town lawyer and part-time writer, to compete with the legendary Tink Thompson? If she had actually rejected me, I would have pleaded with her to change her mind. But Amy's honesty had disarmed me. I began thinking of what was best for *her,* the advantages she'd have as Mrs. Tink Thompson.

I could give her nothing.

He could give her the world.

So I told Amy she should marry him. She asked if I was absolutely certain that this was what she should do.

I said yes, it was the only thing that made sense. Her parents were right. This was a golden opportunity for her, and she must not throw it away. I told her that I'd get over her in time—though I knew I wouldn't. I said that she would get over me. That was how life went, I told her. We had to be realistic about the situation. And so we parted.

Of course, I never did get over her. I later found out that she had never loved Thompson, not even after they had a son together and became the perfect *Screen Stories* family. She *had* deeply loved her son, Larry, but now—suddenly and horribly—he was dead.

9

Feeling somehow responsible for her grief, I just wasn't up to trying to see her, and I couldn't risk complicating her marriage by phoning her. Instead, I mailed a card with a short, socially correct sympathy note inside. And thought: that's the end of it. The past is behind us, and things can never again be the same.

I was soon to learn I'd been mistaken.

A week later, the phone at my desk rang. "Yes?"

"Erle?"

That voice, *her* voice, hit me like a shock wave over the line. I hadn't expected her to call me, wasn't mentally prepared for it. My hands began to shake. "Amy! . . . Are you all right?"

"I received your card, and the note," she said huskily. "It was sweet of you."

"I should have phoned," I said, jerking out the words. "But there was nothing I could have said . . . about Larry, I mean."

"You did exactly right, as always." A hesitation on the line. I heard her sigh deeply. "Larry was the only thing that made my life worth living." Her voice dropped to a harsh whisper. "I'll never forgive Tink! *Never!*"

"Forgive him for what?"

"I can't talk about it over the phone. There's so much I have to tell you . . . and I've made a decision, Erle. I need your help. Can I come to your house tonight?"

"Of course. I'm always here for you. Anything I can do . . ."

"There's a *lot* you can do," she said firmly. "I'll be there at seven."

I sat with the receiver in my hand for a long time after the call ended. The receiver, somehow, was part of Amy.

And I couldn't let go.

TWO

You need to understand what happened with Natalie. And about my daughter, Grace.

When we got married, Natalie and I were in love. We were both convinced our relationship would last a lifetime. Back then we acted like a couple of moonstruck kids, holding hands, gazing into each other's eyes, taking long walks together to Ventura's ocean pier on Front Street. We'd sit with our legs dangling over the edge of the pier, watching the big lumber boats and oil liners come in to dock, listening to the bands play in the balmy sea air. I used to buy roses for her at the El Jardín flower shop on East Main. Then we'd have lunch at Townsend's Café, eating hot roast-beef sandwiches in our favorite booth in the back. How Nat loved those sandwiches!

Good days. Fun days. We both remember them with fondness.

But later, after Grace was born, things began to change. Nat spent most of her time with the baby, while I worked at my office at Main and California. How well I remember walking up the hill to the old county courthouse, where I honed my skills as a trial lawyer.

To be fair, I suppose I was responsible for the erosion of our marriage. I spent too many years completely absorbed in my work. The two prime elements in my life then were the law and my writing, but since I gave up the law in '33 to concentrate on Perry Mason, I haven't really missed it. After more than two decades, I'd had enough of real juries and real courtrooms. I wanted to concentrate on their fictional counterparts.

Not that the law wasn't a satisfying challenge in those early years when I helped the Chinese residents of Oxnard win their cases—and later, when I battled the big insurance companies in Ventura.

I vividly remember the time I went head-to-head with the attorney who repped New York Life in a case against the Magby family. William Magby had been found dead in a closed garage with the engine of his car running. Because he had been depressed and suicidal, the insurance company insisted that his death was self-inflicted. It refused to pay the policy proceeds to his family.

In court, I introduced an official weather report that showed there had been a brisk wind blowing on the day Magby died. My argument was that this wind had blown the garage door closed, resulting in an "accidental death." And this won the case.

I got a big kick out of the rough-and-tumble of a good courtroom fight—breaking down a stubborn witness, pulling off a legal hat trick with the jury at the last moment. A lot of folks swear that Perry Mason is really Erle Stanley Gardner, and in public I always deny it, but there's actually a lot of truth in the claim. Mason wouldn't exist without my long years in law, and I've used several of my court cases as the basis for novels.

But that's normal. Every fiction writer uses his own life as raw material—just the way Dash Hammett used his years as a real-life detective for his crime stories. The "Continental Op" is really a thinly disguised version of Hammett himself when he was an operative for the Pinkerton Detective Agency. Ditto Sam Spade. That's what makes Hammett authentic. He knows street crime and criminals the way I know my way around a courtroom.

When I was practicing law, sometimes the action in a court case would get really hot. Things were different back then; you could get away with a lot more than you can these days. It wasn't unheard of for one attorney to take a roundhouse swing at his opponent, and I recall the time I got knocked flat after winning a particularly heated case in Oxnard. Sported a black eye for a week! But then, I was never popular with the authorities in that town. In defending the underdog Chinese—who were considered trash in the eyes of the "good white folk"—I managed to alienate the district attorney, most of the local cops, and the entire city council. My subsequent move to Ventura proved to be a lot healthier for me.

I need to tell you about my daughter, Grace. She was our only child, a bright-eyed little girl with an immense zest for life. We were emotionally close when she was growing up, and we spent a great deal of time together. I taught her to ride a horse, and to fish from the pier, and to tie slip knots, and to use a bow and arrow—archery has always been a major passion of mine. On weekends, I would take her downtown and buy her candy and a sack of those fat oatmeal-raisin cookies she loved so much.

As she grew up, she became a big fan of my *Black Mask* character, Ed Jenkins, The Phantom Crook. When I'd get an advance copy of the magazine from Joe Shaw in the mail, she would grab it first thing and run off to her room to devour the latest Jenkins adventure.

There was a woman in the series, a rich socialite I named Helen Chadwick, and I had Ed get romantically involved with her. A lot of *Mask*'s readers wrote in demanding that they be married, and I was fool enough to go along with the idea. But once I wrote them as husband and wife, I knew it wouldn't work for my series. The Phantom Crook couldn't operate effectively as a married man. So in the next story, I killed Helen off.

Grace was shocked. Got so mad that she wouldn't speak to me for a month. She was that way, growing up. Really took things to heart.

Grace attended the University of California and majored in English. For a while we thought she would end up teaching in some college, but she surprised us by running off to Reno with Al McKittrick and getting married. They make their home in the Bay Area now, and I always look forward to the times when we can get together.

Grace left in 1933 and by then, I had lost Amy. The zest had gone out of my marriage with Natalie years before. She had never enjoyed camping out under the stars. She used to complain bitterly about the mosquitos, the dirt, the wind, the isolation—and finally, she just refused to go with me. It seems like a small thing in the context of an entire marriage, yet it illustrates what was happening to us. We couldn't continue the way we were, so Natalie and I separated. No anger. No bitterness. Just a clean break.

Later, when I moved to Hollywood, I moved alone. Nat and I had the mutual understanding that if either of us should fall in love with anyone else, the other would agree to a divorce. In this way, Natalie would not have to deal with the social stigma attached to those women who are, tongue-in-cheek, commonly referred to as "gay divorcées." To me, it has never seemed right that divorced males are considered desirable men-about-town, while divorced females are often considered somehow "stained." I had no wish to inflict that embarrassment on Natalie.

Which explains why I was living as a bachelor in the hills above Hollywood when Amy Thompson came to my house that evening. I had dismissed Tomas for the night. I didn't want him to hear what I anticipated was going to be an intensely private conversation.

She arrived just before seven, stepping out of a taxi and walking slowly to the door, her head down, weary and dejected. We hugged each other for a long moment, but when she tried to smile, her lips trembled. Her blue eyes were bloodshot and puffy, surrounded by dark circles. Her willowy figure now seemed almost gaunt. It was obvious that she had slept very little since her son died.

But even under those circumstances, she was still beautiful. Her shining, flaxen-yellow hair, pulled back in a French roll, was still soft as an angel's wing, and her dark knit outfit suggested mourning without being severe.

"It's so *good* to see you again, Erle," she told me as I led her into the sitting room.

"I feel the same way," I said. "It's been too long."

Benny Goodman's band was broadcasting a swing tune on the radio, which was anything but appropriate. I switched it off.

Amy sat down tentatively on my overstuffed sofa; the lamp from the end table illumined her pale ivory skin. Her skin had always glowed with warmth, but now the color seemed to have drained away.

There was an awkward silence between us. I felt the tension that emanated from her, a palpable presence. I knew we couldn't begin by talking about Larry, about her loss. We'd have to ease into this. It was going to be tough for both of us.

"Can I get you anything to drink?"

"Coffee," she said. "You know the way I like it."

"Sure. Half milk with two lumps of sugar."

She nodded, smiling at me again. Her smile was less strained, more self-assured. Our old routine was putting her on safer emotional ground.

However, when I returned from the kitchen with a tray of coffee, she was still in the same position on the sofa, sitting rigidly, head lowered, staring down at her hands.

The coffee seemed to relax and nurture her. Still, she didn't offer more conversation.

I broke the silence between us: "Been keeping up with you," I said. "Reading about you and your husband in the papers. Watching you in the newsreels. I saw the one they filmed last summer, with you and Tink on that island cruise in Hawaii. You've been leading a glamorous life, Amy."

"Glamorous?" She smiled faintly. "I guess you could call it that. On the surface, at least. But there's so much that you don't know, Erle."

I sat down next to her. I wanted to touch her, take her hand in mine, but I didn't. I sat there quietly, sipping my coffee, trying not to pressure her in any way.

15

"I'm going to tell you everything," she said. "From the beginning—right through Larry's death."

"I want to hear every word," I said. And I meant it. Oh God, how I meant it.

I have no doubt you've heard a great deal about Lloyd Hadley Thompson, America's most beloved film star. The easygoing, laid-back crooner with the velvet voice, who got his world-famous nickname after playing Tinkerbell in a grade-school production of *Peter Pan*. That was in Chula Vista, the southern California town near the Mexican border, where Thompson had been born and raised.

A few years later, after he graduated from Chula Vista High School, he entered vaudeville under the name "Tink Thompson," performing a song-and-dance act with his two brothers, Len and Freddie, as the Thompson Trio. They were going nowhere fast until the night Paul Whiteman caught their act in Chicago, met the boys backstage, and invited them to do a guest stint with his band.

When this engagement proved successful, they toured with Whiteman for a couple of years. And then the King of the Silents, Mack Sennett, who was by this time producing talkies, put Tink into a series of musical two-reelers. Thompson was soon attracting the gramophone people. He made some hit recordings, including an impressive number of American standards, got into radio, and then into big-time films. His first major film role was as the romantic lead opposite Carole Lombard, a huge break that catapulted him into a blazing, cometlike climb to the top.

By 1931, Tink Thompson was a household name. When he played the gentle, self-sacrificing parish priest, Father Kelly, who gave up his sight in order to save a starving orphan girl in *Song of St. Margaret's*, the world fell in love with him. Thompson even wrangled a knighthood from the Pope in a well-publicized visit to Rome.

His acting roles expanded; soon he was Hollywood's top romantic lead. No heavies for Tink Thompson. He was every girl's wished-for date, every woman's dream husband, and every matron's fantasy son-in-law—and he was genuinely loved by millions.

When he and Amy got married, on Thanksgiving Day in 1932, it was an international event. "Tink Takes a Wife!" Headlines around the globe. A flood of letters, cards, and gifts. A three-ring circus to celebrate what many filmgoers felt was a major event in their lives.

Amy gave birth less than a year later and the magazines went crazy with cover stories. *Life* devoted five pages to the new parents and their gurgling offspring. Norman Rockwell was commissioned to paint the Thompson family for the cover of the *Saturday Evening Post*'s Christmas issue.

No couple in the world seemed happier.

"It was all a lie," Amy confessed to me that night. "Tink never cared about me . . . or Larry, either. But we were essential for his public image. To him, that's what it was all about."

"Surely, though . . . in the beginning . . . he must have loved you then."

"I told myself he did. Lord knows, he said all the right words. But they were hollow. Like lines in a script." She shifted uncomfortably on the sofa. "I realized right after our marriage that he didn't love me. He wanted me to be the perfect model wife for public occasions, especially when there were any cameras around, but when we were alone . . . he was cold and indifferent."

I didn't break into the flow of her words. She needed to vent her feelings without interruption. Speaking so softly I could barely hear her, Amy continued. "Tink wanted me pregnant. That was very important to him . . . to his public image. He worked very . . . *industriously* to get me pregnant. But as soon as the doctor said I was expecting, the physical side of our marriage was over." She started crying, in painful humiliation. But I remained silent.

She took out a linen handkerchief and dabbed at her eyes, trying to regain composure. "I began lying to myself, pretending that things would get better, that in time I could *make* him love me."

17

I sat there beside her, breathing deeply. When I gave up Amy, the one thing I had been sure of was her future happiness. That certainty had given me the strength to let her go. We'd *both* been deceived by Tink Thompson.

"Why didn't you tell me any of this? I would have—"

"What would you have done? What *could* you have done?" She was nervously twisting her wedding ring. The papers said that Cartier had custom-designed it for Thompson, but to me it was simply hard carbon and cold metal. It didn't belong on Amy's soft, warm hand.

She looked down at the floor. "I had married him and I was pregnant by him. Telling you the truth wouldn't have changed anything. It would have hurt you, and I didn't want to do that." She looked intensely at me. "I never stopped loving you, Erle."

I drew Amy into my arms, holding her close to my chest; I could feel her body trembling. "Me, too," I managed to say thickly. "Always."

Eventually Amy sat up again, pressing her back stiffly against the sofa pillows. She sipped at her coffee, then put it aside. She had a lot more to tell me.

"Tink has his act down pat," she declared. "The fun-loving, easygoing crooner with a friendly word for everyone. Smiling, joking with his cast and crew, delivering his casual wisecracks, making people laugh. They adore him. Everyone adores him.

"He's actually sadistic and cruel. Nothing I do pleases him. He's constantly finding fault with me . . . mostly about my appearance. That's all he cares about." She stopped for a moment, thinking, and then her eyes flashed with anger. "Do you know that he makes me travel up to Carmel for a week each month so I can stay at the Silver Gate health spa? It's a *requirement*; I don't have any choice in the matter. I guess he thinks that if I don't receive constant maintenance, I'll deteriorate, like one of his antique automobiles."

The tight smile again. "You just can't understand how much he loves to parade me in public. I'm his most prized possession."

She hesitated, in obvious pain. "I found out about his vicious temper on our honeymoon . . . how horribly cruel he can be."

My lips tightened. "He beats you?"

She laughed at that, a harsh, mocking sound. "Oh, no! He'd never physically abuse me. Mrs. Tink Thompson couldn't be seen in public with cuts and bruises. I must look *perfect*. After all, there are no dents on his Rolls, no scratches on his paintings. It's all *verbal* abuse. Cutting and savage. Larry was terrified of him."

"He mistreated his own child?"

"From the week Larry was born, Tink was insanely jealous. Odd, isn't it? He'd wanted a child so much—so we could play the perfect American family for his fans—and then, when Larry arrived, Tink saw him as a competitor. When people would fawn over the baby, Tink would be seething inside. He demands that everyone's attention be focused on him. And now, once again, it *will* be. Tink saw to that."

I stared at her. "What do you mean . . . 'saw to that'?"

Her gaze was unwavering. "Tink is directly responsible for the death of our son." Her body began to tremble at the memory. "Larry left one of his toys, a little stuffed rabbit, in the upper hallway. Tink began bellowing at him, raising his fists and moving toward him. Larry ran down the hall in panic. At the head of the stairs, he stumbled and . . ."

Her voice trailed off as the tears came. "With my parents dead . . . and now Larry . . . you're all I have left," she said. Her parents had been killed in a car crash soon after Larry had been born, and Amy had no brothers or sisters. I held her close. We didn't say anything to each other for a long time after that. I just held her, allowing the grief to flow out. Finally, she sat up and dabbed at her eyes again.

"The world should know the truth about this bastard," I said, "that he's the direct cause of your son's death."

"No one would ever believe it," she said, a tone of flat defeat in her voice. "I have no proof. No witnesses. It would just be my word against the word of America's most beloved star. Who would listen to *me*? Especially about Larry. People would think I was crazy if I told them Tink was jealous of his three-year-old son."

"But what about the servants? The maids . . . the cook . . . the gardener? They could testify."

She shook her head again. "No. Tink never yelled at me when the household help was around. It was always when we were alone, behind closed doors . . . after the servants had left for the night, or had their days off. No one lives at the house but us. Even Larry's nanny lived by herself, in an apartment about a half-mile away."

She put her hand on my arm. "I swear to you, Erle, there's nothing I can do—except get away from him. Now that Larry is gone, I just want to get the hell *away* from him."

THREE

I've never been what anyone would call a "ladies' man." Before I met Nat, I didn't have much to do with women. At thirteen, when I first became aware of the opposite sex as an attraction rather than a distraction, I was with my father in the Klondike, where he was employed as a mining engineer. Not until we settled in the small mining town of Oroville, in northern California, and I was attending Oroville Union High School, did I ever have anything to do with girls. Even then, I didn't date, just kidded around with them in the hallways. I had a crush on Martha Ann Loving, and she let me walk her home each afternoon. I'd carry her books. And I did take her to a school dance once, so I guess you could call that a date.

I was pretty much of a rebel in those days, a kind of Peck's Bad Boy. I got kicked out of high school before graduation for making fun of the principal. I transferred to Palo Alto High, near San Francisco, where I managed to graduate.

Then my folks sent me to Valparaiso University in Indiana, but I lasted less than a month there. Knocked down one of the teachers in my dorm during a boxing match. The local police issued a warrant for my arrest and I slipped out of town one jump ahead of the sheriff.

As you can see, I didn't have a lot of time for women. I'd work all day and study all night, with maybe a couple of hours' sleep.

In those days, things were a lot simpler when it came to entering the law profession. You didn't need a university degree. No special schooling. You just apprenticed yourself to an attorney and then, when you felt ready, you took the bar examination. If you passed— bingo! you were a lawyer.

I passed the bar at twenty-one and opened my own one-man office in Merced, a town in central California's San Joaquin Valley. Business was dismal, so I grabbed the chance to work for a corporate attorney in Oxnard, in southern California's Ventura County.

I dated a few times during that period, but I was too broke to spend money on a girl. It was mostly weekend picnics in the local park. Then, later, when I was working in Ventura, Natalie came along. And that was the end of my relationships with other women—until Amy.

Now, sitting there on the sofa beside her, listening to her bitter, pain-filled story that night, I was reminded anew of just how much Amy meant to me, of how vital she was in my life. It was like coming home, seeing her again, and I found myself experiencing a conflicting mixture of anguish and joy.

". . . so I know you'll be able to guide me through this," she was saying. "The divorce is going to be a matter of intense interest to the press, and I want to keep as low a public profile as I possibly can." She sighed deeply, fully aware that she was asking the impossible. Because of Tink Thompson, Amy herself had become a well-known celebrity.

"You'll need legal grounds for a divorce," I told her. "If you can't prove cruelty—"

"I can prove adultery," she said.

"Oh?"

"Tink was never faithful." She looked down at her lap, too hurt to face me. "I'm not even his type. He's always been attracted to Hispanic women, but he knows that the public would never accept him with a Mexican wife, so he's made sure that his various ladyloves are kept offstage. No one in the press suspects a thing—but I know about several of these women, including a serious affair he's been having for some years now."

"How did you find out about it?"

"Tink saves her letters. I was in the attic one morning, looking for a suitcase I needed for my monthly trip to Carmel, and I discovered the letters in an old hatbox. Reading them, I knew there was no question at all of what Tink and this woman were involved in.

"So after that, I began eavesdropping on his telephone conversations with her. I made shorthand notes. Of course, I only heard what *he* was saying, but that was enough. There were photos of this woman along with the letters, so I knew what she looked like. And once, when Tink told me he was going to Chicago, I followed him up to Santa Barbara. He spent a week with her."

"Who is she?"

"Marisol Herrera-Quintano. Of *the* Herrera-Quintanos. A good share of California was given to the family by the king of Spain, back when we were a Spanish colony. This woman and her husband, Fernando, are Californios, direct descendants of the original Spanish land grantees. And they're cousins. Not close enough so their marriage is illegal, but they're related to each other through several different bloodlines. Certainly their marriage did a lot to keep the family landholdings together."

"And they live in Santa Barbara?" I asked.

"Close by. Their main home is in Montecito, just a few miles from Santa Barbara. They have a beautiful old Spanish mansion there, with gardens, a swimming pool, tennis court, stables . . . it's just a gorgeous estate. According to the local history I looked up, the house is built on land that's been in their family since the sixteen hundreds."

Amy took a long, deep breath. Talking about the affair was very difficult for her. "They're extremely rich. A lot richer than Tink. Fernando is an international banker. He travels a lot in Europe, and that's when Tink and this woman get together."

"You talk as if you know the couple," I said.

"I met them once. Fernando invited us up to the Montecito estate for a business conference he was holding there, something about land development in South America. Tink was paid an enormous sum of money to entertain the group. He took his two brothers along and they sang together."

"What did you think of her?"

"She's much more beautiful than her photographs. Long black hair, incredible deep, dark eyes, and skin like . . . slightly beige mother-of-pearl. And her regal bearing! She's a real lady in the grand tradition. Despite myself, I felt overwhelmed in her presence, as if I should curtsy or something."

"You were formally introduced?"

"Oh yes, by her husband. Tink had no idea, of course, that I knew about the affair. And from the way Fernando talked, it was obvious that he had no knowledge of it either. To him, Tink was there to entertain his guests, and nothing more.

"I watched Tink and this woman that night. Once, when they thought no one was looking, they exchanged a knowing glance. And later, when she was selecting dessert from a buffet table, she 'accidentally' brushed against Tink's arm as she offered him a dish of iced fruit. All very casual, but it made me sick."

I thought about what Amy had just told me. "With the letters and photographs, the shorthand notes you've taken of telephone conversations, and your following him that week when he said he was going to Chicago, you definitely have grounds for divorce. Thompson is due for a nasty surprise."

"He deserves it," she said bitterly. "I'll tell him tomorrow."

"Am I the only one who knows about this?"

"Beth knows. Elizabeth Winniger. She's the wife of Jack Winniger, the radio comedian. She and I are very close. But I haven't told anyone else."

"Is there anything more I should know?"

"No." She pressed my hand again, warmly. "Except how much I've missed you. Except what a fool I was to ever leave you for Tink. My God, Erle, we could have—"

I stopped the flow of her words with my lips, pressing them softly against hers. I'd forgotten how incredibly warm and welcoming those lips were.

There was much I had forgotten.

And much that I remembered.

The next morning, when I woke up, Amy was gone. She'd left a note on her pillow:

> Dearest, dearest Erle . . .
>
> Thank you for the most wonderful night of my life! For a few magic hours you took away my pain and frustration, and I didn't think that was possible.
>
> I must return to Tink, but only long enough to set things in motion for the divorce. A week at the most. Then I'll come back to you.
>
> Maybe, when this ugly business is over, things between us can be the way they once were.
>
> Wouldn't that be *wonderful?*
>
> Your loving Amy

I was greatly moved by her note. Our night together had proved that she still loved me as much as I loved her. Maybe things *could* be the way they were five years before. That morning, as I read her words over and over, I believed it.

25

Walking around the office in a happy daze with my mind on the future, I didn't hear the phone ring. Not at first. Then its insistent jangle finally penetrated my thoughts.

"Gardner," I said into the mouthpiece.

"It's Dash. I need to see you. Could you meet me at M-G-M today?"

"Well . . ." I hesitated. "I'm against a deadline on a Paul Pry novelette. And I've promised to meet Joe Shaw in Hollywood at five."

"Won't take long," said Hammett. "You'll have plenty of time to meet Shaw. This is important, Erle. You're in a position to do me a big favor."

"What favor?"

"Tell you all about it when you get here," he said. "There'll be a pass for you at the gate. I'll be at the jungle set on the back lot, near the alligator pool."

"Okay, just this once."

He said, "Thanks, pal," and rang off.

I'd been doing Paul Pry stories since 1930, just one of my bagful of characters for the pulps. Pry is known as "The Crime Buster," and that's what he does: he goes after crooks, hijacks their loot, thwarts their plans, and generally gives them a hard time. An urbane gent, tough and debonair. His weapon is a sword cane, and he can fence like Errol Flynn. I started him out in *Gang World*, then switched him to *Dime Detective* for a better word rate.

Usually when I have a deadline to meet, I don't let anything stand in the way, but Hammett is special. He almost never asks for a favor, and I couldn't say no to this one—whatever it was. We've shared some rambunctious times together: "The Cat's Eye" adventure, when we chased that infernal jeweled skull Hammett used as the basis of his *Maltese Falcon*, and the "Vampire Queen Caper" (as Dash calls it), when Ray Chandler almost got himself killed.

I had read in the Hollywood trade papers about Hammett's current assignment at M-G-M. They'd called him in to rework the latest Tarzan script for Johnny Weissmuller. Hammett's a great script doctor. He knows how to take a weak screenplay, beef it up, strengthen the characters, increase the action, and inject fresh life into it. And he'll take any job that pays him top dollar, which is something I've never been able to understand. His willingness to do hack work, that is.

Of us all—Shaw's "*Black Mask* boys"—Hammett is the most famous, and by far the most respected. I mean, the critics put him right up there with Hemingway. Yet he quit writing novels after finishing *The Thin Man* in '33, and he swears he'll never do another book like it. Hates being pegged as a mystery writer. He talks about doing a big mainstream novel, or a play for Broadway, but that's all it is. Talk. Meanwhile, he's hacking out this junk for Hollywood, taking any job that's offered him.

There's no amount of money that would make me work on these turkeys, and I'm no Hemingway. I've got my limits when it comes to literary prostitution.

Dash is an up-front guy, with plenty of grit and courage, but he's a Hollywood sellout and he knows it. I guess that's what makes him so cynical.

When I drove up to the gate at M-G-M's back lot in Culver City, the guard asked me my name and business. "I'm Erle Gardner," I told him. "Here to see Dashiell Hammett."

"Oh, yeah. I got a call about you," he said as he handed me a lot pass. He was large and beefy, with a pug's face. The metal tag on his shirt read "Joey Devarona." I was tucking the orange slip into my pocket when he told me to leave it in sight on the dashboard when I parked. "That way, your car's legit. We don't hafta tow 'er."

"How do I get to the jungle?" I asked him.

"Go straight past the Egyptian tomb in the Sahara, turn right at the Little Big Horn—where they got all the Indian extras—and keep going past the Civil War. Then you—"

I was confused. "Civil War?"

27

"Yeah, they're gettin' ready for Sherman's march through Georgia on Stage Six. Anyhow, just keep going till you get to the Eiffel Tower. Take a left there, and Africa's dead ahead. Can't miss it."

"Thanks, Joey," I said, heading for Egypt.

Hammett was where he said he'd be, looking gaunt and undernourished, standing next to a pool of rubber alligators. He'd fought off attacks of tuberculosis the whole time he lived in San Francisco (when he was doing all his best work for Joe Shaw), and once he licked the disease, he just never filled out. Dash likes to eat, but it doesn't show. He gave me a thin-fingered handshake.

"Appreciate your coming over," he said. His face was long and solemn, and his prematurely white hair made him look older than he was. He was still handsome, but years of hard drinking had taken their toll. I'd heard he was off the booze, but maybe that was a rumor.

"How's Lily?" I asked him. I was referring to his primary ladylove, writer Lillian Hellman. They'd been an item for some time now. She was ugly as a mud fence, in my opinion, but Dash didn't seem to mind that. At least she wore nice hats.

"Lily's back East, in Westchester, working on a new play," he told me. "Soon as I wind up this lousy job, I'm going to head East myself. But right now, I'm broke."

Seems like Dash is always broke. He spends the money he makes from the studios as fast as it rolls in. And he loves to gamble. I saw him lay five grand on the nose of a twenty-to-one shot at Santa Anita when the sorry nag was lucky to finish last. Dash didn't blink; just shrugged those thin shoulders of his and placed his next bet.

Once, when he was trying to steer a redheaded starlet into bed, he sent her a taxicab full of flowers each day for a week. And one night at the Coconut Grove, when he was plastered, I watched him order every dish on the menu. I remember this long line of waiters, balancing trays, that extended from his table all the way back to the kitchen. God knows what the bill came to.

He'd earned a nice bundle writing an original screen treatment for *After the Thin Man*, but that money was long gone, so here he was doing Tarzan.

The jungle set was impressive. Most of the background trees were papier-mâché, with the real ones rooted in pots. A few (the trees Tarzan had to swing on) were actually planted in solid ground. The prop boys had filled it all in with masses of rubber foliage, creating a thick jungle effect.

Tarzan's tree house was in the foreground. Cheetah the chimp, chained to a tree, was being fed bananas by his trainer. I noticed that the animal was wearing a diaper. I asked Hammett why.

"So he won't crap all over the set," Dash told me. "When they start shooting, they take the diaper off and hope for the best. If he craps on-camera, the scene's a washout."

"Looks as if they've set up a pretty good jungle," I said.

"It'll pass. They'll be filling in with scrap footage from *Trader Horn*. Won't match, but who cares in a Tarzan picture?"

"Does Weissmuller really swing through the trees?"

"His double does most of that," said Hammett. "They've rigged a trapeze disguised as a vine for Johnny to swing on. If you look real close, you can see the trapeze bar."

"Creatively, this must be a tough job for you," I said. "I mean, it must be hard to take seriously."

"The worst part is writing scenes for all the lousy animals. They want new stuff for Tantor the elephant, Numa the lion, and Kala, Tarzan's ape mother. Ever try writing dialogue for an ape?"

"Weissmuller must be a gutsy guy to work with all these wild animals."

"Are you kidding? To play Numa, they brought in this toothless old lion from the Griffith Park Zoo. In the big scene we shot last week, when it was supposed to attack Tarzan in a battle to the death, the lion fell asleep. They ended up using a stuffed one."

I looked around. "I don't see Weissmuller."

"Right now, Johnny's taking a steam bath in a private joint they call 'The Healthatorium' in Newport Beach. He'll show up after lunch. At the moment, the shoot's on hold while Burroughs argues with Louie Mayer in the production building. Big confab."

"Ole Edgar Rice himself is here?"

"Yep. He's real annoyed over the way Tarzan talks. The Tarzan in his books is an English lord, with an aristocratic command of the language. Burroughs is here to complain about the dialogue." Hammett shrugged. "Won't do him any good. The 'me Tarzan, you Jane' lingo is all that Weissmuller can handle. Guy can't act for sour apples. He's a *swimmer*, for God's sake!"

"Does he like playing Tarzan?"

"Well, he's happy about the money they pay him. But he complains a lot about his loincloth. Says it's too tight. Makes his balls ache."

We'd seated ourselves in two of the canvas-backed crew chairs, and Hammett had an unlit cigarette in his mouth. I offered to light it for him.

"Naw, I'm off these coffin nails," he said. "I tried chewing pencils for a while, but that didn't help, so I went back to cigarettes. But I don't light 'em. I just enjoy the tactile pleasure. So far, it's working."

I asked Dash about the title of the picture.

"It's called '*Tarzan and the Snake Apes of Zandor*,'" he said.

"What's a snake ape?"

"This tribe of giant gorillas from the lost city of Zandor—it's on Stage Two—they worship a snake goddess who has hypnotic power over all the apes."

"Is she a snake?"

"No, she's human. But her father was a reptile."

"Then wouldn't she be half snake?"

"Technically, yes. But Mayer wants a classy-looking doll to play the role, and he doesn't want her ass wrapped in snakeskin. Which brings us to the favor I need from you."

"Name it. That's why I'm here."

"I was too embarrassed to tell you over the phone," Dash admitted. "Figured if I did, you'd never say yes."

"A loan? Is that what this is all about?"

"No, that's not it. I need you to sit in for me as a judge."

"A judge of what?"

He stood up, tossed away the unlit cigarette, and spread his hands. "It's a sort of contest. Mayer's idea." He pointed to his left. "See the tall, salmon-colored building? That's Stage Three. Go in and tell 'em Hammett sent you. You'll meet the other two judges and then these girls will come out and do the snake dance and—"

"Aw, c'mon, Dash," I protested. "This is ridiculous!"

"No, no. It's very serious. Mayer set it up personally. The whole plot is built around the snake goddess—and we don't have one picked out yet."

"Why can't *you* be a judge?"

"I've got to stay here and rewrite the alligator scene," he said. "Needs a lot of work and they're shooting it right after lunch—so I just can't get involved in this snake business."

"But why *me?* Get somebody from the studio to fill in for you."

"No good," he said. "Mayer insists that at least one writer take part as a judge. For 'intellectual input.' He's absolutely firm on that. I couldn't reach Ray Chandler and you're the only other intellectual writer I know in L.A." His eyes were pleading. "*Will* you do it, Erle? As a personal favor to me. I can't be in two places at once, and I need this job!"

I sighed. "Okay, okay . . . I'll help pick out Mayer's snake goddess. But I'll feel like a damn fool doing it."

"Knew I could count on you." Hammett grinned broadly. "You're a peach!"

FOUR

It was just after one-thirty when I stepped through the door into Stage Three, which meant there was still plenty of time before I had to drive into Hollywood to meet Joe Shaw.

Still, I was in a grumpy mood, knowing I should have been at home working on the Pry novelette. Dash was right: if he'd told me over the phone about this nutty snake thing, I never would have agreed to participate.

Like all sound stages, this one was huge: an immense concrete-floored arena with enough room for half a dozen standing sets—but most of the area was bare. Just lights and scaffolding and coiled cable. The snake-dancing set, however, which centered around the interior of a fake cave, was ready for action. The stagehands had brought in a truckload of dirt for the cave floor, which was dominated by a ten-foot-tall wood carving of a black python. A male snake god, probably, but you can't tell with snakes. There were papier-mâché rocks for the apes to sit on, and a fake stone platform in the middle, where the snake goddess would do her number.

It was all pretty cheesy.

Off to one side, facing the platform, was a long plywood table laid out with notepads and pencils. There were three chairs, for the judges I guessed, all empty at the moment.

A small fat man waddled toward me like an agitated penguin, waving his arms. "If yer here to play an ape, yer outa luck," he said. "Go back and tell casting to quit sending me ape candidates. Apes I got out the ass!"

"I'm not here to play an ape," I told him. "I'm filling in for Dashiell Hammett. For the audition."

He looked relieved. "Great. We're just about ready to start. The other judges are due any minute, an' I got the girls all lined up, ready to go."

"How many?"

"How many what?" His left eyebrow shot up.

"Girls," I said. "How many will be snake-dancing?"

"Not many. These janes is the ones specially selected from what you'd call your general mass of applicants. Dames from all over L.A.—they flock in. But these is the cream'a the crop."

"How many?" I repeated.

"Fifteen," said the little man.

"That's a lot," I said, thinking of having to sit though fifteen snake dances. And I was also beginning to get concerned about my appointment with Joe Shaw. Five o'clock suddenly seemed a lot closer than it had when I entered the building.

"These is the cream," insisted the fat man. "Absolute top babes. I don't envy you judges, having to pick just one of 'em."

"I don't envy us either," I said.

At that point, another stage door opened behind the cave structure and a pair of shadowed figures walked toward us.

"Great. Here's the other two judges. Now we can get this show on the road."

I didn't recognize the first man, a pasty-faced character in a checkered satin vest and velvet trousers, but I had no doubt about the identity of the second man.

33

Tink Thompson.

We'd never met, and Amy had told me she hadn't mentioned my name to him, so the recognition was all mine. Thompson was in his usual ultra-casual Beverly Hills sports attire, and when the penguin introduced us, Tink gave me a swell-guy smile as he put out his hand.

I hesitated, since I didn't fancy shaking hands with a brute, but I didn't have a choice under the circumstances.

"Erle Gardner," I said.

"And just what is it that you do?" asked Thompson.

"I'm a writer—filling in for Dash Hammett."

"Well now, Erle, I'm doggone glad to meet you. Guess you know all about me?"

"I know enough," I said.

The remark passed right by him.

"This gent with me is Pierre. A dress designer all the way from Gay Paree. Got his own fashion line. Right, Pierre?"

"That is correct, Monsieur Tink," he nodded. Then, turning to me, he said: "Pierre Capillion, Monsieur Gardner."

We shook hands.

The agitated fat man waved us all to the plywood table. "Please, gents, be seated. The babes are ready to perform."

"This ought to be quite entertaining," said Thompson as we sat down. "You know, Garner—"

"It's Gardner," I said.

"Of course, old fellow. As I was saying, Mr. Mayer *personally* chose me to sit in on this. Said he wanted an actor, a writer, and a designer as judges. For the proper balance, he said. Brilliant man, Mr. Mayer, don't you agree?"

"Never met him," I said. "I heard he can be tough."

"Strong-minded is a better term," Thompson said, "Actually, he's been like a father to me."

"That's nice," I said.

34

It was difficult keeping a level tone. I felt like shouting obscenities at him for what he'd done to Amy and to his poor dead son. I'd expected to meet Tink Thompson for the first time in divorce court. That I would be sitting with him at this makeshift table, on an M-G-M sound stage judging a snake dance, was the ultimate irony. Life can be pretty damn strange at times. Especially in southern California.

Thompson turned to Pierre. "So, how do you like L.A.?"

"Ah, eet ees *fantastique*, Monsieur Tink."

The actor grinned at me. "Doncha just *love* that Frenchy accent?"

"Love it," I said.

Thompson leaned toward me. "You know, old fellow, I'm something of a writer myself."

"Really?"

"Poems and essays, mostly. Personal things, dealing with self-improvement. It's something I've studied all my life. We must strive for perfection. Impossible to reach, of course, but that shouldn't discourage us from our quest."

I stared at him. Self-improvement? From Tink Thompson? Unbelievable!

"I think the audition is about to start," I said.

Five musicians, wearing ape costumes and lugging tall skin drums, came around the cave's edge. They sat down on the fake rocks in front of the raised "stone" platform and began to tap out a jungle beat.

The fat man noticed that one of them was smoking a cigar.

"Kill that stogie!" he yelled at the ape.

"But there ain't no cameras," complained the musician, reluctantly stubbing out his cigar. The fat man glared at him, then stepped up to the table. "Gentlemen, I herewith give ya our first dancer . . . Denise Gunderson!"

A busty redhead with wide hips, dead eyes, and a vacuous smile, wearing a fake leopard-skin sarong, came slithering onto the cave floor and launched into a writhing snake number to the rhythm of the beating drums.

It was painful to watch. I lowered my head. Fourteen to go.

I was turning off Hollywood Boulevard, into the parking lot for the Seven Seas Restaurant, before I was able to calm myself. Meeting Thompson, having to sit next to him and listen to the crap he spewed out, had really upset me.

I didn't know why Joe Shaw was so anxious to talk to me, but I looked forward to seeing him; it wasn't often that Joe came in from New York. I was feeling sorry for the guy after what had happened to him. He'd been at the editorial helm of *Black Mask* for a full decade when, last winter, the publisher had booted him out. It wasn't Joe's fault. Late in '26, after Shaw took over from Phil Cody, the magazine's circulation had increased from 66,000 to 80,000 in the first twelve months. By 1930, Shaw had the circulation up to 103,000, but then it began dropping. By the close of '35, *Mask* was selling just 63,000 copies each month. The publisher had to blame somebody, so Shaw took the rap.

Unfortunately, it was the Depression that was behind the slump in sales; lots of other magazines are in trouble in this country for the same reason. Millions of Americans now lack the money to buy food, let alone magazines. There was nothing Shaw could have done to change the situation at *Black Mask*.

Of course, out here in southern California, the entertainment industry is flourishing, in no small part *because* of the Depression. Movies for the masses provide pleasant escape at minimum cost: thirty-five cents for a three-hour double feature. Most Americans can still ante up the two bits and a dime, so as the nation gets poorer, the studios get richer.

Thank God I'm not personally affected. Living here in Hollywood, in the middle of this "golden bubble," it's easy to forget how tough times are for the rest of the country. I just hope that Roosevelt can keep his promises and pull us out of this economic quagmire. If not, our future could be pretty dim.

As a writer, I've always been grateful to Phil Cody, who was the first editor to get behind my stuff. He bought my best stories for *Black Mask*, gave me invaluable editorial advice, and promoted me in a big way with his readers. It is thanks to Cody that I became a major name in the pulps, with *Mask* leading the way. I couldn't have done it without him.

Shaw has never given Cody proper credit. Joe has always claimed that *he* developed the *Black Mask* style, guiding me and Hammett and Carroll John Daly along the path he laid out. It's not true. We all wrote for Cody long before Shaw took over. And whatever his faults as a writer, you have to credit Daly with inventing the hard-boiled private eye (with his characters Terry Mack and Race Williams); Daly did it as early as 1923, the same year Hammett produced his Continental Op. I was in *Mask* with my Bob Larkin stories by '24— so Joe's claims are mostly hogwash.

Which is not to say he wasn't a good editor. He was *very* good, but you have to keep things in perspective; Joe's ego won't allow him to accept the fact that Phil Cody was the real trailblazer. Professionally, that's always been Joe's biggest problem, that ego of his. What he *did* do was move the *Mask* away from its mixed bag of genres and place the editorial focus sharply on what he bannered on the cover as "Gripping, Smashing Detective Stories." This was a major accomplishment, and he deserves full credit for it.

Shaw has always hated the word "pulp." To him, it smacks of cheapness and vulgarity. When he helmed *Mask*, he called it a "rough-paper book." I remember one newsman who referred to him as a "pulp editor" in one of his columns. Joe walked into the guy's office, leaned over his desk, and growled: "I'm a *detective-story* editor, you son of a bitch, and don't you ever call me anything else!"

Another problem for Joe, beyond his ego, has been his desire to be a writer. Not just editorials and story blurbs—but novels. He talked me into reading one, *Blood on the Curb*, and it was god-awful. I told him it "needed work." I don't think he tries to write anymore, which is a blessing for us all.

And then, of course, there's the tragedy of Joe's daughter. Hammett's already written about that case in *The Black Mask Murders*, so I won't repeat the details here. But Joe's been through a lot.

He was a captain in the Great War, which is why most people call him "Cap" Shaw. I never minded being one of his "boys," since he's always been square with me. We get along fine until he starts talking about himself as "the father of the *Black Mask* school." That gets me riled up every time. But I wrote a lot of good stuff for Shaw, seventy stories in all, and I think of him fondly. I hadn't kept track of him since he'd left the *Mask*, so I was curious about what he was currently involved in.

I was about to find out.

When I walked into the Seven Seas at ten minutes to five, Joe was waiting for me at the bar, wearing a summer wool suit and tony striped tie. Very New York.

"Erle!" He hopped off the red bar stool to meet me, shaking my hand vigorously. "How you doing, pal?"

"Doing fine," I said.

He patted the stool next to his. "Sit down. Let's have a drink."

I did that, ordering a Bloody Mary while Joe finished his Scotch.

The Seven Seas lived up to its name. The room-long bar faced a panoramic mural: island palms swayed in the breeze against a background of South Sea mountains, while a luxury ocean liner plied the exotic tropical waters. Bamboo was everywhere in the room: walls, ceiling, tables, chairs. They even had bamboo place mats. And, for your hearing pleasure, there was a recording of tropical rain on a tin roof—a famous house specialty that helped provide the proper atmosphere.

"I've been following your career," said Shaw, smoothing his brush mustache. "You've come a long way up from the rough papers. *This Week* . . . *Liberty* . . . and last month, you made the *Saturday Evening Post* with a Mason. I'm damned impressed."

"Yeah," I said. "The *Post* serialized my 'Case of the Lame Canary,' and they want more. Big break for me. I've been trying to hit them for years."

"Proves that my faith in you was justified."

"You and Phil Cody," I said, and I could tell that he didn't appreciate the correction.

"I see you're still writing for *Mask.*"

"Sure am," I nodded. "Ellsworth is taking everything I send his way."

"Ah, then . . . you've never met?"

"No. We've done everything by mail."

Shaw grinned like a little boy with a wicked secret to share. " 'F. Ellsworth.' That's the name on the masthead. Know what the 'F' stands for?"

I shrugged. "Frank? Frederick? Foster?"

"Wrong," Joe smirked. "The 'F' stands for Fanny."

"A woman?"

"Can you beat that?" Shaw was shaking his head. "Me . . . replaced by a *female!* After ten years of blood and sweat, after making *Mask* the top crime book in America, they kick me out for a dame!"

"I just assumed that Ellsworth was a man," I said.

Joe's face was flushed; a vein pulsed in his forehead as he let his anger and frustration build. "Everybody does. That's why they list her as 'F. Ellsworth'—to fool the readers. To deceive! A woman has no damn business editing a hard-boiled *man's* magazine. Am I right?"

"It's . . . unusual," I admitted.

"Goddam fraud on the reading public, that's what it is!"

"I'm sorry about the way things worked out for you," I told him. "Tough break. But what's done is done."

"I know." He sighed, relaxing. The tension gradually drained from his face. "I've still got a life to live."

I sipped my Bloody Mary. "So . . . what brings you out West?"

"My boys," he said, pulling at his mustache.

I blinked at him.

"My *Black Mask* boys. You . . . Dash . . . Ray Chandler, all of you. I'm here to see my boys."

"Didn't know we were so close to your heart," I said, grinning.

"Well, it's not exactly that," he admitted. "I've come with an offer. A very sound offer. To you first. Then I'll talk to Dash and Ray and some of the others out here on the Coast."

"What kind of offer?"

"I'm starting my own literary agency," Shaw told me. "I'll be based in New York, and in touch with all the publishers. I've already signed up some solid talent. The Shaw Agency is going to be able to get top dollar for its clients."

"And you're offering to take me on as a client?"

"That's it, Erle. I can do wonders for your career. I can—"

"Hold it, Joe." I put up a hand. "I've got an agent."

"I know. Jane Hardy. But I've heard you're not happy with her."

"You heard right," I said. "She took over when my first agent—her husband, Bob—died of cancer. We don't see eye to eye on a lot of things, but she *did* sell 'Lame Canary' to the *Post* for fifteen grand, with an option on the next book for seventeen five."

"That's good money," Shaw agreed.

"I don't like the idea of switching horses—or agents—in midstream," I told him.

"Naturally, I understand your thinking, but—"

"And if I do decide to drop Jane as my agent, I'm quite capable of handling my own sales. I've worked with most of the editors personally, and selling is a game I know a lot about."

"Then you're turning me down flat?"

"I'm sorry, Joe."

"What do you think my chances are with Hammett and Chandler?"

"Hammett doesn't do books anymore. His film agent sets up his assignments out here, so he has no need of a literary agent in New York. Don't know about Ray. He writes like a snail going uphill. Takes him forever to finish a story, and I'd say he's still a long way from tackling a book. Right now he sells only three or four novelettes a year. How could you make any money off him at that rate?"

"You've answered my question," Shaw said, a defeated look in his eyes. He pulled at his mustache. "Guess I'll just forget about Dash and Ray. A waste of time. There are a few of the other boys I can talk to."

"I wish you all the luck in the world with the Shaw Agency," I told him.

"I'll drink to that," he said, raising his glass.

And we drank to that.

FIVE

Two days later, I had the Pry novelette in the mail to *Dime Detective* and was sweating out the plot for my next Perry Mason. In addition to my work for the pulps, I need to keep up my average of at least two Masons each year, which means I'm always on the lookout for fresh locales, colorful new sites I can utilize in these novels. At that moment, I needed to come up with an exotic spot for Mason to meet an upper-crust female client.

Then I recalled what Amy had said about Thompson's insistence that every month she spend at least a week at the Silver Gate, a chichi health resort in Carmel, halfway up the California coast. *Very* upper crust. Many of Hollywood's top stars—Crawford, Dietrich, Shearer, Harlow, and Lombard—show up there on a regular basis. The perfect place for Mason to meet his client.

I determined to scout out the area. My readers demand authenticity, and you can't be authentic about a place you've never seen. So Tomas helped me get ready for an early start the following morning.

It was a full day's drive up the coast highway, so I left Hollywood more than an hour before sunrise. That way, by the time the sun came up, I would be beyond Ventura County—my old stomping grounds as an attorney and certainly not a place I needed to research.

With full daylight dawning around the time I entered Santa Barbara County, I would be in the perfect place to begin serious research. Mason was going to make this trip north, and I needed to see the terrain through *his* eyes.

Santa Barbara marks the beginning of some of the most spectacular scenery in the world. North of Morro Bay, the cliffs of the Santa Lucia Range rise up some four thousand feet from the waters of the Pacific. Closely cradled between them, the coast road—part of the old *El Camino Real*, or King's Highway—twists crazily, carved out of the raw mountainside high above the ocean floor. Not a drive to take if you're queasy about heights, or unsure of the rubber on your tires.

When California belonged to Spain, and then to Mexico, when trips along the more than six-hundred-mile length of the *El Camino Real* were on horseback or by carriage, the twenty-one California missions offered a much-welcomed night's shelter for colonial travelers. Built under the direction of Fray Junipero Serra (and later, Fray de Lasuen, Serra's successor), each was positioned a day's ride apart, from San Diego in the south, all the way up to Mission San Francisco Solano, north of the San Francisco Bay. These varied architectural masterpieces remain a vital, living presence in California life today.

As I approached Mission Santa Barbara, I thought of Amy. Nearby, Marisol Herrera-Quintano, Tink Thompson's mistress, lived on her grand estate in Montecito; it was there that Amy had met her husband's paramour face-to-face.

North of Santa Barbara, the road passes through ranch land that—except for the Burma Shave signs—seems almost untouched by time. I passed yellow rolling hills studded with ancient oak trees, where white-faced cattle drowsed in the ripening summer heat. The mounted ranchers working in the distance could easily have been from an earlier era. From my perspective, there was no difference to be seen between Spanish caballero and American cowboy.

I stopped for fuel in San Luis Obispo, the halfway mark between

Los Angeles and San Francisco. Having traveled this highway several years before, I wasn't sure I would find any more gas stations until Carmel. While the station manager filled my tank and checked my radiator and tires, I caught a truly delicious whiff of just-out-of-the-oven apple pie, set to cool on the kitchen windowsill by the manager's wife. I suddenly realized how hungry I was; I hadn't eaten for over six hours.

La Posada turned out to be an excellent choice; I promptly decided that Mason was going to dine in this same venerable eatery. The restaurant is located in an old adobe building that hasn't been greatly modified since 1772, when Father Serra himself founded the nearby San Luis Obispo Mission. The furniture inside is mission-made, rough-cut from raw timber and sanded smooth by hand, and every table is illuminated by flaming candles set in weathered brass lanterns.

The food turned out to be both simple and excellent: tacos, tamales, and rice, corn tortillas and pinto beans, all washed down with homemade apple cider.

I left San Luis Obispo with a full stomach and a reasonably happy heart. Someday soon, I was going to come back here with Amy. I had a feeling that she would be just as enchanted as I was.

A few miles north, I passed San Simeon, William Randolph Hearst's incredible castle on the hill. Then, suddenly, I was into the mountains. The road took me through deep canyons choked with heavy brush and sun-washed sage, past sandstone cliffs, and into dense growths of redwood and cypress. I arrived at my destination four hours later.

Carmel-by-the-Sea is aptly named. A small village laid out in the midst of a spreading forest of cypress and pine, it stretches down from the highway to the white sand beach of Carmel Bay. The modern town was founded in 1870 as an art colony by creative types—painters, poets, musicians, and writers—and still retains a strong artistic flavor. Portrait galleries, bookshops, and art studios cluster shoulder to shoulder along Ocean Avenue, catering to a genteel upper class whose assets encompass culture as well as monetary wealth. Afternoon high tea, served in the formal English tradition at some of the town's toniest restaurants, is the highlight of many a Carmel matron's day.

The old mission, San Carlos Borromeo de Carmelo, a hundred years older than the village itself, remains the historical heart of Carmel. This was Fray Junipero Serra's favorite mission; it became his final resting place. As I drove by, I could see restoration work continuing on the unique buildings, distinguished by their unusual Gothic and Moorish architectural elements.

I located the Silver Gate at the end of San Carlos Street; it looked more like a Spanish hacienda than a health spa. I used the polished silver knocker on the massive oak door. It was opened by a tall woman with good bones and questing eyes. She gave me her best professional smile. "You must be Elwood T. Wicker," she said in a cultured voice.

"Afraid not," I said. "I'm Erle Gardner."

Her smile faded.

"But we've been expecting Mr. Wicker," she told me. "He is making a special trip here from his home in Oregon to take part in our regimen."

"What regimen is that?"

"Natural food, vigorous exercise, sun, air, and water," she declared briskly. "Nature's path to universal health."

"Well, not only am I not Elwood T. Wicker, but I'm not here to walk nature's path," I told her.

"Then why *are* you here?"

"Have you ever heard of Perry Mason?"

She shook her head. "We have no one registered under that name here at the Gate."

"He's a fictional character," I explained. "Out of my head. I'm a mystery writer."

"Regretfully," she said, "frivolous reading is a luxury I do not allow myself."

"The point is, I'm plotting a new mystery novel and I thought I'd check out your spa for some possible scenes in my book."

She was suspicious. "Just what would you like to check out?"

"I'll need to walk through, get a mental picture of the place. Maybe talk to some of your paying customers."

"*Guests,*" she firmly corrected. "Never customers."

"Fine," I said.

"If you were to write about us, we would need to be assured that you would not hold the Gate up to ridicule, or present our establishment in an unfavorable light. There are so many forces in American society today that work against natural health. Every day we face grave dangers from those who would put us out of business. Do I have your word that you would use your influence as a writer to strengthen rather than destroy our work?"

"You have it," I said.

"And you will not have anyone murdered here in your story?"

"Absolutely not."

"Then you are welcome to enter." And she bowed me inside.

As we walked through the building, she told me her name was Ida Favershim and that the Silver Gate was owned by her father, Dr. Elias Favershim, a "scientific genius in the field of health therapy" who was currently operating another resort on the French Riviera, frequented by playwright George Bernard Shaw and novelist F. Scott Fitzgerald.

"Mr. Fitzgerald tends toward excess," she said. "He often uses Daddy's spa to dry out after a week of alcoholic indulgence. He must be a very sad man."

"All alcoholics are sad," I declared.

We passed areas where guests were being provided with body massages, water exercises, floral vapor baths, herbal beauty treatments, and mud wraps.

"We stress *total* health," she said. "Mind, body, and spirit. In just two weeks, with our help, guests achieve amazing transformations."

"That's wonderful," I said.

"Out of my father's great intellectual gift, he has created natural-food supplements that not only optimize overall health, but greatly reduce the effects of aging, resulting in a much younger physical appearance. That is most important to our guests, of course."

"I'm sure it is," I said.

"Youth-O-Vim, one of our most popular products, is actually a miraculous *internal* cosmetic. It's so effective that in only three days, our guests actually begin to see their skin becoming younger— smoother and finer, with a renaissance of youthful color. Six months later, most of their wrinkles have completely disappeared, and this applies to our *male* guests as well." She lowered her voice. "Of course, I'd never mention any names, but let me assure you that many of Hollywood's leading men depend on our rejuvenating treatments to maintain their manly perfection."

"What's in this Youth-O-Vim?" I asked her.

"Well, the exact formula is a proprietary secret, of course, but I can tell you that it's based on brewer's yeast and an array of rare mountain herbs."

"Sounds awful," I said. "What does it taste like?"

She shrugged her shoulders. "Our guests find that regained youth carries its own sweetness. They soon become accustomed to the taste."

"That bad, eh?" I said.

She laughed. "It's a rather, uh, *intense* drink . . . almost like syrup. Would you like to try a complimentary bottle?"

"I'm rather fond of my wrinkles," I said. "And I'm not the yeast-and-herbs type."

"Well, if you ever change your mind, I suggest that every morning

47

you mix two tablespoons of brewer's yeast flakes into tomato juice, then drink it down as fast as possible. The real secret of Youth-O-Vim is the brewer's yeast. Also, raw vegetables and uncooked fruits should become the foundation of your diet." She smiled. "I seem to be giving away all of our secrets, Mr. Gardner."

"I appreciate your concern," I said, "but I'm not going to promise that I'll ever drink brewer's yeast!"

She laughed. "How did you hear about the Gate?"

"From a friend of mine, Amy Thompson. She's been up here a lot. Or so she told me."

"Of course. Mrs. Thompson is a regular guest of ours. We've been able to do wonders for her skin—thanks to Cleopatra."

"The one from Egypt—*that* Cleopatra?"

"The very same."

"What does Cleopatra have to do with Amy's skin?"

"As queen of Egypt, she commanded that certain vital secrets, which had up to then been kept carefully hidden by the priesthood for over a thousand years, should be revealed. One of those secrets concerned a formula for maintaining the bloom of youthful skin. I'm proud to say that we at the Gate employ this very same formula. Mrs. Thompson has benefited greatly from it."

"What's in this one?" I asked.

Her eyes twinkled. "Sour milk."

"Sour milk?"

"We purchase raw goat milk from a local farmer, add a bit of lemon juice, let it sour, and then use the clabbered solids as a facial cleansing mask. It dissolves the layers of dead skin so the newer, more youthful skin underneath can glow."

Ida paused, her eyes intense. "Is Mrs. Thompson not beautiful, with perfect skin?"

"She's very beautiful," I agreed.

"Her husband has accompanied her here on several occasions.

Such a wonderful man. So gentle and attentive. And what a great wit! He never fails to amuse our other guests. They simply *adore* him. And he insists that we call him Tink. Is Tink . . . uh . . . is Mr. Thompson also a friend of yours?"

"We've met," I said.

Ida sighed deeply. "Mrs. Thompson is *so* fortunate to be the wife of such a rare individual."

"Yeah, he's a rare one," I said, careful to keep contempt out of my tone.

"Well, Mr. Gardner, you've seen everything but the steam room. And it's in use at the moment." Then, suddenly, she giggled. "But I'll just bet they wouldn't mind your going in there."

"Who are 'they'?" I asked.

"I shouldn't say, but with these two . . . Mae West and Gloria Swanson . . . well, both of them have very daring ideas about what is proper—and what is not."

West and Swanson were certainly controversial film stars. Tales of their unconventional behavior had been circulating through Hollywood for years. But whether they'd allow a strange man to join them while they were taking a steam bath was open to question. At any rate, Ida Favershim was greatly amused by the idea.

She led me to a tall wooden door at the end of the corridor and tapped loudly. "Ladies! I have a gentleman here who is researching our premises for a book. He'd like to see the steam room. Are you decent?"

I recognized the unmistakable throaty voice of Mae West: "Dearie, I haven't been decent since I lost my milk teeth."

Swanson chimed in: "We've got towels on, so shoo him in."

Ida opened the door for me. "Go ahead," she said, a twinkle in her eye. "Bon voyage!"

I felt rather silly about this whole thing. After all, I didn't really *need* to see the inside of a steam room. White ceiling, white walls, some wide wooden benches to sit on, and a heavy mist of steam in the air. They're all alike, and this one was no exception. Still, I was intrigued with the idea of encountering two Hollywood legends under such bizarre circumstances. And what better place for Perry Mason to meet his client?

Indeed, as I entered, the ladies *were* wearing towels, fluffy pink ones, tucked into their bustlines and extending just far enough to cover the essentials. It was obvious that Mae West had lost none of her heft, and Gloria Swanson hadn't put on any necessary poundage; she was still too skinny for my taste.

Swanson's eyes were what you noticed: a luminous, penetrating lake-blue, dominating her hawklike face. West's eyes were languorous, half-slitted with calculated sensuality.

I told them who I was and what I was writing.

"I simply *devour* books," Swanson told me. "My house overflows with them. I'll alert my personal bookseller and make a point of reading yours."

"Maybe, if you like what you read, you could write my publisher and say something nice about me," I suggested.

"Oh, no," she said, shaking her head. "I never endorse anything but health products."

"Just a thought," I said.

West didn't seem at all interested in literature. She aimed one of her crooked smiles at me, slurring out her words in a husky tone: "Take off your shirt, darlin'—an' let's have a look at your pectorals."

The heat was intense as steam drifted out of the wall vents like thick smoke. My shirt was already sticking to my chest as I unbuttoned it.

"I'm no muscle man," I said. "So don't expect much."

"A man is a man," Mae said, "and I'm not choosy." She batted her eyes. "I can usually find *something* to admire."

Shirtless, I sat down on a slat bench facing them, trying to accustom myself to the heat and humidity.

"Tell me, Mr. Gardner, do you also write for the screen?" Swanson asked.

"No, just books and stories," I told her. "With a few nonfiction pieces thrown in."

"You should write a book about white sugar," she said vehemently. "It's killing people!"

"Really?" I said.

"The sugar companies take the God-given, nutritious juice of natural cane or beet, refine it to molasses, then refine that to brown sugar, and then refine *that* to white crystals. By then, it's nothing more than chemical poison! Refined sugar is absolutely ruining this country."

"I get all the sugar *I* need from the men in my life," West declared. "But when it comes to food, I don't worry about *anything* I eat, because I get rid of it fast. What you have to do is thoroughly cleanse the bowels each day."

"Mae spends a lot of time in the bathroom," said Gloria.

West rolled her eyes. "I believe in a clean colon . . . and a *dirty* mind."

Swanson chuckled. "How wonderfully vulgar!"

"The censors don't know what to do with me," West declared. "I give 'em fits. I always have at least three outrageous scenes in every picture; that way, they can cut *them* out and be satisfied, so they leave my *other* outrageous scenes alone."

"Mae gets away with the damndest things," Swanson said. She turned to her towel-draped companion. "Tell him the line about the six-foot cowboy."

"Sure, sure," said Mae. "Well, I asked this fella how tall he was, an' he tells me: 'Six feet seven inches, ma'am,' and I come back with: 'Let's forget the six feet and concentrate on the seven inches.' That one slipped right past the censors."

I laughed in genuine amusement. Mae West wasn't anyone I would ever be attracted to, but she was a hell of a raconteur. I stood up and looked down at my sweat-soaked trousers. "Ladies, it's been a real pleasure, but this heat is killing me. I wish you both good health and a long life."

Swanson pointed at me. "Remember what I said about sugar, Mr. Gardner. It's *poison.*"

"I'll keep that in mind," I said, picking up my shirt and moving toward the door.

"The mind has nothing to do with it," Mae declared. "It's all in the bowels."

I couldn't think of a proper exit line, so I nodded to each of them and hurriedly left the steam room.

I now had more than enough for Perry Mason.

SIX

I've never thought of myself as having any psychic ability, but when I returned home late the following day, I was possessed by a sudden sense of foreboding. As if my subconscious mind had locked into a negative vibrational field. And I couldn't seem to shake the dark mood.

I tried to work on my new novel, but couldn't get anywhere with it. Finally gave up.

I'm not a regular filmgoer. Most of the time, I'm too busy writing. On this particular night, however, when I couldn't work, I drove to my neighborhood theater and bought a ticket without bothering to find out what was playing. The film turned out to be *San Francisco*, with Clark Gable and Spencer Tracy, and it was quite well done. The earthquake scenes were particularly impressive, but even an on-screen earthquake couldn't shake me out of my mood. When I left the theater, I was still under a mental cloud.

Something was wrong.

I couldn't get to sleep that night. Just lay there in bed with my hands laced behind my head, staring at the ceiling.

It was barely after four when I got out of bed, dressed, and drove to the all-night newsstand on Hollywood Boulevard, where the morning papers would be out. If my feelings were trustworthy, I thought there was a good chance I'd find a story there that had a direct bearing on my life.

And I did.

FILM IDOL'S WIFE FOUND DEAD

Tink Thompson Discovers Wife's Body in Beverly Hills Home

Oh, no! Christ, no! Not Amy!

I sat in my car, stunned, tears rolling down my cheeks as I read the article.

> Returning to Los Angeles yesterday from a singing engagement in Palm Springs at the Golden Spur Hotel, international film and recording star Lloyd Hadley "Tink" Thompson discovered the body of his wife, Amy Latimer Thompson, sprawled on a living-room sofa in their Beverly Hills home.
>
> Authorities at the scene found no evidence of foul play. There was no indication that an intruder had entered the house.
>
> Los Angeles County Coroner Harold Edgewater will perform an autopsy to determine the cause of death.
>
> This is the second time that tragedy has struck in the brilliant life and career of Tink Thompson. Last month, Lawrence Thompson, the three-year-old son of Mr. and Mrs. Thompson . . .

At this point, I tossed the newspaper aside and began to sob. I just couldn't accept the fact that Amy was gone, that I had lost her again. This time, forever. I felt as if a knife had been driven into my flesh. I was short of breath, my heart was beating erratically, and I was trembling.

It was the worst moment of my life.

Sometime later, I picked up the paper again. A second story caught my eye: an "exclusive interview" with Thompson, in which the actor expressed "profound shock over the sudden death of my beloved wife."

The quote sickened me. Beloved indeed! Thompson was right on form, playing his role of the grieving husband. At this point, I had no doubt that he was greatly relieved to have Amy out of the way. Now no ugly divorce and no negative headlines would tarnish his shining reputation.

And financially, there would be no loss of community property assets, either. For Thompson, there would be a gigantic monetary difference between being a widower (who would inherit everything from his deceased wife) and an ex-husband (who would have been forced by the divorce court to turn over half of his considerable wealth to Amy). With her death, Thompson had effectively doubled his financial assets.

And as the "devoted" widower of a beautiful young woman that the public had come to love, Thompson would forevermore be the beneficiary of enormous media and public sympathy.

Amy's death had just provided Tink Thompson with the career coup of his life.

I continued reading more of the printed interview with mounting anger.

"She seemed so full of joy and vitality," a grief-stricken Thompson declared. "Amy always took wonderful care of herself. Yet, somehow, her heart failed. I'm sure that's what killed my wife—a heart attack. Why the Good Lord chose to take her at this time, we'll never know. We must trust that God has his own reasons. No matter how painful to us, his ways are best. And I am greatly comforted to know that Amy is with our son, Larry, and that they will now be together for eternity."

His voice choked with emotion, Thompson recalled the moment when he discovered his wife's body. "Amy was so beautiful. She was on our rose-colored sofa, looking like a sleeping princess. I will always remember her that way . . . my poor sweet darling Amy."

I couldn't read any more. Disgust welled up in me.

Then, instinctively, I knew how Amy had died. The truth was suddenly crystal-clear in my mind.

It had to be murder.

Once she had informed Thompson that she intended to divorce him, the cold-blooded bastard had killed her. But how? Had he really been in Palm Springs when she died?

I've been writing about murder for over a decade, but my murders have all been fictional. This one was real, painfully real. I needed to talk to someone who had dealt with murder on a professional basis.

I needed to see Dash Hammett.

"So what makes you so sure Thompson killed her?" Hammett asked me. He was in a gray-silk lounging robe, his hair tangled and bags under his eyes. He'd been up late and I'd awakened him early, a bad combination that had left him looking bushed. Now he continued: "Why would the guy risk everything—his life, his career, the whole shebang—just to get rid of a wife who was leaving him anyway?"

"But don't you see?" I countered. "That's exactly why he *did* kill her! Thompson was afraid that Amy would expose him to the world for the monster he really is. She would have shown that he was responsible for the death of their son. She would have revealed his affair with the woman in Santa Barbara, which would have destroyed his public image as the devoted husband. It would have been a disastrous blow to his career. He couldn't risk a public divorce."

We were sitting in Hammett's ice-cream parlor at his leased house in Pacific Palisades. As usual, Dash was living beyond his means. In my opinion, he had no business in this lavish forty-four-room mansion that had once belonged to a rich film comedian who had loved ice cream (which explains why Dash has his own ice-cream parlor in the basement). He'd originally leased it on *Thin Man* money from M-G-M. And now it was Tarzan. Whatever he was getting for the ape-man rewrite, I doubted it was enough to support a fancy place like this.

Plus he was paying for a full-time chauffeur, "Buddy" Desvarieux (Hammett claimed he was unable to pronounce Buddy's Haitian-French first name).

Dash seems to enjoy living life on the edge. Maybe this precarious existence challenges him to survive. Lord knows, throughout his life he's overcome incredible obstacles. In his detective years alone, he'd been knifed, blackjacked, shot at, hit with a brick, and nearly drowned—not to mention his long battle with tuberculosis. Whatever anyone might say about him, Samuel Dashiell Hammett *is* a survivor.

"Could be that you're allowing your negative feelings about Thompson to affect your judgment," Hammett was saying. "You claim he murdered Amy. Yet she died at home, alone. Thompson was singing at a hotel in Palm Springs at the time of her death. Police found no evidence of foul play. How does all this add up to murder?"

"I don't have the answers right now," I admitted, "but I'm gut-certain that this son of a bitch killed her. If I knew *how* he killed her, I wouldn't have come to you at six in the morning."

"Look . . . I want to help, Erle. I really do." Dash spread his thin hands. "And it's likely, from what you've told me about this creep, that he's *capable* of murder. But that doesn't prove he committed it."

"I grant your point, but will you try to look at this from *my* perspective?"

"If I do, then what?"

"Then we need to consider his method. Thompson is a helluva liar. Maybe he wasn't at the Springs when Amy died."

"Did you read the whole article?" Dash asked me, examining the newspaper story I had brought in to show him.

"Not all of it. Made me sick. Disgusted me. They treat him like a god, when he's really filth. I read as much as I could stomach."

"Well, it says here that—according to police sources—the cops phoned the hotel at the Springs to check out Thompson's alibi. He *was* there. The hotel owner, Gus Alberghetti, verified it. Says Thompson did two shows, spent the night there, and drove back to L.A. early yesterday morning."

"So maybe Alberghetti is lying. Maybe he's covering for Thompson."

"That would mean Alberghetti's an accessory to murder," argued Hammett. "Doubtful that anybody would do *that* as a favor to Thompson. And then we come to the method. She wasn't strangled. Her body was unmarked. No bruises. No blood. No gun. No knife. How did he kill her?"

"That's why I came to you. You've dealt with all kinds of murders. So you tell me."

"Well . . . there's always poison," Hammett said. "He might have given her something that triggered a heart attack."

"That's *it!*" I slapped my knee in triumph. "Thompson must have poisoned her!"

"If he did, he's dumber than he sounds. Couple of days and the autopsy report will be in. Poison will show up in her system. The cops will have evidence of murder, and Thompson will be in big trouble."

"But what if he used a poison that isn't detectable?"

"Most killers aren't that knowledgeable," Hammett said. "Thompson would have to be an expert in order to know exactly what wouldn't show up in a toxicology examination. And in addition, he'd need to have access to it."

buttoned leather stools fronted the bar. Rows of tables, now unoccupied, were covered with what looked like large red-checkered bandanas. At the far end of the room, on a raised stage just big enough for a small band and a singer or two, stood the melancholy Dane himself, Hamlet, in full voice. Of course, his outfit was all wrong: stained blue-flannel trousers and an open-necked tennis shirt. The voice was whiskey-slurred, but the delivery was first rate.

"To be or not to be," he intoned. "*That* is the question." He rolled his eyes upward, spreading his hands in a broad theatrical gesture. "Whether 'tis nobler in the mind to suffer the slings and arrows of outrageous fortune, or to take arms against a sea of troubles, and by opposing end them . . ."

A besotted John Barrymore, delivering what is perhaps his most famous soliloquy. I'd read somewhere that Barrymore had played Hamlet on Broadway for something over a hundred consecutive performances, an all-time record. For many years now, he has been widely regarded as the nation's greatest Shakespearean actor. This reputation, along with his best Hollywood films—*Grand Hotel, Dinner at Eight, Twentieth Century,* and *The Sea Beast*—should have placed him at the pinnacle of success.

But he had self-destructed in a heedless life of alcoholic excess and relentless antisocial behavior. Of the many scandalous stories circulating about Barrymore, the one that amused me the most concerned the night he chose to relieve his bladder in the ladies room at an exclusive Beverly Hills restaurant. As he came out of the stall closing his fly, a woman entered and, in a shocked voice, informed him that "This is for the ladies!" Whereupon Barrymore halted, pointed downward, and replied: "And so, madam, is *this!*"

However, here and now, there was nothing amusing about his wasted talent and smashed career. Barrymore's once-handsome face, with its fine aquiline nose, firm chin, and blazing eyes, had won him global fame as "The Great Profile." That face had deteriorated badly; the skin was gray, the cheeks sunken, the eyes lusterless and haunted.

People who knew him had told me that with film and stage offers practically nonexistent, he was spending more and more time here at the Springs, drowning his past in an ocean of booze.

On this particular afternoon, Barrymore was performing for an audience of one: the man I assumed was Alberghetti, who sat at a checkered table directly facing the stage, smiling up at his famous guest. No one else was in the lounge. Just the three of us.

When Barrymore saw me walking toward them, he froze in mid-speech, scowling. "And just who the deuce are you, sir, to intrude on the Bard?"

When I didn't answer, he stumbled from the stage to the table, knocking over a pitcher of water in the process. It spread across the horseshoe-patterned rug.

"I came to see Mr. Alberghetti," I said. "And I apologize for the interruption."

"Ah, it's just as well," he muttered, dropping heavily into a chair. "I've forgotten the rest of the damned speech." He looked up at me with drink-dimmed eyes. Pain was etched in the puffy lines of his face. "I used to know a dozen of Shakespeare's plays by heart . . . every glorious word . . . but now they're all slipping away from me, deserting my mind . . ." His voice trailed off.

"Jack is still a great actor," said Gus Alberghetti, a small round barrel of a man with a vein-reddened face. He wore a neatly pressed beige suit, calfskin boots, and a Western string tie. "Drunk or sober, no one can touch Jack when it comes to sheer talent."

Barrymore shook his head. "That's bloody rot and you know it, Gus. My day is done, dear hearts! The sun has set on Jack Barrymore and henceforth I live only in shadow. Christ help me!"

Following these florid words, he pulled a silver flask from his hip pocket, uncapped it, and tipped it to his lips. He swallowed rapidly.

"All my talent is right here," he said, waving the now-empty flask. "Without this, I cannot live." He swung toward me. "Do you imbibe, sir, if I may be so bold as to inquire?"

"No," I said flatly.

"Then you have absolutely no bloody idea of the hell I'm going through."

"I'm sorry."

He bristled at this. "Sorry? Sorry? By the eternal Christ, sir, don't *ever* be sorry for Jack Barrymore! I reject your bourgeois pity. I may be drunk, sir, but I remain without peer. Who else, pray tell, has played Lear, and Don Juan, and Ahab, and Svengali, and Julius Caesar? Kings, lovers, scoundrels . . . I have mastered them all. I do not require, nor do I accept, your pity." He stood up shakily. "What I *require* is another drink. But first, gentlemen, I must needs to pee."

And he staggered away, weaving between the tables, muttering under his breath.

A sad sight.

With Barrymore gone, I introduced myself to Gus Alberghetti. "I want to ask you about Tink Thompson," I told him.

He shrugged. "What's to ask? I told the cops everything I know. I mean, it's a lousy shame, his finding his wife dead and all. I sure would hate to find *my* wife like that." He took a swig from his coffee mug. "Amy Thompson was first class. Tink used to bring her down here to the Springs a lot. She liked to swim and play golf and ride in the mountains. She liked horses. And people, too. She was always real nice to me. Respectful, you might say. I thought she was a peach."

"Yes," I agreed. "She was wonderful."

"Tink always treated her like a queen," Gus declared. "Couldn't do enough for her. What happened must be tearing him apart."

I leaned across the table, closer to him. "At the time she died, Thompson was singing here at the Lariat?"

"You betcha. I paid an arm and a leg to get him. That mellow voice of his just sends goose bumps up my spine. Some people tell me they prefer Rudy Vallee—but in my opinion, he can't hold a candle to Tink."

"This is your off-season," I said. "Why did you pay so much to hire Thompson when the crowd's not in town?"

"Because he wanted to sing here. I said great. You don't turn down a talent like that. We had an okay crowd, especially considering the season. All around, I made out fine."

"And he did both the early and the late shows?"

"Yeah, right. Both shows. Then I put him up for the night here at the hotel. He drove home yesterday morning."

"Did he seem nervous? Different than usual?"

"No. He was like always. Laughing, kidding around with everybody, telling jokes. Clean ones. No blue stuff for Tink." Then Gus laughed. "He grabbed this big bottle of Scotch from behind the bar and went around the room pouring the stuff into everybody's glass. Didn't matter what they were drinking—vodka or gin or tequila or beer—old Tink topped 'em off with Scotch. He was a riot."

"I'm sure he was," I said.

"There was this little old lady in a wheelchair," Gus continued. "She wanted Tink's autograph. Had a copy of *Collier's* with that article he wrote for 'em, 'A Smile Never Hurts.' "

"Guess I missed that one," I said.

"He not only signed it for her, but he lifted her right out of her chair, set her on the bar top, and sang 'Danny Boy' just for her. I tell ya, that old gal had tears in her eyes when he finished, and so did plenty of other folks."

"A touching story," I said.

"Well . . . that's Tink for you!"

"Were you with him backstage . . . in his dressing room between shows?"

"Sure. A lot of the time. I brought him jelly doughnuts. Tink *loves* jelly doughnuts."

"What was his mood like? Did he seem at all . . . apprehensive? Guilty?"

Alberghetti's eyes took on a hard shine. He stood up. "Are you trying to say that Tink Thompson had something to do with his wife's death?"

"I'm just trying to reach some facts."

Alberghetti's face was flushed. "I want your ass out of my hotel." He pointed toward the bat-wings. "Leave. *Now!*"

I didn't argue with him.

I left.

SEVEN

When I got back to Hollywood, I phoned Hammett to tell him what had happened at the Springs between me and Gus Alberghetti.

"You still think he may be in cahoots with Thompson?" Dash asked me.

"No, not now. I'm sure he told it to me straight. I'm pretty good at reading people. Comes from all my court trials, when I had to know if a witness was lying or telling the truth. Gus thinks Thompson is some kind of saint. Right up there with Jesus. The mere hint from me that Thompson might have been involved in Amy's death sent him up the wall."

"Then I guess you struck out."

"Not exactly," I said. "Gus told me that Thompson *asked* to perform there. Which suggests that he knew Amy would die that night and he wanted to be out of town when she did."

"You're reaching again, Erle. What would Thompson gain by being away?"

"He'd have a perfect alibi, for one thing," I said. "Depending on what killed her."

"Go on."

"Being out of town allowed him to discover the body and play shocked husband. If he'd been home when she died, he'd have a lot of questions to answer."

"Based on your poison theory, right?"

"You don't really think she died of natural causes?"

"We'll *both* know what to think when the autopsy is wrapped up," said Hammett. "Until then, it's all straws in the wind."

I was right. By damn, I was *right!*

Two days later, Harold Edgewater, the Los Angeles county coroner, released the autopsy report. Amy Latimer Thompson had died from poisoning.

The story rated giant headlines:

STAR'S WIFE POISONED
Coroner Finds Amy Thompson
Victim of Possible Homicide

The report was quoted at length. Evidence collected from the Thompson house by the police had included an opened bottle of Youth-O-Vim, manufactured by Dr. Elias Favershim Enterprises. The tall brown bottle that contained the thick brewer's-yeast-and-herbs Youth-O-Vim formula had also included an ingredient never intended by Dr. Favershim: oleander extract. The postmortem examination revealed that Amy had ingested approximately a half-cup of the Youth-O-Vim-and-oleander mixture several hours before Tink Thompson had returned home. The coroner was quoted:

> Oleander is a common flowering plant that grows in profusion throughout southern California. Every part of the oleander plant is toxic, including the fragrance and the roots. In small doses, oleander can cause abdominal pain, nausea, vomiting, and erratic blood pressure. However, in the case of Mrs. Thompson, a substantial amount of oleander was in-

gested. This triggered massive internal injuries, which culminated in a fatal heart attack.

Of course, Thompson feigned shock at the report. According to the news account, when he was questioned at police headquarters about the source of the poison, he denied any knowledge of it. He also professed no knowledge of anyone who would have wanted to murder his wife—a woman who was, as he pointed out, immensely popular throughout the world. In Thompson's quoted words, "Amy had no enemies. This is all an unbelievable nightmare."

The police let him go, with instructions not to leave Los Angeles County without permission. They also questioned Thompson's servants: the maid, cook, gardener, and handyman, as well as the nanny who had taken care of the Thompson child prior to "the tragic accident that resulted in the boy's death." Each of the household employees vigorously denied having had anything to do with Amy Thompson's death.

The article speculated: was it suicide? Could Mrs. Thompson have mixed the lethal dosage herself? This was deemed highly unlikely by the police, but authorities were "thoroughly investigating the entire case."

Thompson remained a prime suspect. The husband always does in a family murder.

I phoned Dash. "Did you read it?" I asked.

"I read it. And it looks as if you were on target, Erle. Death by poison. I guess Thompson *is* dumber than I figured."

"I'd like to get my hands around his throat!" I said, my voice heated with anger. "The bastard actually thought he could get away with it. He obviously hoped the stuff wouldn't show up in an autopsy."

Hammett agreed. "And there's another strong motive you didn't mention the other day. If he'd allowed her to divorce him, he'd have lost half of his fortune under the California community property law."

"Uh-huh, I thought of that," I said. "Also his alibi is no damn good. He could have put the poison in that bottle before leaving town, since he knew she'd be drinking from it in the next twenty-four hours. So the fact that he was at the Springs is meaningless."

"I'd say it's just a matter of time before they charge him with murder," declared Hammett.

"I'll go to the police," I said. "I'll tell them everything that Amy revealed to me about their marriage, and how Thompson was ultimately responsible for his son's death. And about the letters to his mistress in Santa Barbara. Blow the lid off his saintly reputation. It'll give the cops plenty to work with."

"Yeah," said Dash, "all that should help put him away. But before you talk to anybody, we should see Ray Chandler on the poison angle. Get squared away on the oleander. He's an ace on poisons. Really knows the subject."

"Good idea," I said. "Ray's always home, so let's go over now."

"I heard he's moved again," Dash said. "You have his new address?"

I gave it to him—a bungalow court in Santa Monica—and Hammett agreed to meet me there in an hour.

Raymond Chandler is hard to keep track of; he once admitted to me, with a degree of embarrassment, that he and his wife Cissy had moved nine times in the last ten years. Ray finds something wrong with every house or apartment he lives in. Too noisy. Or too windy. Or too many chatty neighbors. Or too much traffic in the area. Or the garage is too small for his Duesenberg. Or there's not enough shelf space in the kitchen. Or the landlord is an impossible idiot. Something.

Always something.

Like an ethereal flower, Cissy drifts from place to place with Ray. She has been almost a total recluse in the years I've known them— a smart, strong-minded, stubborn woman who refuses to socialize. She spends most of her time in their bedroom reading the classics or

69

listening to concert music. She loves to play the piano and is very talented at it.

Cissy is much older than Ray, and she's become self-conscious about their age gap. Ray thinks this is nonsense. He loves her, heart and soul—and age be damned. Ray doesn't mind staying home with Cissy. A natural loner, he enjoys solitude, communicating with the outside world mainly by correspondence. He'll sit up half the night writing to people all over the country. If Chandler likes you, he's warm and loyal. If he doesn't like you, he can be short-tempered and abrasive.

In my case, luckily, he likes me.

Driving to his latest abode in Santa Monica, I thought back to our first contact three years ago. He'd written me a letter, in care of my publisher, congratulating me on Perry Mason (I'd had four Masons out by then) and telling me that he had learned to plot pulp fiction after making a detailed breakdown and analysis of a Rex Kane novelette of mine. He wanted to acknowledge his debt.

We became instant friends.

Ray was born in Chicago, but he was educated in England and spent most of the early part of his life there. He didn't know a thing about the American pulp magazines until he discovered *Black Mask* in 1933. By then, he'd been kicked out of the southern California oil business for some high jinks involving "booze and broads" and had been forced to find another way to make a living.

He found the pulps—and Joe Shaw printed Ray's first story late in '33. Chandler has sold every one he's written since then, but it takes him forever to finish a novelette, and pulp writing pays off only if you're productive. In a single year, I had fifty-five novelettes and twenty-two short stories printed in the pulps. Ray's a perfectionist. He can't let go of a story until every word is as perfect as he can make it. Hell, I've seen him break into a sweat over punctuation.

Because he works so slowly, he's made very little money over the last four years. I know he has some oil stock that helps take up the slack, but things have been tough for him. Once he breaks out with some novels, I think he'll do fine, but so far, the novels are still in his head.

I'm very fond of the guy. He's decent, loyal, and dependable. He'll put his life on the line for a friend; he'd done that for me and Dash. But he'd be a hell of a lot more successful as a writer if he'd just learn to relax and let the words flow.

I pulled up in front of the Riness Court Apartments on 17th Street in Santa Monica. A whitewashed arch led through an iron gate into a circular courtyard surrounded by a group of small, one-bedroom bungalows. A new brick wall at the rear of the property separated the court from its neighbors. The yard and bushes were all neatly trimmed and the bungalows had been freshly painted; everything looked clean and inviting.

I walked under the arch, along a circle of white cement to Number 6, and pressed the buzzer. I was early and had arrived ahead of Hammett. As I waited for Ray to respond, I felt a twinge of guilt. Maybe I should have phoned in advance, since nobody likes people barging in unexpectedly, but Ray hates the sound of a ringing telephone. I'd phoned him many times in the past, and it took him a while to admit how much a ringing phone bothers him. Calls it "a personal assault." I understand, because I'm that way myself. Telephones are a scourge of modern society. Anyhow, Ray finally told me: "Whenever you feel like popping by, don't phone; just come on over."

Yet every time I'd taken him at his word, he'd seemed annoyed by the intrusion. Once I was inside, he'd warm up and be glad to see me. Actually, Ray's life is pretty lonely and he welcomes the chance to talk to a friend.

When Chandler opened the door, he looked sour, as usual. Somehow, he always reminds me of a disgruntled bank manager, with his owlish glasses and solemn eyes. He was wearing a short-sleeved summer shirt and rumpled gray trousers.

71

He stared at me, unsmiling, then said: "I *knew* you'd show up today. Step in."

I entered the bungalow, which smelled of fresh paint. The place had obviously just been renovated. Everything was in off-white.

"How did you know I'd be coming over?"

"Dream," he said. "I trust dreams. They often foretell the future. In this one, you flew over here to see me. I can't remember why."

"Flew?"

"That's right. I dream in Technicolor. You had big feathery yellow wings. Otherwise, you looked normal. You know how dreams are."

"I know."

"Joe Shaw was in it, too," declared Chandler, "but he didn't have any wings."

We went into the living room and I sat down in a large upholstered armchair. Cissy was nowhere in sight. Probably reading a Great Book in the bedroom.

"We keep most of our furniture in storage," Ray told me. "Because we move so much. Someday we'll buy a house and settle down. I'm beginning to feel like a bedouin. Always changing tents."

His dour expression had softened. "Care for some orange juice?"

"No. I just want to talk."

"About what?" He sat down on the sofa, and Taki, his black Persian cat, jumped on his lap. Chandler began stroking the fur on Taki's neck.

"Did you read today's paper?" I asked him.

He shook his head. "I quit reading the papers. They depress me. Too much bad news."

"Okay," I said. "I'll tell you what you need to know."

And I did. All about Amy and me, and what she'd revealed about Thompson, and about her murder, and how I was sure Thompson was the killer.

"How did she die?" Ray asked. "Gun? Knife? How?"

"Oleander poisoning. Which is why I came to see you. Dash tells me you're an expert on poisons. He's due here any minute."

As if on cue, the buzzer announced Hammett. Taki leaped off Ray's lap and scampered for the kitchen.

"She hates the buzzer," said Chandler, going to let Dash in.

They murmured something to each other at the door and then Ray led him into the living room. When Dash accepted Ray's offer of orange juice, I said, what the hell, I'd have some, too.

Chandler brought out a tray from the kitchen. Peanut-butter cookies and a pitcher of freshly squeezed orange juice. We all had some.

"How's Cissy?" Dash asked.

"Fine," said Ray. "She's in the bedroom reading *Great Expectations*, her favorite Dickens. She's read it three times. Finds something new with each reading. Says it's inspirational."

"I've filled Ray in on why we're here," I told Hammett.

Dash looked around the room. "Neat little joint."

"It'll do," nodded Chandler. "Better than our last place in Culver City. Our backyard neighbor played Dixieland jazz day and night. I don't mind Dixieland—but not coming at me day and night. Got so I couldn't get any work done."

"I had a neighbor once who practiced the trumpet," said Hammett. "Used to drive me nuts."

"We keep moving back to Santa Monica," Ray said. He sighed, munching on a cookie. "For a pulp mystery writer, I suppose this is the place to be. Plenty of corruption to write about. In my stories, I call Santa Monica 'Bay City.' My detectives are always getting worked over by Bay City cops."

"Yeah, Santa Monica cops are snake-mean," said Hammett.

"I've got a novel in mind that deals with political corruption," said Ray. "My title is *Law Is Where You Buy It*. My only problem is finding the time to write the book. I have to keep grinding out pulp stories for rent money."

"I'm working on a play," said Hammett. "About some kids that get lost on an island. But I can't get past the first act."

"I thought we came here to talk about poison," I said, attempting to get the conversation back on track.

Chandler smiled. "A fascinating subject." Whereupon he launched into a clinical description of the effects of a viper bite on the curator of the Chicago Zoo. Then he told us that some cases of morphia poisoning can be cured by repeatedly washing out the stomach, and that arsenic is stored in the liver and can circulate from there to the heart.

I cut into his discourse by asking: "What I want to know is, how can one bottle of health elixir contain enough oleander to cause a severe heart attack? You can't stuff roots and leaves into a bottle."

"True enough," Chandler answered. "It would have to be reduced to a liquid form. If you took a cooking pot and filled it with oleander leaves, then added water, and you boiled the leaves for a few hours, adding more water as needed, the resulting liquid would be lethal. I assume that's the method Thompson used. *If* he's the guilty one."

"That bastard's the one all right," I said tightly. "I'm a hundred-percent sure of it."

Chandler shrugged. "From what you've told me, he fits as the killer."

Then he elaborated on oleander: "The plant produces a profusion of innocent-looking pink-and-white flowers that are potentially lethal. Death can result from simply *smelling* the flowers on a regular basis. The smoke from burning oleander is deadly. And boiled down, in concentrated form, oleander is as effective as a bullet to the brain."

"If the stuff is so dangerous, how come there's so much of it around?" Hammett asked.

"Because most homeowners consider it no more than a nice-looking yard plant. It needs practically no water or maintenance, and it grows fast into a thick green bush that serves as either a windbreak or a privacy screen. People have no idea of what this plant is really like."

Hammett had been right; when it comes to poisons, Chandler is an ace.

Of course I attended Amy's funeral. Thank God I received an invitation. Evidently some secretary had gone through Amy's address book and sent invitations to the people who had been part of her personal life.

And of course her funeral was a major media event. The church in Beverly Hills was surrounded by a sea of fans, curiosity seekers, death freaks, and news reporters. It was more like the Academy Awards than a funeral, with limos arriving and celebrities being guided through the crowd into the church: Clark Gable, Charlie Chaplin, Spencer Tracy, William Powell, Bob Hope, Carole Lombard, Douglas Fairbanks, Eddie Cantor, Katherine Hepburn—each entering with solemn dignity, ignoring the popping flashbulbs and the fans shouting for autographs.

Inside, I sat in a pew at the rear of the church. Chandler and Hammett were not in attendance; they hadn't known Amy. By the time I had moved to Hollywood, she was married to Thompson and out of my life.

Thompson himself, his parents and his two brothers, along with other Thompson family members, sat in a reserved pew facing the flower-draped coffin. I was getting my first look at Thompson's two brothers, Len and Freddie; they were big, square-shouldered fellows with hard faces. They resembled a pair of thugs from a Warner Brothers gangster film and had none of the handsome smoothness of their famous brother.

On the other side of the aisle from the Thompson family, in another reserved pew, sat Amy's few remaining relatives, none of whom I recognized.

A portly Episcopal priest, his bald head gleaming in the candlelight, stood at the pulpit. He talked about Amy, describing her as "a rare flower plucked all too soon from the garden of life." He was certain that heaven was now enriched by her presence, and he eulogized her as "a splendid helpmeet to her beloved husband and a paragon of virtue to all."

Then the priest stepped aside and Thompson rose to deliver a tear-drenched tribute in which he claimed to have been blessed with "the finest wife a man could ever have at his side on life's tempestuous journey."

His overcooked performance, broken by chest-racking sobs, was prime schmaltz, as phony as a wooden nickel. However, the crowd bought it and sobbed right along with him.

After the tributes ended, a long line of mourners filed slowly past the open coffin, but I didn't join them. I had no desire to stare down at Amy's dead face. I wanted to remember her in life, not in death. Approaching her coffin was beyond my emotional capacity.

I *did* go to the burial at Oak Hills Cemetery in the San Fernando Valley, standing under a hot afternoon sun at the verge of the grave site to pay my final respects. The tears came then, and it was difficult for me to breathe knowing that I would never again hear her voice, lose myself in the depths of her eyes, or hold her in my arms.

I deliberately avoided looking at Thompson during the burial service. I didn't want my anger and hatred to show. Not here and now. There would be a better time to make him pay for his outrageous crime.

After the service ended and I was walking back to my car, I felt someone grip my left shoulder and spin me around.

Thompson was glaring at me. "I had Mark Silver, the private detective, follow Amy," he said. "I read his report this morning. She was at your house. She stayed with you all night." His mouth twisted. "You slept with my wife!"

"That's right," I admitted. "She asked to stay with me that night. She never loved you, Thompson. And you never loved her."

"That's a damned lie!" he snapped. "What makes you think—"

"She told me all about you," I cut in. "Your marriage was a sham from the beginning. Amy was determined to divorce you. I'm a lawyer and I agreed to help her."

"I'm going to fix you for this, you bastard!" His eyes blazed. "Nobody makes a fool out of me!"

"What movie is that line from?"

Thompson grabbed the front of my shirt and pulled me close to him, his balled right fist raised. His face was flushed with rage.

But at this point, he realized that our heated exchange had drawn a cluster of witnesses. Nervously, Thompson let go of me and stepped back with a forced smile. "Another time, Gardner."

"See you in court," I answered as I got into my car.

He was still smiling as I drove away.

EIGHT

My plan for the day after Amy's funeral was to go to the police and tell them everything I knew about Thompson—including the letters, photos, and notes that related to his Montecito mistress. Unfortunately, I didn't have these items in my possession, but the woman in Montecito was still alive and could probably be made to admit her involvement with Thompson. The police should certainly be told about her. They'd find a way to get at the truth once they were armed with my information.

I had eaten lunch and was ready to leave for police headquarters when the phone rang. I answered, and a brisk voice on the line said, "This is Walter Winchell."

"The newscaster?"

"You got it," said Winchell.

I'd read his newspaper column, and knew that his national radio show had a huge listening audience. Known for his staccato delivery and exclusive stories about the high and mighty, Winchell was a potent force in the news.

"I'm going on the air with a hot scoop and I need a quote from you."

"I'm part of your story?"

He chuckled. "You sure as hell are."

"What's this about?"

"Amy Thompson's will," he said. "It was read aloud early this morning in her attorney's office."

"She told me that Thompson persuaded her to make out a will immediately after their marriage," I said. "It leaves everything to him in the event of her death. So now he's due to collect, right?"

"Wrong," said Winchell. "The early will is no longer valid. She prepared a new one with her own attorney the day before she died. And you're named in it."

"*I'm* in Amy's will?"

"You sure are. Erle Stanley Gardner is sole beneficiary. You get everything, chum. Assets, stocks and bonds, even her jewelry. Plus— and this is the cherry on the soda—*plus* her half of Tink Thompson's fortune under California's community property law."

I sat down, stunned. "I had no idea that I would be named in Amy's will," I told him. "No idea at all."

"Maybe not," Winchell said. "But a lot of people are gonna believe otherwise. Which puts you square on the hot seat."

"What do you mean?"

"Figure it out for yourself. The lady gets poisoned right after she makes out a new will, and you end up with all of her money. I'm talking *motive*, Mr. Gardner. A motive for murder."

"Go to hell!" I snapped, slamming down the phone.

I sat there at my desk, numb with shock. Why would Amy have done such a thing? Then I recalled what she'd said to me on the last night we were together—about having no one else in her life now that her parents and her son were dead, about how she cared only for me. That was why she had changed her will, as a gesture of her love, but of course she hadn't anticipated that Thompson was going to kill her.

I was sure he hadn't known about the new will. He probably assumed that the first will was in force—and that he'd inherit everything at her death. He'd undoubtedly been as surprised as I was to find out that the first will had been superseded.

This second will changed the equation. Winchell was right: from a legal standpoint, the probable motive for Amy's murder had now shifted.

From Tink Thompson to me.

I reacted to a sudden pounding at the front door. A harsh voice from the porch shouted: "Open up! It's the police."

The hot seat.

I was on it for sure at the headquarters of the Beverly Hills Police Department, placed under formal arrest for the murder of Amy Latimer Thompson. I had been photographed, fingerprinted, and thoroughly searched. My personal items had been put into a large envelope and taken away, along with my tie, belt, and shoelaces.

The Homicide Division interrogation room was stark and featureless, its walls and ceiling painted an oppressive gray. The room had one door, no windows, and a standard two-way mirror mounted on the far wall. A timeworn, government-issue wooden table sat in the center of the room, with four straight-back wooden chairs surrounding it. I was seated in one of them, being grilled by a trio of plainclothes dicks. The lad in charge was named Lotcher, and he looked tough enough to chew bricks. He kept leaning into my face, feeding me his foul cigar smoke, trying to force me to confess.

"Make it easy on yourself, Gardner," he was saying. "Just tell us the truth."

I'd *been* telling them the truth for the past hour, about how Amy had come to me to help with her intended divorce and about what kind of man Thompson really was, but all the things I had to say rolled right past them.

A mistress in Montecito? Ridiculous! They'd searched the Thompson house and had found no letters, photos, or shorthand notes. That's because Thompson has obviously destroyed them, I declared.

Had I ever *seen* these items? Well, no, but Amy had intended to bring them to me. Oh, *sure* she did.

And the idea that Thompson verbally brutalized his wife, or that he was jealous of his three-year-old son . . . utter nonsense.

And when I told them that I was certain that Thompson had killed Amy, they laughed like hyenas. Lotcher began yelling at me. I had a helluva nerve, trying to pin the blame for *my* crime on Tink Thompson, an all-around sterling individual who contributed heavily to police charities every year. No finer man walked God's earth—and everyone knew what a great marriage he had. Why, the poor fellow was *shattered* by his wife's death.

As for me, they had more than motive to tie me to the crime. They had a report from Mark Silver, Hollywood's most famous private investigator, that had been turned over to them by Thompson. The report proved that Amy had recently spent a full night at my home. Not only was I conducting a secret adulterous affair with Thompson's wife, but I had obviously convinced Amy to draft a new will, naming me as her sole beneficiary. Once the will was signed, I had killed her, hoping that the poison I'd used would not be discovered. My lust for riches had made me take a stupid risk. I was not only a murderer, I was a fool. They'd already talked to Ida Favershim at the Silver Gate. She had told them about my visit and about my interest in Youth-O-Vim, a product that Amy Thompson conscientiously took every day.

The police were confident they had an airtight case against me. The D.A. had done a radio interview, declaring that "We have our man. And he will pay for his crime. Our office will push for the death sentence."

Lotcher put it a bit more colorfully: "We have your ass in a sling."

"I didn't kill her," I repeated over and over. "I loved Amy."

"What you loved was her money," snarled Lotcher. "Give us a confession and things will go a lot easier for you, chum. If you don't confess, you're gonna be sorry. *Real* sorry."

As he said this, he was tapping a leather blackjack against his open palm. His eyes told me he'd enjoy using it.

I felt like one of Chandler's luckless private eyes in Bay City; these boys were ready to work me over.

"Use that sap on me," I said tightly, "and *you'll* be the one who's sorry. I was a practicing attorney for more than twenty years and I know exactly how to deal with sadistic thugs like you. Start any rough stuff with me, and you'd better go all the way. You'd better kill me— because if you don't, I'll have you hauled into court on assault charges."

I was running a bluff in the hope that they'd back off, that while they might enjoy working me over, they wouldn't dare risk killing me. But I wasn't sure about that, which is why I was sweating through my clothes. I felt like a pig on a spit.

Lotcher glared at me for a long moment, grunted sourly, and slipped the blackjack into his hip pocket. Then he turned to one of the others. "Get this creep outa my sight."

And I was hustled from the room.

I was allowed to make one phone call, and that call went to Hammett. I was to be arraigned in court at noon the next day. As an attorney, I was well aware of the fact that bail is next to impossible to get in a murder case. But there are exceptions to everything. With Tomas unable to access my bank account, I needed a lot of instant cash.

Dash had heard about my arrest over the radio and he readily agreed to post whatever sum was needed. He'd get the money from his bank first thing in the morning and bring it along to court. I could pay him back later.

"I just got a fat check for the Tarzan job," he told me. "And my agent has set me up on a quick polish of a tits-and-sword epic over at Universal. So I'm loaded right now. I'll bring along plenty of jack."

"Really appreciate this, Dash."

"Hey, any time a pal of mine gets jugged, I figure the least I can do is bail him out. Have they got a strong case against you?"

"They think so."

"You'll beat the rap," declared Hammett. "I'd lay odds on it."

"Your faith is inspiring," I said, trying not to sound negative, "but unless we can nail Thompson . . ."

I let the sentence trail off.

"We'll find a way to get the bastard," Hammett said. "What did the cops say when you told them what you know about him?"

"They think I'm trying to drag poor Tink into the case to save my own skin. They don't believe me. How could I say these terrible things about such a great guy? Hell, the police chief is a personal friend of his."

"So you got nowhere with what Amy told you?"

"Yeah, that's where I got. Nowhere."

"I talked to Chandler just before you called. He wants to be in on this."

"There's nothing he can do."

"Well, he's gonna show up tomorrow at your arraignment. Says Cissy is also worried about you."

"It's good to have people who care," I said, meaning it. "Remind me not to complain the next time you ask me to judge a snake-dancing contest."

Hammett chuckled. "See you in court."

"Yeah . . . in court."

The Beverly Hills courtroom was jammed with spectators and reporters when I was led from my cell to face Judge Zebediah B. Carter. The papers had dubbed me "The Poison Slayer"; I had already been tried and convicted by the media. One of my neighbors in the Hollywood Hills (a man I had never met) gave an interview in which he described me as "definitely abnormal" and "more than a little odd." God knows, the photo of me they ran on the front page of the papers fitted the description. I remember when it was taken. By a camper pal of mine who no doubt sold it to the press. It was during a desert outing just after Nat and I got married. I had discovered a baby rattler in our tent, grabbed a gun from our camper, and was going after the damn snake when the picture was taken. I looked wide-eyed and dangerous, and definitely abnormal.

Nat had written me a note to say she couldn't be at my arraignment, but that her thoughts were with me.

Judge Carter used his gavel to call the court to order, scowling down at me with open hostility. Guess he'd been reading the morning papers.

The words "hanging judge" crossed my mind. With his muttonchop whiskers and flowing mustache, His Honor would have been right at home on the bench in old Tombstone.

It was odd and unsettling to be back in court on the wrong side of the law. I'd had dreams about being the accused, but the dreams had always come out okay. I was always set free. Now, in real life, that prospect seemed dim. The hard-set line of his jaw told me I'd get no sympathy from Zebediah Carter.

When he asked me who was representing me as counsel, I said I was representing myself, and that as a practicing attorney for many years, I had a clear understanding of court procedure. He didn't seem to like the answer, but accepted my plea of "not guilty."

During the arraignment process, I saw Hammett enter the courtroom. He gave me a high sign and settled into an aisle seat. It was comforting to know he was there.

The time had come to determine the matter of whether I would be allowed bail; I requested that it be granted.

"Request duly noted," said Carter. He turned to the prosecuting attorney, a fierce-eyed little man in a pin-striped business suit. "Do you have an objection to bail in this case?"

"I most certainly do, Your Honor," said the little man, springing to his feet like a jack-in-the-box. He pointed at me in a sweeping, dramatic gesture. "This man stands accused of the heinous crime of cold-blooded murder. The people will prove that he is responsible for the horrific death of an innocent woman in the prime of her life. He is a public menace and should not be allowed to roam the streets. I most strongly and urgently request that the court withhold bail and keep this man incarcerated, where he belongs."

The judge nodded toward me. "Your response, Mr. Gardner."

"I would point out to the court that I have no previous criminal record. I am, in fact, a respected citizen with an unsullied reputation. I have never been arrested in the past, and I am most certainly not a menace to the public. It is obvious that I pose no threat to anyone. Therefore, I request that bail be granted."

Judge Carter pursed his lips, combing the fingers of his right hand through his mustache. His eyes were hooded, like an angry hawk's, and I had little hope that he would respond favorably to my plea. The thought of spending my future days and nights in a jail cell chilled my blood.

Which is when Ray Chandler stepped forward from the back of the courtroom, where I hadn't noticed him. "I would like a word with Your Honor in chambers," he said. "With Mr. Gardner present."

It was a totally unorthodox request, and I was certain that Judge Carter would sternly reject it.

He stared at Chandler, then rapped his gavel. "The court," he said, "will take a brief recess."

Chandler gripped my shoulder in a gesture of "I'm-here-for-you" friendship as we walked behind the black-robed judge into his chambers. But once the door had closed behind us, the solemn mood evaporated.

Chandler directed a beaming smile at Carter. "Skippers!"

Carter returned the smile in spades. "Boogles!"

And, to my astonishment, they threw their arms around each other in a crushing, prolonged bear hug.

"Great heavens!" exclaimed the beaming Carter. "How wonderful to see you here, old friend! It's been too many years."

Chandler turned to me, still smiling. "Zeb and I went to Dulwich together. In England. In those days, everyone called him 'Skippers.' "

"And they called you 'Boogles,' " said Carter, the glint of nostalgia brightening his eyes.

Again, they embraced.

Although he'd been born in America, I knew that Chandler had attended an upper-class English school into his late teens. I had forgotten the name, but it was Dulwich. Ray never liked to discuss those early years when he'd lived in Europe as a displaced American. He had told me once: "I was miserable. A British-based schoolboy with an American passport. I felt like a misfit, suspended between cultures and countries."

But there was no misery expressed between these two former classmates as they nostalgically recalled their Dulwich days.

"Remember that skinny string bean of a fellow who taught us Greek?" asked Chandler. "The one who kept losing his glasses. He'd stumble around the room, bumping into desks. Blind as a cave bat."

Carter nodded vigorously. "We called him 'Longshanks.' I heard he married the librarian, Miss Cladd, and that they'd moved to Ireland."

"Right," declared Chandler. "To Dublin. They had five children and he became a university professor. Well-respected, I was told."

"Whatever happened to old Hosey, the one who—"

"Died on a ski trail in Switzerland," cut in Chandler. "Freak avalanche. Buried him and his whole party."

"He'd talk for hours about maths," nodded Carter. "Differential equations were a real passion of his. Poor ol' Hosey. Not a bad chap, really."

"Not at all," agreed Chandler.

"Did you ever get into teaching?" asked Carter. "I understood that's what you wanted to do."

"Oh, no," Chandler corrected him. "I'd make a poor teacher. Just don't have the patience for it. Trying to control all those rowdy students . . . not to my taste at all."

"What, then? What did you get into? Forgive my bad manners for asking, Boogles, but we're in America now, and Americans ask each other this sort of thing all the time."

"No offense, old chap. I'm a writer. But the writing I did in Europe was sheer drivel."

"Now that you mention it," said Carter, "I seem to recall you had some verse published in the *Gazette*."

"Deplorable rubbish," nodded Chandler. "I wrote hopelessly pretentious essays, poems, and book reviews for the *Academy*, the *Spectator*, and the *Westminster Gazette*. I can still remember some of those titles . . . 'The Tears That Sweeten Woe' . . . 'The Rose-Leaf Romance' . . . and 'Time Shall Not Die.' Just terrible dreck. I shudder to think of it."

"Are you still writing?"

"Yes, and I'm finally getting the hang of it. I didn't do anything worthwhile until I got out of the oil business here in southern California and began to write pulp detective stories. Have you ever heard of *Black Mask* magazine?"

Carter shook his head. "Can't say that I have."

"Well, doesn't matter. The point is, I'm finally turning out some halfway-decent prose." He paused, grinning. "And someday I might even make some halfway-decent money out of it."

They both chuckled.

"One thing I'm grateful for," said Chandler, seating himself on a black-leather couch while Carter settled into the wing chair behind his desk. "I got a damned good education at Dulwich. Far better than what I would have ended up with over here."

I sat down next to Chandler on the couch. The room was full of sepia-toned hunting prints and framed wall photos of Carter, in full sportsman's regalia, rifle in hand, posing with a variety of dead animals. A stuffed deer head loomed over his desk.

Shooting helpless animals really isn't sport. I often wonder what would happen if the deer had rifles and lived in offices. They might have Judge Carter's stuffed head on the wall.

"I know you spent your early years in Oklahoma with your parents," said Chandler, "but I never was clear on what brought you to Dulwich."

"My father took me to London with him when I was twelve," said Carter. "When he returned to Oklahoma a year later, I stayed on with his sister—my Aunt Ella. She's lived in London since before I was born. It was Aunt Ella who sent me to Dulwich."

"When did you return to the U.S.?" asked Chandler.

"Not for several years after Dulwich," Carter said. "I went up to Oxford and read jurisprudence at Balliol. I got my First and stayed on for a B.C.L., but then I wanted to come back home. I needed to reconnect with my American roots. I thought of looking you up when I got back, but I had no idea where you might be."

"I've been in Los Angeles since nineteen-nineteen," said Chandler. "A stint with the Canadian Highlanders took me away during the war, but I've been in L.A. ever since. I've grown rather fond of the place."

"Ummm," nodded Carter. "Unfortunate, how old school chums drift out of one another's life."

Chandler put a hand on my shoulder. "This fellow is a dear friend, Skippers, and I would appreciate it if you could see your way clear to grant him bail. I can personally vouch for him."

Carter pursed his lips again, deep in thought. "If you vouch for him, Boogles, I'll do it."

Chandler stood up, raising his right fist, the little finger extended. "Dulwich forever!"

"Dulwich!" echoed Carter solemnly, standing to make the same gesture. "Forever!"

And I had my bail.

NINE

Back in the courtroom, Judge Carter set my bail at $5,000—which outraged the D.A.'s people, and which Dash promptly paid in cash.

Before I left the building, I phoned my daughter in the San Francisco Bay area.

"Grace?"

"Oh, Pop! It's so good to hear your voice. All this in the papers . . . about you being arrested. I was so worried! When I phoned your house, Tomas said you were in jail and couldn't take any calls."

"I was arraigned this morning," I told her. "The judge granted bail, so I'm free until the trial."

"But you didn't do anything!"

"It happens all the time. Remember all the clients I defended who were innocent?"

"I remember," Grace said, "but I didn't think my father would someday be one of them!"

"I didn't kill anyone, and I'm sure I'll be able to prove it."

"Mom's been worried, too," she declared.

"Tell Nat I'm fine and that everything is going to work out. Make sure she understands."

"I will. I promise."

"Are things good with you?"

"Oh, yes. I've got a wonderful marriage, Pop. Al and I really love each other."

"Great," I said. "Well, I'd better go. I wanted to call you as soon as possible, so I'm on a public phone here in the courthouse. Dash Hammett and Ray Chandler are waiting for me. They're good pals. They helped me make bail."

"Take care," Grace said, "and let me know what happens."

"I will. 'Bye, honey. I love you."

"I love you too, Pop."

I walked out of the building with Hammett and Chandler and we all climbed into Ray's Duesenberg.

"We need to celebrate your freedom," Dash said to me. "Let's have lunch at Musso's."

"Great," I said, and Chandler nodded agreement.

On the way to Hollywood, we talked about the case. Mostly about how my being named in Amy's new will took all the heat off Thompson as the real killer.

"He must have had a fit when he got that detective's report about her spending the night with you," said Dash. "Guys like that figure it's jake for them to play footsie with other women, but if they catch their wives at the same game, they go nuts."

"Amy's will gave him the chance to lay her murder on you," said Ray. "For him, it was a bonus he hadn't expected. Once you're convicted, her money goes right back in his pocket."

"I don't like the 'once you're convicted' part," I said.

"I just wish she'd had the chance to pass those letters and photos she talked about over to you," said Dash.

"Yeah," I said. "The cops refused to even *consider* the possibility that he has a mistress in Santa Barbara."

"Thompson must have found them when he went through Amy's things," said Ray.

"And burned them," I said. "In a possible homicide, the cops always search the premises. If the letters had survived, the cops would have found 'em."

"Were you the only one Amy confided in?" asked Chandler, sliding the big Duesy through traffic with ease and assurance. We were on Sunset Boulevard, heading east toward Highland Avenue, and the top was down. The sun felt warm and comforting and the sky had never looked so blue. Being in jail tends to sharpen your perceptions.

"She mentioned one other person," I said. "Supposed to be her only close friend."

"Who's that?" Ray asked.

"Can't recall her first name, but she's married to Jack Winniger, the radio comedian."

"I've met her," said Hammett. "Beth Winniger. She was with Jack at a dinner party in Brentwood a few weeks ago. Very fetching lady."

"Amy told me that Beth knows the whole story of her marriage, what Thompson's really like, and about their son's death."

"We should talk to her," Dash said.

"After lunch," I said. "I'm starved. And nobody cooks sand dabs the way they do at Musso's."

"Fine," nodded Dash. "After the sand dabs."

The Winnigers had a beach house in Malibu. Since Hammett knew them, he phoned from Musso's to ask if we might drop by to talk about Amy. Beth told him fine; Jack was in New York doing a show, but she'd be happy to see us. She would leave the highway gate open.

"It's all set," Hammett said. "She wants to talk to us. Beth's been reading about your arrest in the papers, and she listened to the program Winchell did on the case."

"That bastard," I said. "He all but accused me of killing Amy. I'm glad I didn't hear his damn program."

"Winchell's a news vulture," said Ray. "He enjoys seeing people bleed."

"I can imagine what he said about me."

"Better you don't," said Hammett.

We reached the Winniger house by mid-afternoon. The sun was painting the Pacific with gold fire, and a brisk sea breeze tossed white spray off the breaking waves.

The gate was open and we walked down a stone pathway that led to the house. Beth Winniger was waiting for us at the front door. As Hammett had said, she was fetching. About Amy's age, she wore a light sunshine-yellow summer dress, and her dark hair was tied back with a matching ribbon.

After Hammett introduced everyone, Beth led us into the house, to the living room. Beamed ceilings. A large stone fireplace with a feathered war bonnet on the mantel. Navajo rugs on the floor, and Hopi kachina dolls on glass shelves. An Indian blanket was draped over the sofa, and the tall bronze figure of a fighting warrior stood next to the fireplace.

"That's Crazy Horse," Beth told us. "The Sioux chief who defeated Custer at the Little Bighorn. And he *deserved* what he got!"

"Who . . . Crazy Horse?" I asked.

"No, George Armstrong Custer. He was an utterly ruthless man, a warped egomaniac who killed Indians in order to gain political power. He wanted to be president, and was sure that a decisive victory over the Sioux and Cheyenne at the Little Bighorn would be his key to Washington. Their blood would win him the White House."

"A lot of people look at Custer as a hero," I said.

Beth shook her head. "Not if they know the real man. He was anything but heroic. Oh, sure, he led all those wild charges in the Civil War, but that was for personal glory. A hero helps others. Custer thought only of himself."

"Didn't he show courage by leading his men into battle?"

"That was foolhardy, not courageous," she said firmly. "Because of his reckless action at the Little Bighorn, more than two hundred men of the Seventh Cavalry were sacrificed. There was no need for it. Custer was directly to blame for their deaths."

"I take it you think the Indians got a raw deal," said Hammett.

"Our government has broken *every* treaty we made with the Indian nations," declared Beth. "We slaughtered the buffalo they depended upon, sold them rotgut whiskey, stole their land, killed their women and children, and forced them onto reservations, where we fed them poisoned meat. Yes, I'd say they got a raw deal. *Very* raw."

"Speaking of poison," I said, "I assume you know that's what I've been accused of: poisoning your friend. Can we talk about Amy?"

"Of course." Beth spread her hands. "I apologize for my fervor; I always seem to get carried away where the Indians are concerned. Jack and I are both horrified over what this country did to them. Please forgive me. I didn't mean to climb on my soapbox."

"We can appreciate your feelings," I said. "No apology is necessary."

"Amy was very dear to me," declared Beth Winniger. "I still can't believe she's gone. We were so close. Like sisters. She was an extraordinary woman."

"When did you meet her?" asked Hammett.

"In January of nineteen thirty-three," Beth said. "Jack was performing at Ciro's, doing his comedy act there, and Thompson came with Amy. They had arrived in style—in Tink's Rolls Silver Ghost—and had been taken to the best table, right up front. They were treated like royalty. After the show, they both came backstage to see Jack, and that's when I met Amy. She was beautiful. That night she wore an expensive beaded gown from Paris. It was exquisite. Tink always made sure that she dressed in the latest fashion, with cost no object. He must have spent a fortune on her clothes, but he loved showing her off."

"That's what she told me," I said. "But he never loved *her*."

Beth nodded. "I didn't find out the truth about their marriage for some time after Amy and I became friends. It took her a while to trust me."

"She told me you were her only real friend," I said.

"That's probably true," said Beth. "The women who pretended to like her were usually just using her to reach Tink. They didn't give a damn about Amy, and she knew it."

"So . . . she finally opened up to you?" I asked.

"Yes. And then everything came bursting out. She told me what a stinker Tink was, and how their marriage was a phony, and how he had never loved anyone but himself. By that time, though, she was very pregnant with Larry. Amy wanted her baby to have a father." She shook her head. "Some father Tink Thompson turned out to be!"

"She told me that Larry was terrified of him—and that Thompson was responsible for the boy's death," I said.

"Absolutely! Tink is a monster."

"Erle here thinks that Thompson murdered Amy," Dash told her. "Do you believe that?"

"Who else had reason to poison her?" asked Beth. "It's all so obvious. She intended to leave Tink, and, to him, the spectacle of a public divorce was unthinkable. So he killed her."

"I wish I could convince the police of that," I said. "They've got me pegged as the killer."

"I'll be glad to testify at your trial," she said. "What I say will back up what Amy told you."

"Thanks for the offer. Looks as if I'm going to need all the help I can get."

"I assume you heard about Tink's ladylove in Montecito," Beth said.

"Yes. Amy and I talked about her the last night we were together. But again, the police refuse to believe in their affair."

"Makes it easier for them," said Dash. "They discount your story, then they don't have to risk upsetting either Thompson *or* the Herrera-Quintano family with embarrassing questions. Fernando

Herrera-Quintano is a prominent man, with some powerful connections."

"How do you know that?" I asked Hammett.

"Been doing some research on the guy," he said. "Eventually, we're going to have to tell him what's been going on between his wife and Thompson. And confront his wife, too. If the cops won't do it, we'll have to."

"Where will that get us?" asked Chandler.

"Won't know till we have our talk," Dash said. "But it's a lead we need to follow up."

"He's right," I said to Chandler. "We'll have to do this kind of legwork on our own."

I turned to Beth Winniger. "You must know things about Amy that I don't. Can you think of anything that might help me?"

She hesitated, then said: "Just a moment," and left the room.

"I can see why Amy chose Beth as a friend," I said. "She's the genuine goods."

"Her basic honesty comes through," Ray declared. "She's bound to impress a jury."

"Yeah," nodded Hammett. "They'll believe what Beth says."

I shrugged. "Fine. But I'm going to need more than one good woman's testimony to win this case."

"Amen," said Chandler.

Beth returned with a metal box, of the type used for storing family papers. A small silver padlock secured the hasp.

"I keep my important documents in here," she said as she inserted a small key into the lock. "The deed to our house, insurance papers, birth certificates . . . and there's one thing here I think you'll find of special interest."

She opened the box and reached inside, bringing out a cylinder of white paper secured with a green ribbon. She handed it to me.

I untied the ribbon and unrolled the sheet of heavy vellum. What

I read shocked and surprised me. It was a Mexican marriage certificate, issued in the state of Baja California, showing that Lloyd Hadley Thompson and María Teresa Sanchez were wed in San Felipe on February 3, 1917.

"Good God!" I exclaimed. "Is this authentic?"

"Apparently so," said Beth. "Amy brought it to me for safekeeping late last year. She told me to guard it carefully. She didn't want Tink to know she had it."

"Where did she get this?" I asked. Hammett and Chandler were scanning the certificate over my shoulder, but since neither of them read Spanish, they were mostly guessing at its content.

"I have no idea," said Beth. "Amy never told me. I was very curious, naturally, but she wouldn't reveal any details."

I shook my head. "She never mentioned to me that Thompson had been previously married."

"Amy refused to talk about it," Beth said. "And I wasn't supposed to mention it to anyone."

"Did you?

"No. You're the first. She made me promise that I would burn it if she died before I did."

"But you kept it," I said.

"Because of *how* she died . . . she was *murdered*. I didn't feel that I should destroy what might prove to be possible evidence."

"I don't see how this ties in with Amy's death," said Chandler.

"Did you consider turning it over to the police?" I asked Beth.

"I would have if they'd arrested Tink. When they arrested *you,* I wasn't sure what to do. Then, as we were talking, I realized that you should have it. I'm not even certain it's valid here in the U.S.— and even if it is, Tink could have quietly arranged a divorce years ago."

"I need to check this out," I said. "First, I want to talk to María Sanchez."

"How do you know she's still alive?" asked Ray. "The marriage took place twenty years ago. A lot can happen in twenty years."

"The birth date on the certificate shows that she was barely sixteen when she married Thompson," I pointed out. "That would make her just thirty-six now."

"Women die young in Mexico," said Chandler.

"I'm betting she's still alive and living in San Felipe."

"Where is San Felipe?" asked Hammett.

"It's a small fishing village on the Gulf of California, about a hundred miles or so south of Mexicali," I said. "There's not much there—only a few hundred people—and that means it should be easy to locate María Sanchez. Probably everybody in San Felipe is related to her, one way or another."

Chandler began pacing the room, looking agitated. "Under the conditions of your bail," he warned me, "you're not supposed to leave Los Angeles. Dammit, Erle, you can't just go traipsing off to Mexico. I vouched for you with the judge."

I tried to placate him. "It's not as if I'm trying to skip bail," I said. "Believe me, I'll return to L.A. just as soon as I've talked to the Sanchez woman."

"But why do you need to talk to her?" Ray asked. "Even if she's still alive and you do manage to locate her, what good will it do to talk to her?"

"Maybe no good at all," I admitted. "It's just something I have to do. I have a strong feeling about it."

"I'll go with you," said Hammett. "I'd like to see the country. I've never been south of Mexicali."

Chandler was glaring at me. "You're making a serious mistake, Erle. The judge granted you bail on my say-so. If you do this, then you're betraying him—and me."

"I'm sorry, Ray, but I have to go. I won't let you down, or Judge Carter, either. You've got my word on that."

"What if he finds out that you've left the city?" asked Ray.

"He won't," I said. "Not unless you tell him. You're not going to do that, are you, Ray?"

Chandler's jaw tightened. "No, I'm not going to do that." He gave me a hard stare. "But this is not honorable."

"It's clear you don't intend to drive us to San Felipe," Hammett said to Chandler.

"Hell, no! I'm not about to engage in the criminal act of aiding and abetting a fugitive from justice."

"Colorfully put," nodded Dash. He turned to me. "Can you drive us?"

"My camper's on the fritz and my truck overheats on long trips," I told him.

Dash thought for a moment. "It's okay," he said. "I know a guy who'll jump at the chance to drive us down there."

"Who?"

"Barney," Dash said. "Barney Oldfield."

We thanked Beth for her valuable help and left the beach house.

TEN

Berna Eli "Barney" Oldfield has been called many things by the press: "America's Premier Driver" . . . "The Human Comet" . . . "Wizard of the Track" . . . "King of the Dirt" . . . and, most often, "The Daredevil Dean of the Roaring Road."

Oldfield is to automobile racing what Babe Ruth is to baseball, an American legend. His incredible exploits behind the wheel have made him a global celebrity. Every sports fan in the nation knows his name.

In 1902, when he was twenty-four years old, he won his first motor race on a dirt horse track in Michigan, driving Henry Ford's "999," a dangerous, tiller-steered monster that almost killed him. That victory established the Ford Motor Company and launched Oldfield's career. A death-be-damned rebel who defied the rules, Barney was often suspended from official competition by the American Automobile Association. Nevertheless, he went on to become the undisputed master of circus-style racing as he barnstormed the country breaking every track record, from one to one hundred miles.

In March of 1910, at Daytona Beach, driving his ghost-white juggernaut, the *Lightning Benz,* he set a new land-speed record of 131 miles per hour, which made him the official "Speed King of the World."

He drank heavily during his career, survived numerous crashes, earned a reputation as a saloon brawler, and raced his cars against trains and airplanes before he finally retired in 1918.

Along with the rest of the country, I'd followed Oldfield's notorious career in the newspapers—but he'd faded from the headlines after his retirement. Until Hammett mentioned his name, I hadn't thought of him in years. I'd heard that he was racing tractors and setting up thrill shows at county fairs, but that had been some while back. I had no idea what had become of him until Dash filled me in.

"Barney owns a country club now," Hammett told me the next morning over the phone. "Real fancy joint in the San Fernando Valley, catering to the upper crust. I gave him a jingle over there, and he's expecting us."

"Did you tell him why we're coming?"

"Naw. I want Mexico to be a surprise. More fun that way."

"How come Buddy doesn't drive us down to San Felipe in your limo? He takes you everywhere else."

"Last month he asked for some time off," Dash said. "He left yesterday for Frisco. Margaret Stetler is giving a concert there. He's real sweet on her, so I said fine, go ahead."

I had met Margaret at the Chandlers' house last year and I like her. A superb talent on the piano. As a Negro, she's had a tough time breaking into the world of classical music—Negroes not being exactly welcome on the American concert stage—but, hopefully, this is beginning to change. She's already toured Europe to much acclaim, and this appearance in San Francisco could, with luck, do a lot to establish her as an artist in her own country.

"How can you be sure that Oldfield will say yes to the trip?" I asked.

"Are you kidding? I know Barney. He won't be able to resist a chance to hit the open road again. He'll go nuts over the idea."

"You know where his club is?"

"Sure. In Van Nuys. I've played pool with him there. It's [...] layout. You come get me in your truck and we'll go over th[...] noon."

"I'll pick you up just before noon," I said. "We don't have a[...] to lose."

The Barney Oldfield Country Club is indeed "fancy"—just [...] mett had described it. Located in a lush canyon in the [...] boasts twin tennis courts, a softball diamond, six large barbe[...] an Olympic-sized swimming pool, a high-ceilinged ballroo[...] cious clubhouse, and fifteen acres of shaded picnic grounds[...] the club, overlooking the public road, a tall, painted billb[...] tures Barney at the wheel of a touring car, telling the world[...]

BUY POLLY GAS!
IT'S GREAT ON GRADES!

Oldfield met us under a fringed canopy at the club entr[...] sleeves of his white shirt were rolled to the elbows, revealin[...] muscled arms. It requires brute strength to wrestle those ma[...] ing machines around a dirt oval, and Oldfield's thick chest a[...] shoulders testify to his former profession. He smiled broadly a[...] stub of his trademark cigar as he vigorously pumped Hamme[...]

"How the hell are ya, Dash?" he rumbled.

"I *was* dandy," said Hammett, reclaiming his hand. He [...] "But I think you just disabled me."

"Sorry," Barney said. "Guess I don't know my own streng[...] I'd better just *wave* at people!"

Dash introduced me as a "writing colleague," and Oldfiel[...] "Did some writing myself," he said. "For the *Saturday Eve*[...] They printed my life story. Edited me blind, but the facts w[...] All my cars. All my records. You see my life story in the *P*[...]

"Afraid I missed that," I told him, "but I've read a lot about you."

That pleased him. "Step in, gents, and wet your whistles."

Inside, we selected a side booth in the bar, sitting down to a large itcher of foaming brew.

"Fresh from the keg," said Oldfield, taking a deep swig. "By damn, ut that's *good!* Nothing like cold beer on a hot day."

We agreed.

"Well, now . . ." said Barney to Dash. "You have a look in your eye. omethin' is on your mind."

"Are you aware that Erle here is out on bail, pending trial on a urder charge? It's been in all the papers."

"Nah, I just read the racing form," said Barney. "Keep betting on ie nags, but they don't come home for me. You can trust a car, but ou can't ever trust a horse."

"Anyhow, Erle is innocent," continued Dash, "and we have to rove it in court. There's a possible lead in the case we need to check ut. Down in Baja. Ever been there?"

"I've been drunk in most of the border towns," said Barney, "but ve never been deep into the country."

"We need to get to San Felipe, on the Baja peninsula. A long trip,")ash declared. "Lots of open road. How'd you like to drive us down iere?"

Oldfield's eyes grew misty. "Open road, huh?"

"Miles and miles of it," nodded Dash, sipping his brew.

Barney slapped the table. "By God, I've been hibernating in this amn club for too long. I need to stretch my muscles."

"Then you'll take us?" I asked.

"Gents . . . it'll be my great pleasure," smiled Oldfield.

And we all drank to that.

Ever hear of the Cactus Derby?"

The three of us were standing in front of a closed garage at the rear f the club when Barney asked this question.

"No," said Hammett.

"I haven't either," I said. "Sounds like a horse race."

"It was a race, all right," said Oldfield. "But not for horses. For automobiles. From California to Phoenix, Arizona. You had to climb mountains on trails a goat would balk at, ford rivers, charge through cactus and desert, tackle gullies filled with boulders, and fight off sleet and hail and alkali dust. Seven hundred miles of sheer hell!"

"Did you drive in it?" I asked.

"Drive in it? Hell, I *won* it!"

He pulled a large bronze medal from his coat. It was studded with diamonds and bore an inscription. He held it out: "Go ahead, read what the words say."

Dash and I leaned closer to make out the inscription:

To Barney Oldfield
MASTER DRIVER OF THE WORLD

Oldfield chuckled. "Got that for winning the Derby in my wire-wheel Stutz." He gestured toward the closed garage. "And I've still got 'er."

Barney swung back the heavy wooden door to reveal a high-bodied, white racing machine with big wire wheels.

"She took me all the way to Phoenix back in fourteen, and she'll take the three of us to San Felipe."

Hammett put up a hand. "Oh no she won't," he said. "I'm not riding hundreds of miles in an open-cockpit racing car, with rain and wind in my face and no passenger seat. This is a two-man machine. Where would I sit?"

"On Erle's lap," said Barney. "You're so skinny he won't even know you're there."

"Hold it," I said. "Dash is right. Driving the Stutz into Mexico is a daffy idea."

Barney was adamant.

"Okay," said Hammett, "but you realize that none of us will survive the trip."

Oldfield looked at me. "What's he mean?"

"Banditos," said Hammett. "Mexico's full of 'em. And they'd *love* to get their hands on a genuine American racing car."

"Yeah," I added. "They like to sit up on the rocks by the side of the road and pick off gringos in open cars. Most of them are crack shots. We'll make perfect targets."

That argument did the trick. Barney decided it would be wiser to drive to Mexico in his 1932 Packard touring car.

It was a real beauty: a two-door hardtop model, cream-colored, with white walls. Barney showed us the powerful V-12 engine under its long hood. There was a strapped-down spare tire mounted on each side in the front fender wells, and the rear luggage trunk was square and functional.

"Now *this*," said Hammett, grinning, "is more like it!"

We rolled out of Los Angeles that afternoon in the big Packard with me in the backseat. We had a full tank of gas—and a large canvas bag of water gurgling on the rear floor.

"You get the runs if you drink the water in Mexico," said Barney. "Food's bad enough, but we can't do anything about that. No use bein' a damn fool with the water."

He had a fat cigar in his mouth and wore round driving goggles.

"Why wear those in a closed car?" Hammett asked him.

" 'Cuz I wore 'em for seventeen years, wherever and whenever I raced," he said. "Just don't seem natural driving a machine without my goggles."

As we cleared the southern outskirts of Los Angeles, Barney held up his cigar. "Know how I got into these here stogies?"

We said we didn't know.

"The dirt tracks I usta drive on were chopped up pretty good by the horses that ran over 'em. Ended up bein' full of hellish potholes. You'd hit one an' it would rattle your molars. I began jamming a cigar between my teeth to cushion the shock. Turned into a swell stunt. My fans expected me to have a cheroot stuck in my kisser for every race. And people began sending me boxes of 'em in the mail."

"I smoked cigars when I was with Pinkerton," said Dash. "Never got to like them."

Oldfield charged on, unfazed. "In the racing game, you gotta find a way to stand out from the crowd, and my stogies made me special. Look at any picture ever printed of my ugly mug and you'll see a cigar in it. I just wouldn't be ole Barney without my cheroot!"

I looked out at the Pacific Ocean on our right as Barney kept on talking. I had a sneaking suspicion that this was going to be a very long trip.

It took us five hours to reach San Diego. When we got there, we were starved, so we stopped at Mariscos Los Padrinos in Old Town for a last American meal. It was an opportunity to indulge ourselves with San Diego's excellent seafood, caught fresh that morning and grilled Mexican-style, with chili and lime.

An hour later, stuffed to the gills, we were on the highway headed east, toward Calexico and its adjoining town of Mexicali. "Highway" is a rather overblown term for the dirt track we began following through the desert, but it did the job. It was certainly a far better route than our alternative: a Mexican road that connected Tijuana with Mexicali and paralleled us just south of the border. We had to drive more than a hundred miles east to Calexico; there we would cross the international border into Mexicali, then drop straight south to San Felipe. The longer we stayed in the United States, the faster we would get to San Felipe.

When we reached the U.S. border at Calexico, the American immigration officers, who seemed bored and sleepy, waved us on through to Mexicali. We crossed the Rio Nuevo bridge and officially entered Mexico. The Mexican *federales* weren't any more interested in us than the Americans had been.

Barney stopped at a one-pump station so he could top the tank with gas and check the tires. He came back very disturbed.

"Man tells me that San Felipe is four or five hours away, assuming nothin' goes wrong with the car. That's too long. We have to eat."

"What do you mean, *eat?*" Hammett said. "We had what amounts to a Thanksgiving dinner less than three hours ago."

"San Felipe is just too goldarn far away. I say we eat, and *I'm* the one who's driving."

We ate. Or, to be more accurate, Barney ate. He picked out a "restaurant" that consisted of a little cook shack made out of scrap wood and flattened tin cans; several tiny tables for customers were set on the dirt under a big cottonwood tree. Dash and I nursed warm Mexican beer while Barney demolished a platter of goat-meat enchiladas.

He continued relentlessly regaling us with stories of his many exploits, this time about a big racing comeback he had planned in 1931 that didn't pan out, and an accident he'd had on the track in 1917, in which he almost died. "My shirt was on fire by the time I managed to kick open the door. I staggered out just as the gas tank let go—*kablooie!*—which knocked me flat in the mud. I ended up in the hospital. I've had me a lot of smashups, gents, but that was the worst. I even lost my cigar."

"I'll stick to writing," I said. "Books don't explode."

When Oldfield had finished eating, we headed back along the Avenida Cristobal Colon, where we'd left the Packard. A ragged trio of bronze-skinned youngsters offered to sell their sister to us—in exchange for candy, cigarettes, or cash.

"She is *muy bonita*," they insisted. "Very pretty! You can all enjoy her."

We declined the offer, which failed to discourage them. They immediately attached themselves to another group of Americans. Like all border towns, Mexicali was jammed with tourists. Anything and everything was for sale. We passed a gun shop displaying a six-shooter in the window; a placard proclaimed, in English, that it was "The One and Only Original Gun Used by Billy the Kid." I questioned its authenticity, especially after we passed three more gun shops on our way to the Packard, all featuring "the one and only" six-gun used by the Kid.

It was now long after dark. We spent the night in Mexicali (at a fleabag hotel best left undescribed) and got underway again at six the next morning. Even at that early hour, the road was choked with a variety of rusted bicycles, overcrowded buses, horse-drawn wagons, and ancient trucks that emitted noxious clouds of black exhaust as they slowly rumbled forward.

The dirt road south to San Felipe was flat and rutted, but the big Packard smoothly absorbed the bumps as Oldfield gradually increased speed.

We were at eighty when I spotted a cop coming up fast behind us with his red spotlight blinking.

"Got John Law on our tail," I told Barney.

"I see him," nodded Oldfield.

"Better pull over," I said.

He grinned around his cigar. "Why should I? This chariot is fast enough to lose him."

"Nix on that," declared Hammett. "We don't want some damn roadblock stopping us later. Do what Erle said, pull over."

Barney scowled and braked the car to a gravel-grinding stop. "Wait here," he said as he took out his wallet and extracted a five-dollar bill. He opened the car door and walked back to the uniformed officer.

I couldn't hear their muttered conversation, but I saw Barney pass over the five dollars, along with a fresh cigar. The two men shook hands and then Oldfield walked back to us, grinning broadly.

"One thing I learned in the border towns," he said. "Ain't a cop in

Mexico you can't buy off with a five-buck bill. That one wishes us well on our trip, and threw in the blessing of the Virgin Mary as a kind of bonus. Maybe he knows her personally."

For a while after this, Barney drove a little slower, but only a little. He couldn't resist upping our speed mile by mile. As Hammett had said, Oldfield loves the open road—almost as much as he loves to talk.

Dash and I settled back, a captive audience, as Barney rambled on. I was learning a lot more about his life than I cared to know.

ELEVEN

The amazing thing about Oldfield was his total self-obsession. Here I was, accused of murder, breaking bail to follow a lead deep into Mexico, and all Barney wanted to talk about was himself. So far, he had never asked about my case, or about the person I was supposed to have killed, nor had he shown any interest whatever in who we were going to see in San Felipe, or for what reason. Amazing!

Maybe this would change. Maybe he'd become curious once we reached our destination, but at the moment, all Barney Oldfield wanted to talk about was Barney Oldfield.

"When you race automobiles," he was saying as he drove, "the gals just flock around. It's the danger that heats 'em up, the idea that you could be dead before the next race is over. They go for the thrills—and racing makes 'em wild. Which has always been fine by me, 'cuz I *appreciate* wild women. And I've had me my share!" He chuckled.

We were passing a large cemetery that flanked the road. Pink and blue gravestones. Marble saints. Lots of flowers. Dash asked Oldfield to slow down so he could study the place.

"I've never seen a Mexican cemetery," said Hammett.

A black-clad family had gathered around a freshly dug grave site and I saw a small wooden coffin being lowered into the ground. A child. The family had lost a child.

This depressed me. Children shouldn't die. But in a poor country like Mexico—with not enough food, improper sanitation, and a lack of modern medical facilities—many children fail to reach adulthood. A sad situation.

"Should I stop?" Barney asked.

"No," I told him. "They don't need us to watch them bury their dead."

"Yeah," nodded Hammett. "Move on."

And the Packard resumed speed.

After the cemetery, we drove in silence. Seeing the dead child had reawakened the pain of Amy's death—and her own loss at the death of Larry.

Dark thunderheads had rolled in from the west. A tropical storm was gathering over the mountains, and the great gray cloud masses cloaked the sky.

"We're due for some bad weather," said Oldfield. "Storm brewing up ahead."

"And you wanted to take that damn open Stutz," Dash chided. "We'd have ended up like drowned rats."

"You're right," Barney admitted. "I've heard tell that summer storms in Mexico can be rough."

We were closing in on the mountains, moving past rolling sand dunes, when the horizon turned charcoal-black and the rain began its assault. That's the word for it—a direct assault from the sky. I've spent a lot of time in the desert and have survived my share of fierce rainstorms, but this one was truly incredible.

The heavens seemed to split apart, releasing a sudden downpour that drummed the roof of the Packard with a thousand beating fists.

"Gents, we're into it now," said Oldfield, stripping off his goggles for a clearer view of the road.

"Maybe we should turn around," I suggested. "Go back to the nearest town until this blows over. Road's going to turn to mud."

Hammett was consulting a map he'd spread across his lap. "According to this, the nearest town—or village, actually—is *ahead* of us. Better if we keep going."

"But if we turn back, there's a chance we can outrun the storm," I said.

"No good," declared Barney. "Seems to be slowly passing us. At least, that's how the clouds are moving. Dash is right. Our best bet is to just keep on goin'."

Sudden turbulence rocked the Packard. Oldfield fought to keep the car moving in a straight line.

"Wind's come up," he said, peering ahead. The wipers were waging a losing battle to keep the glass clear. "And take a gander at that lightning!"

Bright bolts illumined the sky in sporadic flashes. Long electric whips of lightning sizzled down, and cannon bursts of thunder gave greater voice to the quickly building storm.

Oldfield had reduced our speed to fifteen miles an hour. He was hunched over the wheel, squinting to see through the blowing curtain of rain.

The faint sound of an auto horn barely penetrated the storm's roar and I looked back. Behind us, in the grayness, a truck was blinking its headlights.

"The damn fool's right on my tail," growled Barney, raising his voice to be heard above the drumming rain. "Hell, if I go any faster, we'll slide off the road."

Dash looked back, frowning. "Let him go by. He'll see for himself that nobody can drive fast in this stuff."

Oldfield nodded, easing the big Packard to the right so the other vehicle could pass.

The truck was an open-bed Ford, loaded with tied-down chicken crates. I made out three figures in the cab: an old white-haired man behind the wheel, and two kids. The Ford was badly rusted, scored with dents, and the right front fender was missing. The vehicle swayed erratically as it rumbled past us.

"What's his big hurry?" asked Barney.

"His livelihood probably depends on those chickens," I said. "He's afraid they'll die in the storm, so he's pushing hard to reach the next village before that happens."

"Yeah," said Barney, "and if he don't slow down, he'll lose more than his chickens."

But the truck didn't slow down. I lost sight of it as the taillights dimmed to vanishing red dots in the opaque downpour.

The storm increased in fury. Sand began washing onto the road, along with giant tumbleweeds that rolled like white ghosts in front of the Packard.

The clouds and rain had turned sunny afternoon into gray twilight. The landscape had taken on a surreal aspect as the mountains loomed closer, thrusting up their jagged shoulders against the horizon.

"Sure don't feel like the storm's passin' us by," Barney remarked.

"Maybe it decided to stick around just to give us fits," said Dash.

Oldfield shook his head. "Well, she's a real humdinger."

We were coming up to a narrow bridge that spanned what was normally a dry riverbed. Now the rain had turned it into a fast-rising stream.

Hammett pointed ahead. "The truck!"

"Yeah," said Barney, "and just lookee what's happened to it."

On its fast approach, the Ford had missed the bridge and plunged off the mud-slick road into the riverbed, where it was mired hub-deep. The water was shallow, yet the truck could not gain traction in the shifting river sand.

Barney stopped the Packard at the edge of the road, cutting the engine. Now there was only the sound of the rain beating heavily against the roof.

"Looks like they're gonna need some muscle," Barney declared. "Two kids and one old man can't do the job."

"The three of us ought to make up the difference," I said. "We can push them out."

"Not in this kind of muck," said Hammett. He turned to Barney. "Got a rope or a chain in the trunk?"

"Rope," Barney told him.

"Okay, then," said Dash. "We tie one end to the truck and the other end to the Packard."

"Drag 'em out—like I had a mule team drag me out of New River back in fourteen," exclaimed Barney.

"Good plan," I agreed. "So, who's going to tie the rope?"

"I will," declared Oldfield. "I can stand some exercise. You two stay put. No use all of us gettin' soaked to the bone."

He climbed out of the car, shut the door and, bowing under the force of the pounding rain, made his way to the Packard's trunk.

"I'd like to help!" I told Hammett.

"Nothing we can do at the moment," Dash said. "Barney wants to try this on his own. Let's wait and see what develops."

Oldfield had the rope now and was wading out into the swirling river. Rain had already soaked through his coat and shirt. He looked miserable.

"I feel guilty just sitting here," I said.

Dash shrugged. "If Barney needs us, he'll let us know."

The old man stepped down into the shallow water from the driver's side of the truck to meet Oldfield, waving the two children back. Barney was heading toward the rear of the Ford with the rope.

Hammett was peering ahead. "Oh, hell!"

"What's wrong?" I asked.

"You wanted to help. Well, now's your chance," he said urgently. "We need to get out there. They don't see it."

"See what?"

"Flash flood. Runoff from the mountains. Their backs are to it. *Hurry!*"

I saw what he meant: a swift-running wall of floodwater at the far end of the riverbed, closing fast.

By now, Hammett was halfway to the truck, and I was right behind him. In the river, the mire sucked at our shoes, while the rain slashed us with brutal force, like something alive.

Hammett cupped his hands and began shouting: "Flood! Get out!" But his words were snatched away by the wind. Thunder kettle-drummed the sky as the lightning lashed down from fat-bellied black clouds.

"They can't hear me," Dash yelled in my ear. "Once that current hits, it'll take them with it, truck and all."

We were closer now—and Barney finally saw us coming. As did the old man.

Hammett pointed upriver, to the looming wall of water. Cacti and mesquite and tumbleweeds were being whirled along by the swift tide. In the course of its run from the mountains, the rampaging current had uprooted trees and boulders. The flood's destructive power was awesome. Nothing could stand in its path.

"The kids!" shouted Hammett. Oldfield coiled the rope over his shoulder and we all plowed forward toward the truck, with the river suddenly deeper, wilder, surging to our waists.

I could see that we weren't going to make it. The wall of water would be on top of us before we could reach the truck. But we had to keep trying.

By this point, the children were screaming—a boy and a girl, both about ten, their faces flaring paste-white under the flashes of lightning. They could see the floodwaters rushing at them, and they were terrified.

I was plenty scared myself. The flood was swift and deadly, an unstoppable force of nature descending on us like the fist of God.

Then, with a jungle roar, it hit us—and we were suddenly floundering in the swirl of current, trying to keep our heads above water. The truck was rocking wildly, like a cork in a bathtub, as the flood battered it. Within seconds, it would overturn and be swept downriver. The wooden crates in the open truck bed had split open, spilling out their cargo of hysterically squawking chickens, while the two children had climbed to the cab's roof.

Oldfield headed straight for them, swimming strongly. Instead of trying to save himself, he was going for the kids, and I was stirred by his courage.

The old man was sucked under, sputtering and choking. Hammett grabbed him by the hair, pulling him to the surface. With one arm around the old man's sagging shoulders, Dash attempted to swim for the dirt shore, but I knew he'd never make it. I reached the pair of them, and together we got the old man to the riverbank.

On shore, he was barely conscious, babbling in Spanish as Hammett helped him to sit up. He spat out a lungful of water and coughed raggedly. The storm was still fierce and the rain continued its unrelenting attack. I was soaked and shivering, desperately cold. The wind felt like spears of ice driving through my body.

I looked up to see the truck tipping and rolling in the current. The two youngsters had been pitched into the water, but they had managed to grip the edge of the cab's passenger door just as Oldfield reached them.

Now they seemed to have a chance. Barney had them put their arms around his neck while he swam for shore. And despite the pull of the current, he was making headway, using his remarkable upper-body strength to maximum advantage.

"I think he'll make it," I yelled to Dash.

"No! Can't!" Hammett shook his head. "Current's too strong!"

And he was right. Oldfield was weakening, unable to overcome the power of the flood. He and the children were being swept downriver.

Leaving the old man, who was recovering rapidly, Hammett and I ran along the dirt bank, trying to keep the swimmers in sight. My God, what could we do?

"There," shouted Dash, pointing.

A hundred yards ahead of us, a large pine tree had jammed against the shore, extending into mid-river. Would they see it in time? Would they be able to reach it before being sucked under?

As we climbed over the dirt bank, great chunks of earth were breaking off, ripped away by the savage current. We were both shouting at Oldfield, pointing to the tree, but we knew he couldn't hear us, and he was far too busy trying to stay alive to see where we were pointing.

Too late? No, no!

Seeing the pine tree, like a life raft in the boiling froth of water, Barney acted. He grabbed one of the heavy branches with his right hand, then reached back with his left to gather in the two flailing children.

The current fought to dislodge them, but Barney's strength prevailed. He managed to wrestle them atop the heavy trunk, then pulled himself alongside.

"They're safe!" I yelled to Hammett.

Again, he shook his head. "Not yet!"

I groaned. The tree was breaking up under the water's brutal assault. Branches were splitting and being carried away.

"Now!" Hammett shouted. "Go!"

And he leaped for the edge of the trunk where it touched the shore. We scrambled out along the unstable mass, which was being violently rocked by the surging flood. It was extremely dangerous; we knew that the tree could roll at any moment, spilling all five of us into the river.

The roar of water and wind was deafening. The storm was angry. It didn't want us to reach Barney and the children. It hungered to claim us, to suck us down into its swirling black depths.

"No, dammit!" I found myself shouting irrationally at it. "You're not going to win!"

We were very close to them now. I could hear Barney's voice above the storm: "¡Poco más! ¡Más!" He was telling the kids to hang on. Now Hammett reached the girl. He extended his right hand and the child's fingers closed around it. She was wide-eyed with shock and cold. "Hold on tight," Hammett told her.

Oldfield was clutching the boy, and I could see blood pulsing from a deep cut on his left leg, just above the knee. Most of his pants leg was missing.

"You take him," Barney shouted to me. "I can't walk."

I gripped the boy's hand, very small in my own. It was icy and he was trembling.

"How will you get back to shore?" I yelled to Barney.

"I'll crawl!"

"Then go first," Dash shouted, allowing him to move past us.

We started back, reversing our direction along the slippery bark surface, balancing against the wind, with Barney on all fours ahead of us. He still had the coiled rope over his shoulder and I thought how long ago it seemed since he'd left with it for the truck. The storm had distorted my time sense. Time, in fact, had lost all meaning out there on the river. All that mattered was survival. Nothing else.

The wind cut into my flesh and I had to clench my jaw to keep my teeth from chattering. If the rain would just stop hammering at us!

Incredibly, we all managed to stay on the shifting trunk, making solid progress. The shoreline loomed ahead. Barney was the first to touch ground and he sat there gasping and spent, waving us on.

That's when the boulder struck. A giant piece of volcanic rock that had been caught up in the current slammed heavily into the tree, dislodging it from the shore.

Hammett and I and both of the children were thrown into the swirling water, and for the first time, I experienced the awesome power of the current. It swept me under in a froth of bubbles.

117

When I came up, choking and sputtering, I was close to shore. Barney pulled me in. I could see Hammett and the kids off to my left, being carried rapidly downriver. With the increased speed of the current, we could never hope to pace them on foot. But I had a plan that might work.

"The Packard," I shouted. "Can you get to it?" And I gestured toward his wounded leg.

He nodded. I helped him back to the car. The old man was inside, out of the rain in the back seat.

"*¡Mis nietos!*" He looked stricken. "*¿Dónde están mis nietos?*"

"We'll save them," I said in Spanish as Barney took over the wheel. I looked directly into the old man's eyes, trying to reassure him.

"Are you sure you can handle the car?" I asked Oldfield.

"Yeah," he said tightly. "I'm sure." And he fired up the engine.

"Drive as fast as possible along the bank," I said. "We need to get ahead of them. Keep going until I tell you to stop."

It was a rough ride, with the big car slipping and bumping over the riverbank, and it took all of Oldfield's skill to keep us from ending up in the river. But at least we were moving faster than the current.

"Reminds me of the Cactus Derby," said Oldfield as he jammed a cellophane-wrapped cigar into his mouth and bit down on it.

After about a mile, I had Barney pull over.

"The rope," I said. "Give it to me."

He got the idea and shook his head. "I can handle it."

"Not with that bad leg, you can't. The rope!"

Without further argument, he handed it over. I ran back to tie one end securely to the Packard's rear bumper. Then I slid down the dirt embankment and waded out into the cold river, oblivious to the wind and rain. The flood swirled madly around my waist as the current rocked me, seriously threatening my balance. It was extremely difficult to maintain footing, but I had to be as far out into the water as possible.

Hammett and the two children, holding desperately to one another, were now in view upriver. Would they see me? Or would they sweep blindly past me in the rampaging floodwater?

Then, as I waved and shouted, I saw Dash raise an arm to acknowledge me. Yes!

I'd done some rope work on our desert outings, trick stuff to amuse Natalie, so I knew how to knot a proper loop. Something for Hammett to hold onto if I could get it to him.

If.

They were almost directly across from me when I made the toss. The rope snaked out above the seething river.

There, by God! Hammett's fingers closed over the looped end. With the children clinging to him, he began, hand over hand, to pull the three of them toward the shore.

It was over.

The storm had not won.

TWELVE

Once past the mountains, we put the storm behind us. The road became passable again and I felt liberated. No more drumming rain. No more thunder and lightning. No more battering wind. No more flash floods. The world was stable again.

The sun was still up when we reached the village of La Ventana, home of the old man and his two grandchildren. When we said good-bye, his eyes filmed with tears of gratitude as he patted us on the back and blessed us in Spanish for saving his kids. God would reward us, he said. We would achieve a high place in heaven, seated on golden thrones. Barney told him, in broken Spanish, that we were in no hurry to get there, but were relieved to know we'd be welcome.

I wondered how the old guy would make out after losing his truck, so I slipped him some money. Not a lot, but at least he could buy some more chickens. Later, I found out that Barney and Dash had also slipped him some cash.

No wonder he was smiling when we left him.

The village itself was no more than a rude scatter of tin shacks, and there seemed to be more dogs than people. They followed the car in a snarling pack, barking crazily, biting at our tires.

Lucky for us, since we were low on fuel, La Ventana *did* have a gas station—with the word *"Petróleos"* painted in red on its single rusted pump. The owner, a little fat man with two gold teeth, told us his name was Armando Vasquez. He was delighted to see us. Ours was the first automobile to stop at his station all day, and he simply couldn't do enough for us—checking the water and oil, wiping the windshield, even cleaning the mud off our headlights. He offered to sell us a can of worms for bait, but we let him know we weren't down here to fish.

In contrast to its high-energy owner, the ancient pump worked slowly in filling the Packard's tank, each liter of gas marked by a chiming bell.

As Barney was paying Vasquez in pesos, Dash said, "I could use some chow. Saving kids from flooded rivers gives me an appetite."

Barney asked Armando about a good place to eat. The reply was negative.

"What'd he say?" asked Hammett.

"He says we oughta wait till we hit San Felipe," declared Oldfield. "The food here is likely to kill us."

"A good reason to wait," I said.

My Spanish was much better than Barney's, but I let him ask the questions. He needed the practice.

"Another thirty miles," Oldfield said. "We gotta pass one more range of mountains. Should make it in before dark."

"Great," said Hammett. "These Mexican goat trails aren't designed for night driving."

When we drove out of La Ventana into the long-shadowed afternoon, I was finally able to tell Barney about my case, about Amy's murder, about Tink Thompson, and about the woman we wanted to see in San Felipe. Suddenly, he was curious about everything.

Maybe our shared river adventure had helped him lose his usual self-absorption. Maybe I had come to mean something to him in a personal way. Whatever the reason, I was glad to answer his questions. A bond had formed between us. Behind the bluster and bombast, Oldfield is a decent fellow, and I was pleased with our new relationship.

"Just what are you lookin' to get out of this Sanchez gal?" asked Barney.

"I wish I knew," I answered. "Somehow, I just felt it was vital that I see her. What she'll tell us is anybody's guess."

"*If* she's still alive," added Dash. "And *if* she's still in San Felipe."

"It's a gamble," I admitted.

"What isn't?" And Barney grinned.

The daylight was almost gone by the time we passed the final range of mountains and rolled into San Felipe. The road dead-ended at a sandy stretch of open beach that faced the deep blue expanse of the Gulf of California.

It was a spectacular view. The sun was setting behind the western mountains and their peaks were silhouetted against the sky like paper cutouts. On the wide plain of darkening water, several fishing boats were bringing in their day's catch. The rolling cloud masses to the west were dipped in gold, and the horizon was edged in rich purple. I experienced a sense of utter tranquillity, as if we'd discovered a fresh new world.

The predominant feature of San Felipe was the number of fishermen's shacks scattered along a mile or so of shoreline—tin-roofed, ramshackle affairs built of sea-weathered boards nailed together in seemingly haphazard fashion.

There were no docks; the boats were simply pulled up on the sand and tied there. Several of the local fishermen, all wearing wide straw sombreros, were repairing their nets, ignoring us as we drove past them to the main street of the village. Just another car full of gringo tourists. Nothing to get excited about.

Half a dozen older-model automobiles and trucks were parked along the dirt street, their paint badly eroded by wind and salt. The carcass of an abandoned bus, with all four wheels missing, occupied a corner lot. Mexican children were climbing in and out of its empty windows, giggling and punching one another.

Barney stopped in front of a curio shop with a cracked wooden sign, in English, propped in front: LEATHERS PURSE. Its specialty seemed to consist of seashell sculptures in a wide variety of shapes and colors.

The street's only theater, the Cinema Jimenez, was next to the curio shop. It was no longer in operation. The entrance doors had been nailed shut, and a dusty poster of Greta Garbo was peeling from the lobby wall that faced the closed box office. Obviously, there were not enough movie patrons in San Felipe to support such an establishment. The sand-pitted marquee still retained the title of the theater's last film: *El Rey de Tomate. The King of Tomatoes*. I doubted that Garbo had been in that one.

"Well, gents, where do we start?" asked Barney, surveying this alien landscape.

"We start with some food," said Dash. "Right now I could eat a Mexican burro, hooves and all."

I chuckled. "Maybe that's what they serve around here—*burro con chiquetes.*"

"There's a cantina at the end of the street," Barney said. "Looks like our best bet."

The two-story building that housed the cantina had been built Spanish-style, its wooden balcony now rain-warped. It was painted in gaudy Easter-egg colors of pink and green. There was a rusty-red Coca-Cola sign tacked to the door, just above a cardboard placard lettered in sun-faded Spanish.

"What's it say?" asked Hammett.

I translated. "It says 'Good Food Inside,' plus they serve cold beer."

"Okay," said Dash. "Let's try it."

We entered the cantina and were instantly welcomed by the

123

owner. "I'm José Cardenas. Call me Joe! All the gringos do." He was massive, tall and wide-bodied, with a roll of double chin and shiny shoe-button eyes that seemed to dance in his head.

Cardenas spoke fluent English. He assured us that it would be his very great pleasure to serve us and that we should feel at home here in his cantina, that he would personally see to our comfort.

"We're not after comfort," said Hammett. "We just want to eat."

"Ah, but of course," nodded Cardenas. "Food for the belly and a song for the heart." He waved a guitar player in our direction.

"It's the belly we're concerned with," said Hammett. "You can skip the songs."

"As you wish. Please follow me, gentlemen, to your table. We serve the finest food in San Felipe."

Which, considering the size of this village, wouldn't be that difficult, I thought. We followed him to a large table at the rear of the cantina.

There was a shark's head mounted on the wall above our table. A mean-looking critter with a lot of very sharp teeth.

"One of our fishermen caught him in the Gulf," said Cardenas. "Fought with him for a long time. The whole village turned out to watch him bring this shark in."

"At least he's able to get some sleep," I said.

"Sleep . . . for the fisherman?"

"No, for the shark. They never sleep . . . just keep swimming day and night, prowling for prey."

"Yeah," said Dash. "Our motto at Pinkerton's was 'We Never Sleep.' The Pinkerton logo was a wide-open eye with the motto underneath. Sharks and crime are alike; they never sleep."

The room wasn't crowded—just a few locals, eating quietly—but it was hot and smoky. Too many Mexican cigarettes and not enough ventilation. However, the sharp, spicy odors that drifted out to us from the kitchen were promising.

The menu was chalked on an old school blackboard that had been nailed to the wall. As expected, there was a lot of fish on it. Cardenas began telling us about San Felipe's primary business.

"The good men of our village venture out each day into the Gulf waters to bring back white sea bass, cabrilla, and corbina, under the divine protection of Our Blessed Lady, the Virgin of Guadalupe, whose shrine overlooks this village. It is she who—"

"Look," cut in Hammett. "All this history is swell, but could we just order some food?"

"Ah, but of course," Cardenas said, nodding. "And I shall have the honor of personally seeing to your service."

We ordered grilled sea bass, which came with a fire-blackened iron pot of stewed pinto beans, a huge basket of toasted corn tortillas, and a stone dish filled with a fresh chili-pepper-and-tomato salsa that seared our gullets. It was delicious. We didn't say much to each other until we'd satisfied our hunger. Then I leaned back in my chair. "That sign is right . . . 'Good Food Inside.' " I patted my stomach. "And that's where it is."

We were all sipping cold beer when Cardenas returned to our table to make sure that everything was satisfactory. We told him it was, and then I asked: "Have you ever heard of a woman named María Sanchez?"

His dark eyes flashed knowingly. "*Heard* of her! María works here."

"In this cantina?"

He smiled slyly. "Ah, but of course. You came for María. *She* is the reason for your visit."

"We had no way of knowing—"

"María is upstairs," he told us. "I'll summon her. And I guarantee, gentlemen, that she will not disappoint you."

Cardenas walked over to a stairway that led up to the second floor and clapped his hands. "María!" he shouted. "You have company."

A woman's voice murmured from above and Cardenas nodded. He walked back to our table, literally beaming. "She will be right down."

"Good," I said. This was turning out to be far easier than I had anticipated.

"It is not every day that a fine gringo gentleman such as yourself wishes to engage the services of our María. I am confident that she will live up to your expectations."

I didn't get the full meaning of his words until María Sanchez walked up to us. She wore garish makeup, and her low-cut peasant blouse exposed the full upper slopes of her heavy breasts. A tight red skirt revealed ample hips, and her jet-black hair was held in place by a Spanish comb. She looked tired, shopworn, and the smile she gave us was strained and artificial.

Her job at the cantina was obvious.

"My room is upstairs," she said. "Which one of you is first?"

"We all want to talk to you," I told her.

"I don't see three men at once." Her eyes were impassive, like flat stones.

"We're not here for sex," I said, and Oldfield agreed.

She looked confused. "But . . . if you do not wish sex . . ." Then she nodded. "Oh, I understand. You wish to watch me. That will be all right, but I must charge the same price."

"You don't understand," I said. "We just want to *talk* to you, nothing else."

She stared at me for a long moment. "Men do not visit María to talk."

"This is different," Dash said. "We came all the way down here from Los Angeles to ask you some questions."

"What kind of questions?" She was suddenly wary, suspicious. "About what?"

"We need to speak to you in private," I said.

"You will still have to pay, whether you want sex or not," she declared. "José gets half, and he will want his share."

"That's okay," I told her. "The money is no problem."

"Then . . . come with me."

We followed her upstairs.

María's room, at the end of a dim hallway, was stark and functional. Bed. Dressing table. Washstand. Wardrobe. Two wooden chairs and a standing lamp. The only "decoration" was a framed copy of a painting of the Baby Jesus, with his tiny hands pressed to his bleeding heart. A small candle burned on a shelf just beneath the picture.

Hammett and Oldfield took the two chairs, while I sat down on the bed next to María. She was nervous and uncertain; her bed had never served such a purpose before.

She edged away from me, pressing back against the pillows. Her eyes searched my face. "What is it? What do you wish to ask of me?"

I told her our names and said we had come to ask about Tink Thompson. I didn't say why.

"Tink?" She looked uncertain.

"It's what people call him," I said. "A nickname. *Apodo*," I translated, fearing that "nickname" was a word she wouldn't understand. "Lloyd Hadley Thompson."

Her eyes flashed with recognition and she visibly relaxed against the pillows. "Yes, I knew Lloyd. Long ago." The muscles in her face shifted, and her lips formed a gentle Mona Lisa smile.

My God, I thought. She's still in love with him! "I've seen your marriage certificate," I told her. "You married Thompson in February of nineteen-seventeen, right here in San Felipe."

"That is true," she said softly.

"Please tell me everything you can remember about him. When and how you met . . . what he was doing down here in Mexico . . . everything."

"Why do you wish to know these things?"

"It's very important to me," I said. "I have reasons . . . personal ones."

She didn't pursue the matter. She *wanted* to talk about Thompson, wanted—if only for a moment—to relive her life with him. And we were paying for this information; the fact that money was involved made our visit seem more normal in her mind.

"San Felipe was much smaller in those days," she said. "A tiny village, with few people. The roads were very bad, and there were no tourists. I grew up here, but I can barely remember my mother. She came and went, I don't know where. My father died when I was young. He was a hard-working man with a bad heart, a fisherman. We lived in a little shack near the water. His boat was old; it would leak and he would have to repair it. My older sister, Rosita, and I used to help our father with the nets."

"Must have been a tough life," said Oldfield.

"Perhaps, but I knew no other. My father was good to us. We always had fish to eat."

"What happened after your father died?" I asked.

"My sister married Luis Barela, the *curador* here in San Felipe, and her son, Miguel, was born soon after."

"*Curador?*" asked Hammett, glancing at me.

"A folk healer," I said. "Someone who cures people with herbs and plants."

Turning back to María, I asked: "What about you and Thompson? When did he come to San Felipe?"

"Late in January of nineteen-seventeen," she said. "He had just graduated from a school in your country . . . from Chula Vista, which is near the border. He came here right after."

"But why?" I questioned. "With the roads like they were, why did he come all the way to this village?"

"He told me it was to have an adventure. He had been curious about Mexico, so he came down here on his shiny motorcycle. It was very loud." She smiled faintly. "I had not seen many gringos, and never one as handsome as Lloyd."

"How did you meet?"

"He saw me walking along the sand." She lowered her eyes. "It was

128

told to me by others that I was very beautiful then. I was sixteen . . . and a virgin."

"Was your father alive then?"

She looked up at me, shocked. "Oh, no. He would never have approved of my being with a gringo."

"What made you get married?" I wanted to know. "How did that happen?"

"Lloyd very much desired me, and I would not give in to him. It was a sin. I have a great devotion to Our Lady of Guadalupe. I went often to our small church here in San Felipe to pray to her. So I would not do what he wanted."

"Then Thompson married you for sex?" Dash asked her.

"Yes," she replied softly. "A week after we met, we were married, here in the village church. I was very happy. Lloyd was the man I had dreamed of . . . and he taught me about love."

"You mean physical love?" I asked.

"There was no other kind between us. At least, not from him."

"Then *you* loved Thompson?"

"Yes, very much. He spoke Spanish, the kind people use along the border. He would tell me wonderful stories about your great country. He seemed gentle and considerate—but then, one day, he rode away on his shiny motorcycle, and I never saw him again."

"The son of a bitch!" muttered Oldfield.

"I felt my heart would break in two," said María. "I cried for many days. I even . . ." Her voice faltered, and she clasped her hands tightly together.

I stared at her. "You even what?"

Her voice dropped to a near whisper. ". . . tried to do away with myself. But Our Lady came to me in a vision and said that it was a great sin to do this thing . . . to end my life."

Silence in the room. We could all feel her loneliness and pain.

Then Barney asked, "Did he leave you any money?"

"No, nothing. I lived off scraps in the village. Finally, I was hired here at the cantina, waiting on tables and cleaning the kitchen. I have been here ever since."

"When did you become . . ." I couldn't say the word.

"A prostitute? Is that what you are asking me?"

I nodded.

"It was a natural thing," she said. "Men found me attractive. They put their hands on me. I resisted, but then they offered me money, many pesos for my favors—and finally I took the money. That was how it began. Later, as the gringo tourists came to San Felipe, I learned from them to speak English."

"You speak it well," I said.

She lifted her chin in a defiant gesture. "I am not proud of what I do. I only hope that the Baby Jesus and Our Blessed Lady can forgive my sins and allow me to repent before I die."

"Did you hear from Thompson after he left?" Dash asked her.

She shook her head. "I was a toy for him to play with while he was here in San Felipe. Our marriage meant nothing to him. He forgot about me."

"Did you ever try to get a divorce?" I asked.

"Oh, no! Such a thing is forbidden by Holy Mother Church." She put her hands to her face, turning away from me. "I am so ashamed of my life. So deeply ashamed."

She began sobbing into the pillow.

I put a hand on her shoulder. "It's not your fault, María. You had no other choice."

She snuffled, swallowing her grief, composing herself. "There has not always been unhappiness in my life. When I became pregnant with *mi hijo* . . . my Antonio . . . he brought me much joy. Would you like to see his photograph?"

She didn't wait for a reply, but hurried to the dressing table, opened a drawer and brought out a small photograph. Of a chubby boy who appeared to be about six years old playing on the beach, smiling into the lens.

"My son!" she said proudly, handing me the photo. We all looked at it.

I wondered which of the many men who had paid for her body had fathered this boy, but I didn't ask. I doubted that she knew.

María put the photo back into the drawer and turned to face us.

"I must work now," she said. "There is nothing more I can tell you." She put out her hand, naming a sum in pesos.

We paid more than she asked and left the cantina.

It was dark in San Felipe.

THIRTEEN

We spent the night at the La Posada motor court, San Felipe's only hostelry. Each of our rooms boasted a single metal cot and a chamber pot. Genuine Gulf of California sand had been included between the sheets at no additional cost. Washing and toilet facilities were located in a separate building near the beach.

Barney's heavy snoring, which penetrated the paper-thin wall of the room adjacent to mine, kept me awake most of the night. I lay there thinking sadly of Amy, and then about Tink Thompson and María Sanchez. Barney's rhythmic snores and the nearby sound of incoming waves eventually blended, contributing a unique musical cacophony to my unsettled thoughts.

Hours later, when the sky outside had begun its transition into dawn, I heard Barney's cot creak as he got up, on his way to the outside toilet. I walked out to join him and found Dash there, too. Our thoughts were unanimous: we all wanted to leave as soon as possible. We returned to our rooms and quickly made ourselves ready for the trip back to Los Angeles.

On our way out of town, we had coffee and Mexican sweetbread at San Felipe's only market; at that early hour, it was already crowded with fishermen getting ready for their day at sea. Barney

bought gas for the Packard and we were soon on the ro
Mexicali.

The trip back was without incident. No flash floods. N
saved. No banditos. And despite the uneven lurching c
the storm-rutted road, I was finally able to sleep.

When we arrived in Mexicali, the state capital of Baj
I made inquiries and located the town's most prestigiou
showed him the certificate Beth Winniger had given n
him to verify the legality of Thompson's marriage to Ma
He told me that yes, the marriage was entirely legal un
law and—in the absence of a divorce—was still in effect
myself, I knew that such a marriage, if it was legal in Me:
legal in the States.

Which meant that unless I could find evidence of a c
Thompson was not only a murderer, he was also a bigam
a bigamist, that is, until Amy was conveniently killed
marriage had never been valid. And since Amy h
Thompson's legal spouse, she had no claim to half of hi
California's community property law.

Now I understood why Amy—a legal secretary whei
had not told me about Thompson's first marriage. As
torney, I am an officer of the court; I have legal obligat
sometimes transcend the duties I owe to my client. A
of this, and must have worried that if I knew about Tho
riage to María Sanchez, I might be legally obligated to
formation. If I had done so, she would never have rec
share of Thompson's property. After giving up her
Thompson, she couldn't take the chance that she wou
thing once they parted.

On the other hand, Thompson himself had probably
that he was, in fact, a bigamist. People commonly thi
can marriages aren't legal, but they're wrong, and Am
known the facts. All she could do was to keep the certi

ice with Beth Winniger and hope that no one ever discovered that nk Thompson was already married to another woman.

She would have likely informed Thompson that he had two oices: either pretend their marriage was legal and go through with e divorce, granting her half of his assets without a fight . . . or else through the process of a very public annulment, which—once the rticulars of his first marriage were known—would destroy his ca- er. Regardless of Thompson's universal popularity, if he had ever en revealed to the public as a bigamist—especially with a legal fe who had been forced by his desertion to become a prostitute— s career would be over. Walter Winchell, Louella Parsons, and edda Hopper would have seen to that.

hen we reached Los Angeles, Oldfield dropped me off at my house Hollywood and then took Dash back to the Palisades. Before eaking up, we thanked Barney for his expert driving in our behalf. e said that he'd had himself "a jim-dandy time" and would be proud drive us anywhere we might want to go in the future.

The first thing I did when I got to my desk was to phone Chandler.

"The prodigal son has returned," I told him.

"That's good to hear," Ray said. "If Mexican bandits had killed u down there, I'd have a hell of a time explaining it to the judge."

I filled him in on what we'd discovered, and recounted our inter- ew with María.

"She sounds like a very sad lady," Ray declared.

"Well, she's not happy as paid meat, that's for sure," I said. "But iat else can she do to earn a living in a place like San Felipe?"

"She could leave."

"And go where? Do what? Besides, I very much doubt that she has ough money to quit. Her boss collects half of what she earns, and probably charges her for room and board. A village that size isn't actly swarming with paying customers, even when you count in the urists. María is trapped there, and she knows it."

"A crummy situation," said Chandler.

"Yeah, crummy. But that's the game. Life dealt her a rough hand and she's having to play it out."

"You're beginning to talk like Hammett."

"He's rubbed off on me. Too many days together."

"How'd you get along with Oldfield?"

"Great," I said. "Barney's an incredible character. At first he was boring us to death with all of his racing jabber, but when he helped us save the old man and the two kids from the flash flood, I—"

"Whoa!" broke in Chandler. "*What* flash flood?"

I told him the story in full detail.

"Hey," he said after I'd finished, "I might be able to use the flood in one of my stories. Change the setting to the Mojave Desert."

"Nix," I said. "I'm using it myself. After all, *I* almost drowned in that damned river."

"A point well taken," said Ray. "The flood's all yours. What about Thompson? Do you plan to confront the bastard with what you've found out about his first marriage?"

"Do you think I ought to? Would it do any good?"

"Maybe. Who knows? Seems to me you've nothing to lose by facing up to him with everything you know, including the personal things Amy told you. About his son . . . how Amy blamed him for the boy's death . . . everything. It could throw him off balance, and he just might blurt out something you could use in court. Never know until you try."

"That's not a bad idea," I said. "I'll go over to Thompson's house in the morning. See if I can shake him up."

"But don't expect a confession."

"He'd have to be nuts to confess to me. The most I can hope for is that I'll be able to rattle him, make him say something he wouldn't say otherwise. I used to do that in court with hostile witnesses."

"I'll keep my fingers crossed," Ray promised.

"Do that," I said, "and cross your toes while you're at it."

I learned, via Hedda Hopper, that Thompson was at home. In her gossip column, she reported that "everybody's favorite singing star, Tink Thompson, is recording all the new songs for his latest album in his private soundproof studio inside his posh Beverly Hills mansion. And don't we *all* wish we could work at home. Happy vocal chords, Tink!"

I'd driven by the Thompson house, which was north of Sunset, several times in the past, and although a locked gate with a newly hired inside guard protected the place from strangers, I planned an elaborate method of entrance.

From the magazine articles I'd read about Thompson, I knew that he was an avid collector of rare birds. He maintained a large aviary at the back of his estate, with many birds from around the world.

That collection was my key. I knew that if I phoned the house and managed to get Thompson on the line, he'd hang up on me. His dead wife's lover! Go to hell, Gardner! So the plan I worked out seemed to be my only chance.

The repairs on the clutch of my camper had been finished while I was in Mexico. Tomas, my houseboy, drove me over to pick it up. On the way back, I purchased a birdcage, a cage cover, some paints and brushes, and a book on rare bird species.

In my driveway, while Tomas, curious, watched my activities from the kitchen window (having no idea of what I was up to), I lettered a sign on each side of the camper and on both doors:

RILEY'S INTERNATIONAL
Exotic Pets Our Specialty

Once this was done, I dug out a pair of blue coveralls that I kept in the garage and a peaked yachting cap from my closet. Together, they would serve as a suitable uniform.

Everything was set. I'd planned it as carefully as an armored-car heist. I'd drive up to the gate and tell the guard I had a special item for Mr. Lloyd Thompson that I must deliver to him personally.

What do you have?

A very rare talking parrot from South America. A gift from Mr. Walter Winchell. For Mr. Thompson's collection. Then I'd display the draped birdcage. Naturally, the guard would check with the Thompson house by phone and they would, of course, say fine, let him through.

I'd play the game right up to the point where I met Thompson himself. Then he'd *have* to talk to me.

It would work. I *knew* it would work.

That afternoon, in my Riley's "uniform," wearing dark glasses, I rolled up to the Thompson gate—but the hired guard didn't come out to meet me. A Beverly Hills police officer had taken his place. I was puzzled. Why was a uniformed cop on guard duty at a private home?

Beyond the gate I could see several police cars parked on the long, upward curve of the driveway. Other cops were milling around, looking grim and official.

Something was very wrong.

"What do you want?" demanded the gate cop, looking at me with hard, unblinking eyes.

This was obviously not the time to play my game, so I looked confused and pretended to check a clipboard. "Uh . . . I don't think I have the right address. Is this the Edward Chapman house?"

"Naw," growled the cop. "There's no Chapman here."

"Sorry," I said, putting the camper into reverse. "I'll phone the office and get this straightened out. Sorry to have bothered you."

He just stared at me.

I drove out of there.

When I arrived back in Hollywood, I stopped at a newsstand on Highland and bought a copy of the afternoon *Herald*. Front-page headlines in all the papers, as big as those used to announce a war, told me why all the cops were at Thompson's house:

TINK THOMPSON MURDERED
Beloved Star Fatally Stabbed
at Beverly Hills Home

There was a picture of Thompson in a recording studio, holding some sheet music and singing into a microphone. It was captioned: "Everybody's Favorite."

I was stunned. Thompson murdered!

Incredible.

And totally unexpected.

> The body of Lloyd Hadley "Tink" Thompson, world-famous entertainer and star of screen, stage, and radio, was found today sprawled across the floor of his study at his home in Beverly Hills. The 37-year-old actor had been fatally stabbed and his throat had been slashed. According to authorities at the scene, the multiple knife wounds in Thompson's body offered clear evidence of a particularly brutal attack, although there was no sign of a struggle.
>
> Thompson's body was discovered by an employee at the estate, Carlos Montoya, who immediately summoned police.
>
> The murder weapon was not found and no valuables appeared to be missing from the house.
>
> Authorities refused to speculate on whether Thompson's death was in any way related to the recent murder of his wife, Amy Latimer Thompson, who was found . . .

I quit reading, in a daze. Only half aware of other traffic, I drove to Pacific Palisades. To Hammett's house. Maybe he could make some sense out of all this.

A woman answered the door. In her early twenties, attractive, blond, full-figured. She wore a tight-fitting knit dress and her eyes were cat-green. I wondered who she was. So far as I knew, Dash didn't have anyone but Buddy working for him.

"Is Mr. Hammett at home?" I asked her.

"Not yet," she told me, "but I expect him any minute. He's on his way from M-G-M. Who are you?"

"Erle Gardner," I said. "A friend. Do you work for Mr. Hammett?"

She smiled suggestively, pushing back a strand of blonde hair. "I will be when he gets here. He gave me a key and told me to come in, make myself comfy, and wait for him."

I had known about Hammett's "casual ladies" (as he calls them), but I hadn't expected to encounter one today. We walked into the living room. Her purse was on the sofa. I handed it to her with a twenty-dollar bill. "You'd better leave. I have to talk to Mr. Hammett alone."

She looked indignant. "Dash never told me anything about—"

I took her elbow and propelled her toward the door. "Just leave," I said firmly.

"Okay, Buster," she sniffed, jamming the bill into her purse. "But he's gonna be plenty pissed when he finds out that you—"

"Leave! *Now!*"

I pushed her out the door and slammed it behind her.

On a day like this, I didn't intend to argue with a hooker.

Dash arrived fifteen minutes later, stepping out of the limo before Buddy took it around to the garage.

"Bet you're surprised to see me," I said at the door.

He shrugged. "What happened to my blonde?"

"I shooed her away," I said as we went inside. "We need to talk."

"I know what you want to talk about," he said, moving to the liquor cabinet and pouring himself a bourbon. "First shot I've had all day. I'm cutting down on this stuff."

"Glad to hear it," I told him.

"Care for anything?"

"No, nothing for me."

He nodded, taking the drink with him to the sofa. "Sit down, Erle, you make me nervous."

I was pacing the room. "I'm too upset to sit," I declared. "So . . . if you're such a mind reader, tell me why I'm here."

"Thompson's murder," he said. "I don't read minds, but I *do* listen to the radio. It's on all the stations. Major news. America's beloved star butchered in his own home. Tragic loss to the world of entertainment. The passing of a legend. Blah, blah, blah."

"Okay," I said. "This thing flummoxes me. I just can't figure it."

"You want to know who I think might have killed him, right? Assuming, of course, that you didn't."

I glared at him. "Don't joke with me, dammit! This isn't the time for your cynical humor."

"Okay, okay," said Dash, sipping his drink. "So we'll play it serious. *If* you'll quit pacing. You're wearing out the rug."

I sat down in a chair near the large fieldstone fireplace. "Got any ginger ale?"

"Sure," said Dash. "Anything with it?"

"No thanks."

He got me a ginger ale. My throat was dry and it eased things. Ginger ale has always calmed me. "I had him tabbed for Amy's murder," I said, "but that doesn't make much sense now."

"Yeah," nodded Dash. "What does make sense is that the same person who killed Amy also got rid of Thompson."

"I was so *sure* he was guilty," I admitted. "Not a doubt in my mind. I went over there today to try and shake him up with what I know about him, but the place was swarming with cops."

"Did they question you?"

"No. I was in disguise."

"What?"

"I figured it was the only way I could see Thompson. I fixed myself up as a pet-service deliveryman. When I saw that something was wrong at the gate, I gave the cop a phony story and left."

Hammett lowered his head, thinking. "María Sanchez could have iced Thompson," he said. "Except that she was in San Felipe and he was in Beverly Hills."

"Is that supposed to be funny? Are you joking again?"

"No, I'm trying to think of who might have had a motive for killing this creep. María certainly had one."

"I'll grant that, but what good does it do to talk about her when we *know* she couldn't have done it?"

Dash finished his bourbon, setting the glass down on the coffee table in front of him. He leaned back on the sofa and crossed his thin legs. "In a murder case," he said, "you look at all the angles. Even the ones that seem pointless. María could have arranged to have someone else kill Thompson for her."

"That's crazy," I snapped. "She has no connections in California. From the way she talked, she's never been north of the border. Besides which, she doesn't have the kind of money to pay someone to do a job like this. The whole idea is crazy."

"Okay, so we scratch Señorita Sanchez. Who does that leave?"

"You tell me," I said. "You're the ex-detective."

Hammett fished out a pipe, walked to a corner table, took the lid off a lacquered-wood tobacco humidor, and dipped into the bowl. He tamped down the tobacco, struck a match, and lit the pipe. It took a few seconds before it began to draw properly. Then he turned to me, exhaling a cloud of blue smoke.

"I thought you gave up tobacco."

"I gave up cigarettes. Not pipes."

"It's still tobacco."

"Yeah, but different. I used to smoke a pipe back in Frisco about the time I married José. I quit for cigarettes. Now it's the other way around."

"Suit yourself," I said.

"So, let's revisit the subject of Mr. Thompson's violent demise," said Dash, puffing away as he returned to the sofa.

"Despite his angelic image, I'm sure he made enemies," I said. "Every public figure makes enemies. And one of them could have killed him."

"Maybe," nodded Hammett. "And maybe someone a lot closer to him did the job."

"Like who?"

He smiled tightly. "Like Marisol Herrera-Quintano."

I stared at him through the pipe smoke.

FOURTEEN

Montecito is located ninety miles upcoast from Los Angeles, at the foot of the Santa Ynez Mountains in Santa Barbara County. Early morning fog rolls in from the Pacific to the south, while to the north, the chaparral-covered mountains dramatically rise some four thousand feet into the California sky. On most days, the area is flooded with brilliant sunshine and warm sea breezes by mid-morning. The mild Mediterranean climate supports an amazing variety of plant life and attracts nature lovers from around the globe.

Dante would have called it paradise.

Although the area has always been proud of its colonial Spanish aristocracy, since the 1890s Montecito has become home to some of the wealthiest Anglo families in North America. These expansive estates, each with its own vast gardens, reflect the British, French, Italian, Spanish, and German origin of their original owners, and offer a gracious lifestyle without parallel. And without intrusion; Montecito's estates are some of the most private in the world.

Chandler had phoned Dash to discuss Tink Thompson's murder; when he found out we were going north to talk to Thompson's mistress, he got upset. I took over the phone.

"What's the problem, Ray?"

"You're doing it again! You're leaving Los Angeles! You're jumping bail!"

"You know damn well I'm not," I told him. "I'll be back in town tonight. Dash and I want to check this out."

"Then I'm coming along. To keep track of you."

"Bushwah!" I said. "You want to come along because you think it would be swell fun to meet Thompson's mistress. And you want to see what it's like inside a Montecito estate."

"That too," he admitted.

"So, okay. Pick us up in the Duesy and we'll all go up together."

And that's what we did: we all drove up to Montecito together in Ray's big Duesenberg.

The Herrera-Quintano estate was hidden from the road by high, ivy-covered walls that seemed to continue forever as we searched for the entrance gate.

Hammett had telephoned ahead from his house in the Palisades; when he got Marisol on the line, he told her he was doing a piece for *Collier's* on Montecito, and that he planned to feature the Herrera-Quintano estate in his article. However, he was working against a tight deadline and needed to see her this afternoon. Would that be all right? She told him *The Maltese Falcon* was her favorite mystery, that she practically knew it by heart, and to certainly please come. Would he also be bringing along a photographer?

No, not today, he said, but he *was* bringing two other writers with him. She said that was fine; she loved meeting writers. Just buzz the gate when he got there.

"If she *is* the one who killed Thompson, how are we going to find that out?" asked Ray as we motored along the walled road. He addressed the question to Hammett.

"I have no idea," Dash said. "The best we can hope for is that she'll admit to her affair with Thompson when Erle tells her what Amy told him."

144

"Right," I agreed. "This is a fishing expedition. We need to meet her, find out what she's like. She may say something to implicate herself in Thompson's murder."

"That's a long shot," said Chandler.

"Sure," I declared. "But sometimes long shots pay off."

We finally reached a tall iron gate draped in a spill of crimson bougainvillea. A metal speaker-box was mounted to the left side of the gate, a black button in its center. Hammett walked over and pressed it.

A voice from the box: "Yes?"

"It's the Hammett party," Dash said.

"Of course. Please drive in."

The iron gate swung back to admit us.

A graded road, bordered by massed oak trees, gradually climbed to the main house. Afternoon sunlight filtered through the leaves, creating the effect of a long, green tunnel. I felt as if we had entered another world.

The climbing road ended in a wide forecourt; Ray stopped the car in the adjoining brick-paved parking circle.

As expected, the rambling two-story house was imposing. Whitewashed adobe exterior, scrolled with Spanish ivy. Red tile roof, a gracefully arched Moorish entrance, ornamental balconies, and elaborate Castillian ironwork outside each window.

Marisol Herrera-Quintano was waiting for us at the door. Smiling, she put out her hand to Dash as he stepped forward. "Mr. Hammett. What a pleasure to meet you in person."

Dash introduced Ray and me, and we each kissed her hand. I don't generally kiss a woman's hand, but she was so regal that the gesture seemed appropriate.

Amy had described her perfectly. Translucent, beiged-pearl skin. Dark, liquid eyes. Shining black hair. All of this, combined with an aura of elegance and poise that had obviously been bred into her genes. Her makeup was spare, delicately accenting her polished natural beauty, and she wore a deceptively simple black-silk afternoon dress that had probably cost more than most men earn in a year. Classic gold filigree circled her neck and dangled from her ears, looking as if it had been in the family for generations.

She radiated an aura of inner strength. I sensed banked fire underneath her cool poise; I suspected that fire became an inferno when she allowed herself to let go. No wonder Thompson had been attracted to her. It was difficult to believe that this exquisite creature was capable of murder. But then again . . .

She turned toward Hammett. "My husband is in Europe, but I will be happy to show you around the estate."

"Swell," said Dash.

She led us through the house into a large breakfast room. A giant bowl of white gardenias, exactly centered on a glass table, scented the air, and open French doors offered a spectacular view of the mountains.

"I adore the fragrance of gardenias," said Marisol as we all stood at the windows gazing out at the mountains, now glowing pink in the afternoon sun.

"Yeah, smells good in here," Dash said.

"Mr. Hammett," she said. "Might I ask you something I've been dying to know in relation to your *Maltese Falcon?*"

"Shoot," Dash said.

"*Did* Brigid and Sam Spade ever get together again after she served her prison term?"

Dash ran a finger along his mustache. "Uh . . . I'd say they did . . . sure."

"I know they truly loved one another. You made that very clear."

"That's right," nodded Hammett. "Sam just refused to play the sap for her after she killed his partner." He looked steadily into her dark eyes. "You can't let a woman get away with murder."

We waited tensely for her reply. If she *had* killed Thompson, would she react to such a pointed comment?

She smiled, betraying no trace of hidden guilt. "I agree, of course. Brigid had to take full responsibility for her crime." She sighed. "I'm just glad to know that Sam forgave her and that they were finally able to be together."

"True love will always find a way," Ray declared.

"Well, then," Marisol said as she mentally changed gears. "Back to business. What would you like to see? We have the swimming pool, the tennis courts, the stables, an exercise ring for the horses . . . even our own golf course. My husband, Fernando, is a passionate golfer. He designed the course himself."

"Why don't we take a walk down to the gardens," suggested Hammett.

"Wonderful. I'm sure you'll be impressed," she said. "We're quite proud of what we've accomplished in the years since we inherited the estate. It's taken a tremendous amount of time and effort. We have almost every variety of flower and tree that is capable of being grown in this climate. I like to think of the estate as a botanical resource, something that will live long after Fernando and I are gone. A legacy for the future from the Herrera-Quintano family."

"I'm impressed already," said Hammett.

"As you'll see, we're growing Spanish dagger . . . wild grape . . . California orange poppies, that's our state flower, you know . . . foxglove . . . and more than three dozen varieties of cactus, some of them extremely rare and precious. Here, let me show you."

She led us out to the large rear patio; it was shaded by tall date palms and flanked by statues of Greek athletes and Roman emperors. On the other side, a cobbled path wound downward through a grove of olive trees, heavy with green fruit, and then toward a neatly trimmed boxwood hedge at least ten feet high.

"Spanish gardens are meant to be somewhat mysterious," she said. "Space is segmented; the garden unfolds area by area, so that the visitor constantly discovers something new."

"English gardens are sometimes like that," said Chandler.

"Yes, of course. But I think English gardens are intended mainly as a feast for the eye. Spanish gardens, on the other hand, stimulate all of our human senses. Not just sight, but touch . . . smell . . . even hearing, as we listen for the subtle differences in sound between the rustle of eucalyptus leaves and the whisper of palm fronds."

"What you've done here is certainly more complex than what I knew in England," Ray observed.

"A fully realized garden is balm for the soul. It teaches the lesson of tranquillity. Hopefully, it brings inner peace. That is the goal we strive for."

"Are you at peace?" Dash asked.

"So far as a busy world allows me to be, yes, I am," she answered. "When life becomes too intense, I come out here, to one of our gardens, and I contemplate the beauty and perfection of nature. It restores my spirit, and then I continue on with the things, both good and bad, that life entails."

We entered a walled courtyard that had been tiled in the bright geometric patterns of Andalusia. A bubbling stone fountain in its center was surrounded by a group of bronze water nymphs. Then, immediately beyond the courtyard, we stepped through an arched hedge into what Marisol called "our topiary garden."

It was fantastic. Like something out of a child's storybook. A gardener's shears had cleverly sculpted ducks, horses, rabbits, lions, bears, seals . . . even a giraffe; all had been formed from cypress, eugenias, and junipers. The topiary creatures were lifelike to the smallest detail.

"Pure genius," marveled Chandler. "I've never seen anything to match these. Not even in England, and the English—as I'm sure you know—love topiary."

Marisol smiled in appreciation. "We call them our 'plant children,' " she declared. "We're quite proud of the artistry."

"You should be," said Chandler. "They must require a great deal of upkeep."

"Luckily, we have families working for us who love the gardens as much as we do, so maintenance is never a problem." She nodded ahead. "Come . . . I'll show you our Blue Garden."

We walked through another courtyard, past a terraced waterfall and a white-painted gazebo draped in purple wisteria. Another arched hedge led us into the aptly named Blue Garden.

"Everything here is in complementary hues," she told us as she pointed. "Those are blue fan and *Erythea armata* palms. We have cedar and blue spruce to provide shade for our blue furcraeas. Over there is gray-blue ice plant, and then we have the blue fescue grass as our base. In the moonlight, the various shades of blue are breathtaking."

I know quite a bit about flowers and trees, but much of this plant life was alien to me. And, in a sense, frustrating. We had come here to confront Thompson's mistress, to ascertain her possible guilt in two murders, and instead, we had discovered a woman of exceptional depth and sensitivity. I didn't know what to think, and I wondered when—or *if*—Hammett would turn the conversation toward Tink Thompson. But he was in charge at the moment and I had to be patient.

"The cactus garden is next," she said, leading us down a black-and-white pebbled walk, past a huge fern grotto inhabited by real African flamingos and some albino peacocks, then past a lily pond graced by white swans, and finally, through an unusual pergola with a Victorian glass dome.

As we entered a floral-tiled courtyard furnished with garden chairs, Hammett paused. "Could we cool our heels for a while?" he asked. "I'm not used to all this walking."

"Of course," agreed Marisol. "This is an ideal place to rest."

We sat down in chairs that had been arranged into a conversational grouping around a low table. A series of artfully trimmed boxwood hedges ringed the courtyard's perimeter.

There was a long moment of silence. Then Marisol looked at Dash intently. "You didn't come here to talk about gardens, Mr. Hammett. Isn't that true?"

"That's true," he said. "How did you guess?"

"You haven't taken any notes. You aren't asking any questions, let alone the kind of questions journalists ask. Your mind is elsewhere. So why *did* you come?"

"To talk about someone you knew . . . Tink Thompson."

She winced, and then ran a nervous tongue over her upper lip. "What about him?"

"For one thing," I said, "he's just been murdered."

"Isn't that simply terrible? I was extremely upset when I heard the news on the radio. Mr. Thompson had a wonderful singing voice. I have all of his albums."

Dash pressed on. "You *did* know him personally?"

She nodded. "Oh, yes. He and I were acquainted."

"You were a lot more than that, from what Erle tells me," said Hammett.

"A *lot* more," I added.

She turned toward me, her jaw set. Her dark eyes seemed to burn. "What do you *think* you know of my relationship with Lloyd Thompson?"

"Everything," I said. "His wife, Amy, told me all about your affair. She read the letters you wrote to him, and saw the photos you sent. She overheard your phone conversations. She knew that he stayed here with you when your husband was away. She had planned to use all this as evidence against him in divorce court, but someone killed her before she could do that."

Marisol nodded calmly. "Where is this so-called evidence now?"

"It's in safekeeping," I dissembled.

"Nonsense! There *are* no letters or photos. They don't exist. His wife lied to you. What she said about Lloyd and me . . . all lies."

I met her angry gaze. "Then you deny having had an affair with Tink Thompson?"

"Of course I deny it! We were acquaintences, nothing more. And no one can prove otherwise."

"You seem awfully sure of yourself," I said. "As if you *know* that the letters and photos are no longer any threat to you. The only way you could be certain of that is if you'd destroyed them."

"That's ridiculous," she declared. "They never existed."

"Where were you the night Thompson was killed?" Ray asked her.

"That's none of your business," she said tightly.

"It could be the business of the police," I said. "It could be that you decided to get rid of Amy Thompson while her husband was in Palm Springs. That would have been when you destroyed the letters. Maybe Thompson suspected that you'd killed his wife, so he broke off the affair; he could have threatened to tell the police. Then you would have been forced to kill him, too."

She stood up, her eyes sparking with anger. "You invade my privacy, gain access to my home under false pretenses, and then, without a *shred* of proof, accuse me of murdering two people." Her voice was shrill. "Get out! Get off my property or I will have you *thrown* off!"

"Okay," said Dash. "Sorry to have disturbed your inner peace and tranquillity. But in my book, sister, you're still an ace suspect for having iced Tink and Amy Thompson."

We left her to contemplate the beauty of nature.

FIFTEEN

After leaving the Herrera-Quintano estate, we drove the short distance north to Santa Barbara for dinner. Once, years before, I had taken Amy to Biancheri's Ristorante on Stearn's Wharf for her birthday. It was a place I'd known from my years as an attorney; my partner and I had sometimes entertained important clients at Biancheri's. Although it was far from being the most expensive restaurant in Santa Barbara, its unique setting was one of the most spectacular. I told Hammett and Chandler that Biancheri's had great food and they agreed that it sounded like a swell choice for dinner.

Stearn's Wharf is a Santa Barbara landmark. Built in 1926, largely with money donated by millionaire Max Fleischmann so he could have a place to anchor his yacht, the wharf extends over the Pacific for the length of several city blocks. Biancheri's occupies a handsome building at the far end, out where the pelicans and sea gulls make the wharf their home. The ocean breeze was gusting as we walked straight into the sunset along the wooden boardwalk, high above the gold-washed surf.

Biancheri's was exactly as I remembered it. Following my lead, Dash and Ray ordered shrimp scampi. I confessed somewhat sheepishly that I'd never tried anything but scampi on Biancheri's menu, and I knew from experience that it was primo.

As we ate our way through the antipasto, we talked about Marisol. "Maybe the police will do better than we did when they get around to her," I said. "Even if they refuse to believe my story about Thompson's affair, they'll still be asking her some serious questions about his death."

"So she'll just deny everything, the same way she did with us," Ray said. "And they'll walk away."

"Maybe," I said, polishing off some focaccia bread and tomato checca.

"At least we cracked that queenly façade of hers," said Hammett as the waiter approached with our scampi. "Could be the cops will come up with something. You never know."

The shrimps were just as good as I remembered. Conversation lagged as we chewed crustaceans and sopped up garlic sauce with hunks of crusty, just-out-of-the-oven Italian bread.

Afterward, as we lingered over cups of strong Italian coffee, conversation resumed. I could see the waiter bringing our check just as Ray said: "Well, if *she* didn't kill Tink Thompson, who did?"

As the waiter laid the check on the tablecloth, he hesitated. "I don't mean to intrude, but I can answer the gentleman's question—about who killed Mr. Thompson."

We all stared up at him. I muttered, "*You* know who killed Tink Thompson?"

"Oh, yes sir, I do. It's been on the radio all afternoon. The police found the knife with his blood on it in this guy's camper truck."

"What guy?" asked Dash.

"He's a writer. Does those Perry Mason books. But it looks like he skipped town. The police have a warrant out for him."

"Christ!" I said.

"You look kinda funny, mister," said the waiter. "Are you all right?"

My voice was hoarse. "I . . . uh . . . I'm fine. Maybe just a reaction to the shrimp."

"We guarantee it's fresh, sir. Like all our fish. If there's a problem—"

"No problem," I said.

We paid the bill and left.

Quickly.

Outside, in the Duesenberg, I began shaking. "My God!" I moaned. "Somebody put the murder knife in my camper."

Chandler nodded. "Has to be the same person who killed Thompson and Amy."

"Which lets Marisol off the hook," Dash said. "We were with her in Montecito when the knife was planted."

"She could have had someone put it there," said Ray.

"Possible," admitted Hammett.

"But why *me?*" I asked. "Why pin the Thompson killing on *me?*"

"Simple," said Dash. "You've already been charged with Amy's murder, so you're the perfect patsy to take a fall for the Thompson job."

I felt numb. My heart was pumping fast. "What'll I do?"

"You can't go back to your place. They'll have it staked out." Dash thought for a moment. "Look . . . come home with me. I'll hide you in the basement."

"The police know we're friends," I said. "They're bound to show up at your place too."

"Sure, but they won't find you," he said. "The original owner had a hidden room built next to the ice-cream parlor. He stored his valuables there. Nobody knows about it."

"I'm not sure hiding out is a good idea," Ray told me. "Maybe it would make more sense to turn yourself in to the police. Being a fugitive will just make things worse."

"Worse than what?" I snapped. "They already think I killed Amy, and now they find this murder weapon covered with Thompson's blood in my camper. What chance will I have if I turn myself in?"

"What chance will you have if you don't?" Chandler countered.

"Maybe, somehow, I can trace the killer," I said. "I can't do that from a jail cell."

Chandler shook his head. "How can you find the killer? Where will you start?"

"How the hell do I know?" My tone was heated, intense. "But I'm not giving myself up. I'm not going to roll over and play dead for the cops on two murders I never committed."

"All right," sighed Chandler. "I suppose things can't get much worse if you run."

"Drive us to my place," Hammett said to Ray.

"What if they've got your house staked out too?"

"We'll deal with that situation when we get there," said Dash. "Just drive."

Chandler started the engine and eased the big Duesenberg onto the coast highway, headed south.

Raymond Chandler has many eccentricities; among them is the firm opinion that only specific gas stations (and their Chandler-approved personnel) are qualified to provide gasoline for a Duesenberg. His preferred station is a Texaco at Fifth and Wilshire in Santa Monica. By the time we got back to Los Angeles, the Duesenberg was running on fumes because Ray had refused to stop at any of the stations we had passed on the way. So we drove *past* the turnoff to Dash's Pacific Palisades house in order to obtain gas five miles farther on, in Santa Monica. Despite the near-empty gas tank, we arrived at the approved Texaco pumps without incident, but by the time we got there, I badly needed to visit the men's room.

Dash and Ray said they'd wait for me in the car.

"You guys must have cast-iron kidneys," I told them. "Are you sure you don't want to use the facilities?"

"We control our urinary process through yoga," said Hammett.

"That's right," nodded Chandler. "A case of mind over bladder."

Despite how lousy I felt, that got a laugh out of me. I walked to the rear of the station and entered the rest room. It was clean and brightly lit. Texaco service in action!

Moments later, the door opened behind me—and there they were: Tink's two surly looking brothers, Len and Freddie Thompson.

"Hiya, pal," said Len. He was an inch taller than Freddie (who was a six-footer) and had squinty, pale-blue eyes and a broken nose, with the thick neck and heavy shoulders of a professional boxer. No wonder he never made it as a matinee idol.

I couldn't see brother Freddie's eyes. He wore dark glasses and had his sleeves rolled up. Muscles. They both had plenty of bulging muscles. And they were both glaring at me.

"You killed Tink," Freddie said in his flat, matter-of-fact tone. "You used a knife on our brother."

"The knife was planted," I told them. "I never killed anybody. Someone's trying to frame me for your brother's death."

They ignored this—as if I'd never spoken.

"Tink had Mark Silver following you," Len said. "Private dicks learn a lot. He made notes on who your pals are. Found out that Chandler always gets his gas here—so we figured that sooner or later, he'd show up, and then we'd follow him to you. Turns out he brought you to us."

"Yeah," said Freddie. "So here we are, come to pay our respects."

I backed slowly toward the sink. Nothing I said to them would matter, but I said it anyway: "I know you think I'm lying when I tell you I didn't kill your brother, but it's God's truth. I'm innocent. I swear it."

"And I'm Little Bo Peep," said Len. "I swear it."

"Time to quit stalling," snapped Freddie.

"What are you going to do?" There was a note of panic in my voice. I felt like a trapped animal.

"First, we'll beat the living crap out of you," said Len.

"Break a few bones." Freddie smiled.

"Then we'll turn over what's left of you to the cops," said Len. "They'll do the rest."

Before I could reply, Len Thompson hit me with the Empire State Building. At least, that's how his fist felt smashing into my face.

Then Freddie stepped up, slammed my head against the wall and drove his knee into my stomach.

I was gasping for breath and blood was dripping from my upper lip when they stepped back.

Freddie grinned. "We'll tell the cops you had an accident on the way to headquarters."

"A real bad one," added Len. "Busted you all up."

He brought out a woven-leather blackjack and slapped it against his open palm. "This little baby has lead inside. I'm gonna give you what I've got—a broken nose. For starters, that is. Then I'll break your jaw."

"Drop it!"

They had their backs to the door and hadn't seen Hammett as he came in. He was holding a leveled .38 in his right hand.

The two of them turned to face him. Len allowed the leaded sap to slip from his fingers.

"Get behind me, Erle," said Dash.

"We're makin' a citizen's arrest here," said Freddie. "Your pal is wanted for murder. We're doing our civic duty."

Len was glaring at Hammett. "You'd better stow the heater before we take it away from you and shove it up your ass."

Hammett smiled tightly; he was enjoying himself. "The last poor son of a bitch who tried to take a gun away from me ended up with his brains all over the wall. I'm sure you wouldn't want me to mess up

this pristine crapper by sending a .38 slug through your thick skull."
Then, to me, but never taking his eyes off the Thompson brothers:
"Go back to the car, Erle. I'll deal with this."

I walked out unsteadily, nursing my cut lip. Behind me, from inside, I heard scuffling, then thudding sounds. Dash came out with the gun in his hand.

"What happened?" I asked him.

"I cold-cocked both of 'em with the .38," he told me. "They're sleeping like two babes in the woods."

"I didn't know you still carried a gun."

"Usually I don't," he said, pulling up his left trouser leg. A spring-clip holster was strapped to his calf. He replaced the .38. "But I didn't know what to expect on this trip, so I brought one along. When I worked for Pinkerton, I learned that if you're going to beard a killer, you go armed. And when we started out today, it looked as if Marisol might be a killer."

We walked back to the car.

"What was that all about?" Ray asked.

"The Thompson boys paid me a little visit," I told him. "They're convinced I killed their brother. They were going to work me over . . . then Dash showed up."

"Are they dead?" Ray asked Hammett.

"Naw. Not by a long shot. They'll wake up with a doozy of a headache, but that's all."

"They'll tell the police that you guys were with me in the Duesenberg," I said. "Aiding a fugitive at large. It could be rough for you."

Hammett shrugged. "I'll say we were taking you to headquarters so you could turn yourself in; then these two jumped you. After I got back to the car, you were gone."

"What about the gun?" asked Ray.

"I never had one."

"They'll say you did."

"And I'll say I didn't. They can't prove it. And they won't want me to talk about that leaded sap of theirs."

I sighed. "Well, one thing's for certain—now that I've been seen with you, the cops will scour your place from top to bottom."

"Let 'em," shrugged Hammett. "They won't find you."

"Okay, then," I said to Chandler. "On to the Palisades!"

SIXTEEN

Two blocks short of Hammett's place, Dash and I got out of the car and waited in the thick shadow of a pepper tree while Chandler drove past the house, scouting out the situation. He circled the block and came back to us.

"Well?" asked Dash. "Did you spot anything?"

"There's a black Plymouth parked across the street from your place with two men in it," said Ray. "If they aren't cops, I'll eat my shirt."

Dash nodded. "Yeah . . . plainclothes on stakeout. Which means we don't go in that way."

"Then how *do* we get in?" I asked.

"From the rear," said Hammett. "There's a hill directly behind my house with a path that leads down to the yard. We'll park on the street above the hill. I have a key to the back door."

"What if they've got a man waiting inside the house?" asked Ray.

"They can't enter without a search warrant," said Dash. "And if they had one, they'd be swarming all over the place by now. We still have time to get inside. And once we're in, we'll keep the lights off. They'll never know we're there."

"Let's do it," I said.

And we did.

Chandler stopped the Duesenberg on the street behind Hammett's place and we checked the terrain. The area was deserted. A dog barked in the distance; then there was only the nocturnal chirping of summer crickets.

An overhead streetlight cast our shadows ahead of us as we left the car.

"You go on back home to Cissy," Dash told Chandler. "I'll phone you tomorrow."

"Can you go by my place first?" I asked Ray. "Tell Tomas that I'm safe, and to please hold the fort for me. I'll contact him as soon as I can. But don't tell him where I am."

"This is all so damned bizarre," Ray said to me. "Every cop in L.A. is after you for a killing you had nothing to do with. And not a single clue as to the real killer's identity. It's insane!"

"I can handle it," I said. "You just go ahead . . . and thanks for everything."

"Well, then . . . good luck," said Ray, putting the Duesy in gear. The big car drifted away into the darkness.

It was a clear night. I looked up at the glittering spangle of stars. "Maybe I should have been born on another planet," I said.

And we headed down the hill.

Everything went smoothly. We got into the house through the door that led to the kitchen. No cops were inside. We were alone.

"Where's Buddy?" I asked.

"I knew we'd be late getting back," Dash said, "so I told him to show up tomorrow. He didn't argue. He didn't tell me where he was going, either, but I'd lay odds that he's with Margaret. I just hope I don't lose my chauffeur when they finally get married."

"Has he proposed yet?"

"I dunno. He's kind of closemouthed about his personal life. I know there are some problems that have to be solved first. His family doesn't want him to marry an American, even if she *is* a damned fine classical pianist. We'll just have to wait and see what happens."

"When he returns tomorrow, won't the cops see him come in?"

"Doesn't matter. You'll be well hidden, so I won't mind giving them a tour of the place. They won't even need a search warrant. It was us getting past them tonight that counted."

The house was dark inside. Dash took my elbow and led me toward the basement. We descended a flight of wooden stairs to the ice-cream parlor. "You can have all the strawberry sodas you can drink—complete with whipped cream and a cherry on top. Nobody makes better strawberry ice-cream sodas than Dash Hammett." He grinned at me.

"I prefer chocolate."

"You'll take what you get," he said.

I grinned back at him.

Dash walked behind the counter and pushed a large storage cabinet to one side. He pressed a section of molding at the base of the wall. A door slid open, revealing the hidden room. It was bare and windowless; the air inside smelled unpleasantly stale.

"You're right," I said. "The cops will never find me here. But it's a good thing I'm not claustrophobic."

"I've got a cot upstairs I can bring down, along with some sheets, blankets, and a pillow," said Dash. "I've also got a portable radio to keep you company. You can listen to all the soap operas."

"Great. I can catch up on Ma Perkins. There *is* a problem, though."

"What's that?"

"Ventilation. I could suffocate in there."

"You can keep the door open unless I let you know that cops are in the house. Also, there's a bathroom down here you can use."

"How long do I have to stay cooped up?"

"For as long as it takes us to figure out what to do next. I'm thirsty. How about a soda?"

"It's dark down here," I said.

"I can still fix sodas," Dash answered.

While Dash set to work behind the ice-cream counter, I sat on a stool, thinking.

"I've got a 'what if' question for you," I said.

"Shoot."

"What if those two bruisers, Len and Freddie, knifed their brother? What if *they* did the job on Thompson?"

"What would be their motive?"

"Well . . . the three of them began their careers *together* as the Thompson Trio, but only Tink got famous and hit the big time. He made all the money, won all those millions of fans. Nobody's ever heard of Len or Freddie."

"So they put a knife in brother Tink," said Hammett. "How's that going to help them get famous?"

"That wouldn't have been their motive."

"Then *what?*"

"Jealousy. Maybe they grew to hate their brother for hogging the limelight. Maybe they asked for a cut of his earnings and he turned them down. Maybe they got into an argument and it ended with them killing him."

"That's a lot of maybes," said Dash.

"There's also the money angle. Of course there's no way of telling how much the brothers know about Thompson's estate planning, but they must be named somewhere in his will, for something. I can't imagine that anyone as rich as Tink Thompson would leave his own brothers out for no reason."

"It's possible," Dash said, "but anything they would get from Thompson's estate would probably be only a small percentage of what he was worth."

"That would have been true if Amy had been alive when Thompson died. In that case, she would have inherited the bulk of Thompson's estate and the brothers would have had to be content with presumably minor bequests. But that's not what happened. Instead, Amy died first. That changes everything," I said.

"How?"

"Well, Len and Freddie certainly didn't know anything about Amy changing her will. They would have been under the impression that once she was dead, her half of Thompson's estate would go right back to him, effectively doubling his assets."

"Okay. So where does that take us?" asked Hammett.

I was concentrating hard, back in my legal mode, thinking strategy. "It means Len and Freddie thought that killing Amy would result in Tink Thompson regaining all of his estate."

"You think the brothers poisoned Amy?" Hammett asked.

"It's possible."

Hammett put an ice-cream soda in front of me. "Okay," he said, "Then Len and Freddie kill Thompson. What about María Sanchez?"

I sipped my soda. It was strawberry, but Hammett was right. It was good. I continued: "Let's assume that Len and Freddie didn't know about Thompson's first marriage to María. So they believed that Amy was Thompson's legal wife—just like everyone else did. With Amy dead, *they* inherit."

Dash started to say something, but I kept talking. "Or—let's take another tack—maybe, being brothers, they *did* know about the first marriage, but they also knew that Thompson had gotten a divorce somewhere along the line—a divorce that we don't know about. That would make his marriage to Amy legal. Again, with Amy dead, *they* inherit."

Dash nodded, considering the implications.

"Or—third possibility—they know about the marriage to María Sanchez, and they also know that Thompson *didn't* get a divorce, but they think nobody else will ever find out."

Dash nodded. He was tracking along with me.

"One of the three possibilities has to be the truth, and they all lead to the same bottom line: from the standpoint of Len and Fred-

die, María Sanchez is irrelevant. The death of Amy means money for them. With Amy and her son dead, then under California law, Len and Freddie, along with their parents, move to the front of Tink Thompson's inheritance line. Apart from minor bequests that Tink may have made to servants or friends, the Thompson clan inherits everything."

Dash was troubled. "All your theories involve premeditation. Len and Freddie would have had to really think this out beforehand. That means detailed plans. And these two bozos just don't seem like the 'planning' type."

"Yeah," I admitted. "I'm not so sure they're the type to commit cold-blooded murder. Especially of their brother. He may have had more money than they did, but I've never heard about any deep problems between them."

"As you said, there's always sibling rivalry," Dash countered.

"Well, *somebody* killed Tink Thompson," I said.

"Right," Dash said, nodding. "Somebody sure did. And all we have to do to save your neck is find out who that somebody is, establish the motive, and offer proof of guilt."

"You make it sound impossible."

"I'm a cynic, remember?" he said with a grin. "But believe me, Erle, in this crazy world, nothing is impossible."

I tried to believe him.

Two long days passed. Buddy returned. The cops searched the house. I actually *did* listen to Ma Perkins as I hid in my little room. I also listened to the news broadcasts and discovered that I was being portrayed as the most notorious criminal since Dillinger—with the Hearst empire leading the charge to have me lynched. Tomas phoned Chandler to tell him that people were starting to show up at my house just to stare.

And Walter Winchell reported that the California Bar Association had met in emergency session to suspend my law license, which was

165

ridiculous. I hadn't practiced law since I'd become a full-time writer, and as one of America's most wanted criminals, I certainly wasn't about to return to my former profession now.

M-G-M loaned Dash to 20th Century Fox to write a Charlie Chan script, so Buddy drove him to 20th every day.

The hours crawled by, and my fears and frustrations mounted. I couldn't come up with anything that promised even a hope of finding out who the real murderer was.

Early on the morning of the third day, the phone rang. The police again? Dash hadn't left yet for 20th, so he answered. It wasn't the cops.

"For you," he said, handing over the receiver.

I was shocked by his action. No one was supposed to know I was here. I put my hand over the phone. "Are you nuts? I can't talk to *anybody.*"

"You can talk to her," he said.

"Her?"

"It's Natalie."

"Nat?" I said into the phone.

"Erle! Thank God I finally reached you. When Tomas said he didn't know where you were, I began phoning all over town . . . all your friends. I even called your publisher in New York."

"I've been hiding out here," I told her. "You know why."

"I know what the papers are saying . . . that you murdered two people. But that isn't true."

"No, it isn't," I said. "Someone is trying to frame me."

"Grace just phoned," Nat said. "She's beside herself with worry."

"Tell her everything is going to be all right," I said. "It's just a matter of putting this puzzle together. And right now, I don't have all the pieces."

Her voice was strained. "I just don't understand how you could have—"

"I can't explain over the phone. You'll just have to take my word that I'll come out of this okay." I was telling her something I wasn't sure of myself. "I've handled tougher cases and won. I'll win this one."

"I still love you, Erle . . . even if we can't be together."

"And I still love you, Nat. I care a lot about you and Grace."

"I know," she said softly.

"Give Grace my love," I said.

"I will."

"And tell her to quit worrying."

"I doubt that my telling her will do much good." A hesitation on the line. "Are you going to keep running, Erle?"

"For now, I have to," I said.

"I'll pray for you."

"You do that. And . . . thanks for caring. It means a lot to me, Nat."

"Bless you, Erle."

And the call ended.

Dash came home that afternoon with news. "You won't believe who phoned me today," he said.

"I'm ready to believe anything."

"Marisol's coming here. This afternoon. She's driving down from Montecito right now."

"Why?"

"A good question. We'll have to wait and find out."

"We can't let her know I'm in the house," I said. "But I sure would like to hear what she has to say."

"You can," said Dash. "Follow me."

He took me into the sitting room and pointed to a wall. "Look at that," he said.

"The painting?"

He indicated a beautifully framed oil painting of a flowered meadow. Alpine trees were ringed around the perimeter, while snow-topped mountains soared in the background. It looked vaguely European, like some artist's version of Switzerland.

Then Dash led me into the adjoining room, a library, and pointed at the wall. I saw the same picture, in reverse.

"It's hand-painted on window glass," he said. "You can see it from either side of the wall." He closed the library's dark blue drapes. "If this side of the painting is dark and the other side is well-lit, then it functions like a two-way mirror. If you stand here, and Marisol and I sit out there, then you can see and hear our entire conversation."

"Dash, I'd say you rented a nifty house."

"Remember that the next time you think I live beyond my means."

And we grinned at each other.

SEVENTEEN

By the time Marisol arrived, Dash and I had arranged the drapes in the library so that not even a sliver of sunlight entered the room. We had also rearranged the furniture in the sitting room, creating a little nook of chairs and tables in the afternoon sunshine near the window; it became the only logical place for Hammett and Marisol to have their chat. Buddy arranged a silver tea service on the coffee table in front of the chairs and then brought in a fresh pot of hot tea that he set on top of a chafing dish.

Everything was ready.

Some minutes later, we heard a smoothly purring automobile enter the driveway. Buddy looked out the window and said it was a Rolls-Royce, with a dark-haired woman driving.

The game was afoot.

Marisol Herrera-Quintano had dressed in a gray shantung-silk suit that would have complimented Queen Mary. Pearls surrounded her neck, hung from her ears, and were looped around her black-gloved wrist. The saying is that you can always tell a lady by her leather; Marisol's black shoes and purse were simple in design, yet elegant. She was hatless, and her thick, shining hair tumbled to her shoulders. The effect was electrifying.

"Thank you for seeing me, Mr. Hammett," she said. "I deeply apologize for my previous rudeness. It was unforgivable."

"Nonsense," he said. "You were under a great deal of stress. There's nothing to forgive. And please call me Dash. All my friends do."

She smiled. Hammett had unobtrusively guided her in the direction of the conversation nook we had created and she took the bait, sitting down in the exact chair we'd hoped she would choose. Dash offered her a cup of tea; she accepted. As he poured, she looked down at the rug. I was reminded of that night with Amy, when she finally told me the truth about her marriage to Tink Thompson. It was obvious to me that I was about to hear a similar story from Marisol.

"I think I should first say that despite what the papers and the radio have reported, I do not believe that your friend, Mr. Gardner, killed Lloyd. I have no proof of this, of course, but I do have a full measure of feminine intuition and I am an excellent observer of human character. Your friend never killed anyone."

"You've got that right," said Dash.

"I hope he will be able to clear himself of the charge. You *are* helping him to do this, aren't you?"

"I'm trying," Dash replied. "But right now, it looks pretty hopeless. You came down here to tell me something. Maybe what you came to say will help Erle."

"Perhaps. I certainly don't know who killed Lloyd. But I'll tell you what I *do* know."

"Okay," said Dash. "I want to hear everything."

"Before I begin, I need your promise that what I tell you will never be repeated to anyone unless I give you my permission. I am going to provide you with information that could hurt me terribly if it was revealed. Do I have your promise?"

"I'll need to tell Erle and Ray Chandler. Otherwise, you have my promise."

"Very well." She hesitated, took a sip of tea, looked down again at the rug. It was that night with Amy, all over again.

"I lied to you when you came to Montecito," she said. "I . . . I *did* have an affair with Lloyd Thompson. I loved him. Very much."

She took another sip of tea, a gesture to cover her nervous confession.

"You need to understand my marriage, Mr. Hammett. Fernando and I are cousins. Not first cousins, but in many ways we're even more closely related than first cousins. Virtually all of our relatives are blood-related to both of us. Fernando's aunt on his mother's side is my cousin on my father's side—that sort of thing. From the moment we were born, our families hoped that eventually we would marry each other.

"Since the Americans conquered California in eighteen forty-six, all of the ancestral Spanish land has been under continuous siege. I mean no disrespect, Mr. Hammett, but Anglos are rapacious. And relentless. With each new generation, the old Spanish families lose more of their land, and there doesn't seem to be anything much we can do about it.

"Before Fernando and I got married, even in my own family people were beginning to 'marry out.' To marry Anglos. Wealthy Anglos, to be sure, but Anglos nonetheless.

"I loved my grandparents enormously. We were extremely close when I was growing up. Their biggest fear was that I might 'marry out.' This would have resulted in Herrera-Quintano land being divided, and eventually—inevitably—going to the Anglos.

"Fernando was under the same pressure when he was growing up. We weren't *forced* to marry each other, but it was made clear to us that our marriage was important.

"So we were wed. It was a happy occasion for us—and for all of the family. Fernando and I had grown up together; we had always been best friends. I trusted him as he trusted me. When I was a girl, I was something of a tomboy; this scandalized many of my relatives. But Fernando had always encouraged me in my childhood adventures, so when we wed, I thought I had truly married the perfect man.

171

"Unfortunately, as a bride, I was much more of an adolescent than a grown woman. I had no understanding of adult love—of what genuine love between a man and a woman is truly like.

"Fernando and I were never blessed with children. We tried, but we were not successful. And as the years passed, although our friendship grew, we both realized that we had married to fulfill family expectations, not because we were deeply in love.

"At some point, without ever discussing it, we reached an understanding. Fernando began spending a great deal of time traveling in connection with his business. I doubt that he is alone on all of his travels, and that is acceptable to me.

"And though I have never told him about my relationship with Lloyd, I would be very surprised if he thought that I remained alone all the time he is abroad. Fernando is careful to provide me with detailed plans of his future travels. He never returns early. When he does return, I am always at the door waiting for him. It may not be a perfect marriage, Mr. Hammett, but it *is* a good one."

"So your husband has no idea that you and Thompson were involved?" Dash asked.

"No," she replied. "I'm sure he hasn't."

"How did you meet Tink Thompson?"

"Every summer, Santa Barbara celebrates La Fiesta. This is a very important event for everyone, but it is especially important for the old Spanish families. It is the only time of the year that we are specifically honored by the Anglos for our historical contributions to the community. Despite our considerable wealth and the prestige that attaches to our family names, we are well aware that Anglos often look down on us. But during La Fiesta, we are fully accepted as the most important people in the area, the ones who have more right to be in Santa Barbara than anybody else.

"Six summers ago, Lloyd was offered the position of honorary sheriff of the celebration. It was a great distinction, an opportunity for him to become personally known to the wealthiest, most powerful individuals in the county. That means—to a large extent, of course—the wealthiest, most powerful people in North America. He accepted the offer.

"We were introduced at the *Damas y Caballeros* Ball. Fernando was on a trip to Europe that year; I had been escorted to the ball by my cousin, Rodrigo, an influential member of the La Fiesta Committee. He had been instrumental in offering the honorary sheriff position to Lloyd. Well, Rodrigo was most interested in a woman on the Committee—an Anglo, I might point out—and was quite content to leave me with Lloyd when it appeared that we got on well together.

"And we did. A woman knows when a man is interested in her, and I can tell you, Mr. Hammett, Lloyd was *very* interested in me. I had never felt so sophisticated, or so beautiful, or so exciting as I did that evening. Lloyd made me feel that way." She sighed. "It was the most magical night of my life.

"He knew I was married—and that my husband was in Europe. I knew he had been invited to stay at the Montecito estate that borders our own on the south; the husband of that family headed the Committee that year. So that night, after Rodrigo brought me home, the doorbell rang. I think you can imagine the rest."

"Was Thompson in love with you?"

She winced, closing her eyes. "I think he loved me as much as he could love anyone. But there were problems."

"His career." Hammett made it a statement, not a question.

"Yes. Lloyd was achieving amazing success in Hollywood, and he felt that a 'Mexican' wife would never be accepted by the American public. The fact that my family is of aristocratic Spanish descent meant nothing.

"And then, a year after our affair began, he informed me that Louis B. Mayer—a very important man in Lloyd's career—told him that he should get married and have a family as quickly as possible. His wife should be someone Americans would love as much as they did Lloyd. She should be kind, have a warm personality, be exceptionally beautiful—and should preferably be a natural blonde."

"Tink Thompson *told* you this?" Dash was incredulous.

"I'm not saying it didn't hurt, Mr. Hammett. But I *did* understand, more than most women would have. Remember, I myself married for reasons other than true love." She hesitated. "A few months later, Lloyd began courting Amy Latimer."

"When she was murdered, did that change things between you and Thompson?"

"No, not really. I knew he would never marry me. If Lloyd had lived, I'm sure he would have remarried; I think his new wife would have been a younger, blonder version of Amy." She sighed. "And of course, if he had done that, the relationship that existed between us could not have survived."

She took another sip of tea, and when Dash offered to refill her cup, she waved him away.

"If our relationship had ended, I think Lloyd would also have been looking for another . . . *mistress* . . . a younger, darker-haired version of *me*. My hairdresser does a wonderful job of covering it up, but gray hairs have been appearing at my temples for a couple of years now. My replacement would have been Spanish or Mexican. I think Hispanics were the only women Lloyd truly found sexually attractive."

"And despite all this, you loved him?"

"I did. We had wonderful times together. Lloyd could always make me laugh. And he would sing the most beautiful love songs to me. Songs from his films, but he sang them just for *me*."

She studied the rug again. "He was a very passionate man sexually. He . . . *awakened* me to physical sensations I hadn't known existed, and that meant a great deal, Mr. Hammett. I used to tell myself that things would somehow work out between us, but I know now that I was living an illusion.

"I'm sorry he's dead. I miss him terribly. His death has left a dark hole in my life. I think about him constantly. And I still love him.

"But he *is* dead. And next week, when my husband returns, I am going to tell Fernando this story, very much as I have told it to you. I have no doubt that he will tell me a similar story. And then we will go on."

"How did you know that we hadn't actually seen the letters and photos you sent Thompson?"

"Lloyd phoned me after Amy died. He had gone through her things and found what she had hidden. He told me that he had destroyed everything, and should anyone ask about our relationship, I should deny it."

"And you have no idea who might have killed him?" asked Hammett.

"None at all. I wish I did."

The sun had now dipped below the horizon.

"I had better go now, Mr. Hammett. I want to get back to Montecito before it gets too late." She stood up.

They walked out of the darkened sitting room. I left the library and watched as she drove away. When Dash returned to the house, he looked thoughtful.

"I believe her," he said.

"So do I."

"If she had ended up bitter and angry about their affair, then she might have had a reason to kill him. But I think we can eliminate her as a suspect."

He was right.

Marisol Herrera-Quintano was a victim of Tink Thompson, not his murderer.

EIGHTEEN

I couldn't risk going upstairs to the kitchen, so the following morning I was making chocolate milk shakes for breakfast when Hammett descended the basement stairs.

"We need to go back to San Felipe," I said, pouring the thick chocolate mixture into tall glasses. I handed one to Dash.

He was startled by my statement. "Why? María Sanchez told us all she knew. There's nothing more she can say."

"I think there is," I answered.

"What?"

"Something has been bothering me about our visit with her; it's been gnawing at the edge of my mind. When I woke up this morning, I had the answer."

Hammett perched on one of the tall counter stools and took a sip of chocolate, his eyes intense on mine.

"It's her kid," I said.

"María's son?"

I nodded. "We never asked her a single question about him."

"So? Why should we? A child his age doesn't have any bearing on the case."

"That's just it . . . how do we know *when* that snapshot was taken? It could have been years ago."

"I'm still not following you," he said.

"Suppose the photo was taken, say, ten years back. Her son would be in his late teens now. And he'd have good reason to be upset over what this man Thompson did to his mother."

"Assuming she even told him about her marriage—or about how the bastard walked out on her."

"That's one of the questions I want to ask," I said. "*Did* she tell him? If she did, and if this kid is older now, there's a good chance he could have headed here, to L.A., with an intent to kill."

Dash finished his shake and wiped the chocolate from his mustache with a paper napkin. "Are you suggesting that María's son murdered Amy first, and then went after Thompson?"

"Exactly. He'd hate the woman who took his mother's place. And, naturally, he'd hate Thompson too. It all fits."

"And what if he's just a six-year-old?" Dash asked.

"Then my theory's shot and we're back to square one. But I've got a feeling I'm onto something—and I won't know for sure until we talk to María again."

"Okay, I'm game for a return trip," Dash said. "Barney can drive us back down there. He said he'd be happy to take us anywhere, anytime."

Dash walked over to a table phone near the stairs. "I'll call him now and set it up."

He made the call, reached Oldfield's country club—and was told that Barney was in the hospital.

"Why?" asked Hammett. "What happened to him?" A pause, then: "You don't know. Okay, where is he, what hospital is he in?"

Dash jotted down the address on a notepad, then stuffed the page in his pocket. "They've got him at Hollywood Memorial," he told me. "Let's go over there."

"How can I show up in Hollywood? Every cop in L.A. has my photo."

"Don't worry," Dash assured me. "I've got a makeup kit upstairs that I brought home from the studio. I thought it might come in handy with you in hiding. Lon Chaney used it for *The Phantom of the Opera*. You can wear a fake beard and mustache. Plus a wig. I guarantee your own mother won't be able to recognize you."

"My mother is dead."

"I didn't mean that literally," said Hammett. "The point is, no cop will give you a second look."

"How do we get out of here without being spotted?"

"I'll have Buddy bring the limo up behind the house and we'll leave the same way we came in."

I didn't argue with that; I just wanted out of Hammett's basement. Dash headed for the stairs. "Back in a jiffy. We'll transform you. You'll be a new man."

"Swell," I said. "I'm getting tired of the old one."

Wearing my wig, beard, and mustache, I felt like a Halloween freak, but I had to admit that Dash had done a terrific job. I *was* transformed. I looked more like a college professor from Austria than the creator of Perry Mason. Facing my reflection in the mirror, I saw a total stranger. Eerie, but reassuring.

Buddy drove us over to the hospital.

"If Mr. Oldfield isn't up to it, I can chauffeur you down to San Felipe," he said.

"You may have to," said Hammett. "First, we need to check out Barney's condition."

Dash was so sure of my disguise that he conducted a nerve-racking test. Buddy had stopped for a traffic light on Sunset; a motor cop on the limo's passenger side was also waiting for the light to change.

Dash leaned out the car window to ask for directions to Hollywood Memorial.

"It's between Franklin and Hollywood Boulevard on Wilcox," he was told. "Big white building. Just opened last week."

I was sitting in the front seat between Buddy and Dash, and I felt like ducking as the cop stared at me. Or at least he *seemed* to be staring. Had he penetrated my disguise? Was I about to be arrested?

The light changed to green.

"Thanks, Officer," said Dash.

"Glad to help," said the cop, gunning his cycle through the intersection.

We continued east on Sunset, toward Hollywood.

Dash grinned at me. "What did I tell you? He saw you sitting right here and he didn't suspect a thing."

"I wish you hadn't done that," I said. "Took ten years off my life."

"Nerts," said Hammett. "It was a valid test. And you passed with flying colors."

When we reached Hollywood Memorial Hospital, Buddy pulled up to the front entrance. "I'll wait for you in the lot," he said. "Do you know how long you're going to be?"

"No idea," said Hammett, "but we'll find you."

"Then I'll read," said Buddy. "Margaret gave me a new book that just came out, *Of Mice and Men,* by John Steinbeck."

I was reminded again of how extraordinary Buddy was; I'd never met anyone like him before. The offspring of an immensely powerful and wealthy Haitian clan, heir to the family fortune, a graduate of the Sorbonne in literature and philosophy—and because of his principled independence, the family's fallen angel.

Some years ago, after he had earned his university degree in Paris, Buddy had come to the United States to fulfill a childhood dream. This hadn't sat well with his parents, who cut off the family funds in retaliation. But Buddy didn't let that stop him. Instead, he did what few wealthy, indulged sons have ever done voluntarily: he began supporting himself with menial jobs.

Eventually, he wound up as Hammett's chauffeur, a position that

179

is surprisingly ideal for Buddy's needs. He gets free room and board with Dash, so that he can always be on call; therefore, his salary goes a long way. And there is always plenty of time for him to read. On normal weekdays, when Dash is working at the studio, Buddy can read all day long if he wants to.

Why Hammett needs a chauffeur is another story. In the First World War, Dash went into the service to fight for his country, same as everyone else. But after he enlisted, he was forced into becoming an ambulance driver by the blockheaded military officials who assign jobs to their recruits. It was a poor match. I don't know all the details, but once, while he was driving a full ambulance, there was a bad accident; all of Hammett's patients were spilled out onto the road. Because of it, Hammett vowed that he would never drive again. To the best of my knowledge, he never has.

Buddy held up *Of Mice and Men*. "Do you like Steinbeck?" he asked.

"He's an okay writer," said Dash. "I liked his *Pastures of Heaven.*"

"This one is about a big retarded guy named Lennie who doesn't know his own strength," said Buddy.

"Yeah," I said. "Met him in a Texaco men's room the other day."

Buddy laughed. "I heard about the Thompson brothers. I'm glad you came out in one piece."

"Thanks to Hammett and his trusty thirty-eight," I said.

"Enough gab," said Dash. "Let's go find out what happened to Barney."

"So . . ." Oldfield was saying, "I'm havin' me a quiet drink at the bar when this bald-headed gink comes up to me an' says he saw me race once at a dirt track in Ohio, an' how he figgers his grandma could of beat me in her wheelchair."

We were standing next to Oldfield's bed. He was propped against three pillows, his abdomen swathed in jumbo-sized adhesive bandages, telling us how he ended up here.

"What this bald fella said got me riled, an' I took a swing at him."
Barney raised a fist. "Hit him smack on the button and he goes back-
wards into a table. Knocked all the drinks off it, spilling beer every
which way. Well, next thing I know, he grabs up a cue stick from the
pool table and lets me have it." Barney pointed to the bandages.
"Cracked three ribs."

"What happened to baldie?" asked Dash.

"He got away clean," said Oldfield. "Didn't even have to pay for
the spilled beer."

"A clear case of injustice," said Hammett.

"Goldern right!" agreed Barney. He turned his head toward me.
"What's all this I hear about you puttin' a knife into this big-shot
movie star? Is that why you're sportin' all the phony face hair?"

"Shhh!" I put a finger to my lips. "Somebody could hear you. I've
been framed for his murder. The police are looking for me, so Dash
fixed me up with this disguise." I cautioned him again. "But just keep
your voice down. I don't want some nurse running for the law."

"Sorry about all this, Erle," said Barney. "I know you're a right guy,
an' I appreciate your comin' to see me, you bein' a fugitive an' all."

"We need to go back to San Felipe," said Hammett. "To question
the Sanchez woman again. We were going to ask you to drive us
down there."

"Woulda been my pleasure," said Barney. "But with these busted
ribs . . ."

"Don't worry about it," said Hammett. "When they said you were
in the hospital, I didn't know what to think. We just wanted to make
sure you were okay."

"Mighty thoughtful of you," said Oldfield. "I'll be hunky-dory in no
time. Me an' hospitals are old pals. I been in a lot of 'em, what with
all the smashups I usta have. It's almost like bein' at home."

When we got back to the limo, Buddy was well into *Of Mice and
Men* and he said that so far, it was great.

"Seems like you'll be driving us to San Felipe," said Dash.

"I was hoping I would," said Buddy. "I've never seen Baja California. When do we leave?"

"Sooner the better," said Hammett.

We decided that a return to Hammett's Palisades house was too risky. By now, the police might be watching the rear entrance. We could pick up supplies at a local store. Buddy took care of this while I called Chandler from a pay phone and brought him up to date.

"You're really going back there?" Ray asked.

"We're leaving right away. Barney's laid up with some broken ribs, so Buddy is taking us."

"Swing by the corner of Wilshire and Fifth. I'm sure I can slip away from the house without being seen. I'll walk up the street a few blocks, grab a taxi, and meet you there. If the cops see me leave in the Duesenberg, they'll suspect something is up."

"Wait a minute!" I said. "You mean to go with us?"

"Exactly."

"I thought you were dead set against my leaving L.A."

"That was earlier, when you were out on bail," he said. "With the Thompson murder, things are different. You're a wanted man, and by helping you, I've already broken both the law and my personal promise to Judge Carter. So why should you guys have all the fun? I want in on the adventure."

"What adventure? And we're not going to San Felipe to have fun. This is serious business."

"I know, I know," said Chandler, "I didn't mean it that way. But I want to be part of this, Erle. I deserve it. I got you out on bail in the first place, didn't I?"

"Okay, fine. If you want to tag along, you're welcome," I told him. "Ever been to Mexico?"

"Never. I hear it's a beautiful country."

"You heard right," I admitted.

"Then for me, it *will* be an adventure. Cissy won't want me to go, but I'll tell her not to worry. This takes a bit of doing on my part, because I'm actually a very timid man."

I laughed. "We'll pick you up at the corner of Wilshire and Fifth in about thirty minutes. Will that give you enough time?"

"Yes," he said. "I'll be waiting."

It meant another risk, picking up Ray. What if he wasn't able to leave the house without being seen? What if the cops followed him—to Dash's limo, no less? Then we'd all be in the soup.

Hammett wasn't happy with the extra stop, but I reminded him that Ray had been in on this from the beginning, and that without him, I'd still be sitting in a jail cell. So Hammett reluctantly agreed to the pickup, and told Buddy to head for Wilshire Boulevard.

When we got there, Chandler was waiting, but we drove by him the first time and scouted the streets for any sign of the police. We didn't spot anything suspicious. The area seemed safe enough.

"Stop for him," Dash ordered.

Buddy pulled up sharply to the curb and Ray scrambled into the limo's backseat. We were rolling again within seconds.

"See any cars following us?" Hammett asked.

Buddy scanned the rearview mirror. "It looks like we're in the clear."

"Then head for the border," said Dash, "and let's get this show on the road."

I could relate some highly dramatic incidents about the trip back to San Felipe: how we were ambushed by a gang of banditos and barely escaped by shooting our way out . . . how we were pursued by Mexican *federales*, and with Buddy's expert driving, were able to outrun their police car . . . how another flash flood sent a deadly tide of water rushing through the streets of a small village and how we gallantly rescued most of the population.

But I'd be lying. None of these things happened. Instead, the trip was smooth and uneventful. Chandler called the scenery "spectacular"—a true observation—but all Dash and I wanted to do was to get to San Felipe, and scenery be damned.

We arrived just after midnight. Nothing had changed in the village; nothing ever did. The landscape seemed to be frozen under a pale wash of starlight. It felt as if we were on the dark side of the moon.

"Not much of a place," said Chandler.

"Now you can understand how María could be trapped here," I said. "Once you're born into a village like this, there's no getting out."

Chandler nodded. "Yes, I can see that."

Buddy stayed with the limo while the three of us walked toward the glowing lights of the cantina. The surrounding shops were all shuttered. No one was on the street. San Felipe was dark and empty.

Before dawn, the fishing boats would leave for their day's run on the Gulf. But dawn was still five hours away and now, in the starlit dead of night, the village was tomb-silent, with the scuffling of our footsteps the only sounds on the street.

As we got closer to Joe's cantina, the faint music of a guitar drifted out to us, along with the muted sound of men's laughter and the soft tinkle of glassware.

"I never thought I'd be down here again," I admitted. "But at least the local cops don't have a warrant for my arrest."

It was a relief, not having to wear a disguise. The beard, wig, and mustache were back in the limo and I was myself once again.

Joe Cardenas was happy to have us back and greeted me and Dash like old friends. He pumped Chandler's hand when we introduced him as a fellow writer. "Three gringo writers!" he said, his eyes dancing with pleasure. "My cantina is honored by your presence. You are here, no doubt, to write a book about our fine village of San Felipe."

"Not exactly," said Chandler.

"Another gringo writer came here once," Cardenas said. "Perhaps you know of him . . . a Mr. Papa."

"You mean Ernest Hemingway?" asked Dash.

"Yes," he nodded. "That was his other name."

"I met him," said Dash. "He threw a punch at me."

Cardenas smiled. "Ah, he *was* very macho. After drinking much of my tequila, he challenged three of our strongest fishermen to box with him."

"What happened?" I wanted to know.

"Mr. Papa disposed of the first two in splendid fashion," he related, "but the third man, he . . . how do you say? . . . placed him upon the deck."

"You mean, the guy decked him," said Hammett.

"That, indeed, is the proper expression. Mr. Papa was very upset and left San Felipe soon after."

"Yeah," Dash said. "Hem can be a sore loser."

"We've come to see María," I said. "Is she upstairs?"

Cardenas looked puzzled. "She told me that you did not wish to utilize her services, that you paid only for her voice. Is it true that you have come all this way once again only to *talk* with our María?"

"That's right," said Hammett. "We need to talk to her again."

"Concerning what?"

"It's a personal matter," said Hammett. "But don't worry, we'll pay her the standard rate."

I repeated my question: "Is she upstairs?"

"Yes. In her room."

"Anyone with her?" asked Hammett.

"No. She is not presently engaged."

"Fine," I said. "Then we'll go on up."

Cardenas continued to look puzzled. "I suppose . . ." he said in a hesitant tone ". . . that it will be all right."

"It'll be swell," Hammett assured him.

And we headed for the stairs.

NINETEEN

At the end of the upper hallway I tapped lightly on María's door. When she opened it, her eyes widened in surprised recognition.

"Hello, María," I said. "How are you?"

"I am as always," she replied. "I never expected to see you again, Señor Gardner." And, glancing at Dash: "Or you, Señor Hammett."

"This is our friend, Raymond Chandler," I said, and Ray nodded to her.

"You have more questions for María?" she asked as we entered her room. "Or this time . . . have you come for my . . . services?"

Hammett smiled, shaking his head. "You are a most attractive woman, María—but we are not here for that. You're right, though, about the questions. We do need to know more."

"But what more is there? I have told you everything."

"May we sit down?" Dash nodded toward the two chairs.

"Certainly. But, again . . . you must pay me for my time," she said.

"We will," I told her.

Hammett and Chandler took the two chairs, while I sat on the foot of the bed. She chose to stand, obviously uncertain of what new questions we would be asking.

"It's about your son," Dash began.

"Antonio?" She looked at us with sudden fire in her eyes. "You have word of my son?"

"That photograph you showed us," I said. "When was it taken?"

"Many years ago," she said.

I nodded; what I had suspected had now been confirmed. "How many years ago, exactly?"

She hesitated as she did the computation in her head. "Thirteen years. In nineteen twenty-four."

Hammett ran a slow finger along his mustache. "And your son was about six years old then?"

"Yes."

"Then Antonio was born in . . ."

"Nineteen-seventeen," she replied. "My son will be twenty years old this year." Her face flushed with pride. "He is a fine young man. Tall and strong and handsome . . . like his father."

I leaned forward and asked, as gently as I could: "Do you know who his father was?"

"Of course!" Her answer was firm and direct: "Antonio's father was my husband . . . Lloyd Thompson."

"Why didn't you tell us that when we came here the first time?" I asked.

"You had little interest in my son," she said. "You did not ask about his father. Had you done so, I would have answered as I have an-swered you now."

My voice was intense: "Did Thompson know about Antonio?"

"No. He left me before I could tell him that we were to have a child. I was pregnant with Antonio when my husband rode away on his motorcycle."

"Did you write to him?" asked Chandler. "Did you let Thompson know that he was a father?"

"How? I had no idea of where he had gone. There was no way for me to reach him."

Dash looked angry. "And the bastard never contacted you?"

"No, never." She twisted her hands in her skirt, her eyes reflecting painful memories. "I gave Antonio my father's name, to make it easier for him to grow up here in Mexico. I did not want people to make fun of him because he is what we call a *coyote* . . . I do not know what you call this in English . . ."

"A half-breed," I said.

"Yes. I did not want people to make jokes about my Antonio being a half-breed. But I told him that his father's name was Lloyd Thompson. Many years later, when he was ready to take his place among the men, he saw a magazine that had been sent from Mexico City. It was about film stars. Inside this magazine was a story with many pictures about my husband.

"Antonio read the magazine out loud to me. It said that Lloyd was a famous person, a movie star, and lived in your Beverly Hills. I knew it was Lloyd because of the photographs. But there was no address, and by then . . ." She sat down wearily on the bed. "By then, it no longer mattered."

"And Antonio grew up here in this village?" I asked.

"Yes. He became a fisherman like his grandfather. He was able to buy a boat for very little money from a widow whose husband had been killed in a storm."

"Where is Antonio now?" Dash asked her.

"He went to your country . . . to your Los Angeles. He wanted very much to go north, but he would not tell me why. I did nothing to stop him. He is a man now, and has the right to act as a man."

Dash leaned toward her. "Have you heard from him since he left?"

"He mailed a postcard here, to the cantina. José read the words to me." She got up, opened a lower drawer in the wardrobe, and took out a postcard.

On it was a picture of Grauman's Chinese Theater, with powerful kleig lights spearing the night sky above the theater's multicolored pagoda forecourt. I turned it over.

Mama,
> *Estoy bien aquí en Los Angeles. Tengo trabajo. No se preocupe.*
>
> > *Con cariño para siempre,*
> > Antonio

I translated it out loud, so that Dash and Ray could understand what it said:

Mama,
> I am well here in Los Angeles. I have work. Do not worry.
>
> > With love always,
> > Antonio

María shook her head sadly. "Each time when the mail is delivered to San Felipe—it comes to us from Mexicali—I hope that there will be a letter from my Antonio. Perhaps he has not sent another card because he knows that I cannot read. Maybe he does not realize that José can read to me what he writes. Today, when you talked of my son, I thought that you might have word of him."

I knew I was going to have to ask more questions that would disturb her. Once again I tried to be as gentle as possible.

"María, when you saw the photographs in that Mexican movie magazine . . . were they *just* of Lloyd Thompson?"

Tears began to form in her eyes and she swallowed several times before she was able to answer. "No, Señor. The pictures were of Lloyd with a very beautiful gringa . . . and a little boy. Antonio read the magazine to me. It said that Lloyd was married to this gringa and that the boy was their son."

"So Antonio knew about his father's other wife," I said. "He knew about Amy Thompson?"

"Oh, yes. And then later, when she came here to San Felipe, I naturally told Antonio about her visit."

I was startled at her words. "Amy came *here?* To this cantina?"

María's eyes softened. "She was so beautiful . . . like a shining flame on the top of a candle. She made me think of Our Blessed Lady, who is, as you know, also very beautiful. And she was so kind, so . . . *simpático.*"

I was still shaken. "You never mentioned Amy when we talked to you before."

She frowned in irritation. "I cannot answer what I am not asked."

"How did she find out about you?"

"She said that Lloyd had boasted to her about how he had seduced me when I said that I would not sleep with him unless we were married. He told her that our marriage had meant nothing . . ." her voice was strained and unsteady ". . . that it was done only to obtain my virginity. When she asked him for proof of what he was saying, he told her there was no proof. He had no papers, and no one else would ever know what had happened between him and me here in San Felipe."

"When Amy came to see you, what did she want?" I knew that María was telling the truth, but I was still having difficulty believing that Amy had come all the way to San Felipe. She must have driven herself down, I thought. For myself, I'm an experienced traveler, and yet I would not have driven the dangerous road deep into Mexico alone. For the first time, I realized the depth of desperation Amy had felt in her marriage.

"She wanted to know if what Lloyd had told her was true. I said it was, and showed her my marriage certificate to prove my words."

"And you gave her the certificate when she left?"

María shrugged. "She took it with her, but she had paid me well for it."

"Amy *bought* the certificate from you?"

"Yes. She gave me one thousand American dollars for it. I had never before seen so great an amount of money. José also, was much impressed. He took the money from me to make sure no one would steal it. He assured me that he would keep it safe."

Yeah, sure, I thought. Safe for himself. But I didn't say this. Instead, I asked: "Did Antonio see you sell the certificate to her?"

"No, Señor. He was out on the Gulf in his boat, fishing. When he returned that night, I told him about this woman. How she had paid me for the certificate and then driven away in her big yellow American automobile."

"What was his reaction?" I asked.

"He was angry. The paper proved that Lloyd and I were married. When I told him about her rich clothing and her jeweled watch and ring, he said that such things should be mine, that his father had given me nothing. He spoke bitterly of Lloyd."

"How soon after that did he leave for Los Angeles?"

"The next month. His cousin Miguel, who had been to Los Angeles before, went with him. Miguel is a good boy, Señor, but he was often in trouble with your police when he would go north, so he would return to San Felipe. I think they want to arrest him because of something he stole, but even so, when Antonio decided to go north, Miguel wanted to go with him. The truck driver who brings groceries to San Felipe took them to the border. That was just after Christmas last year. Then the word came about his job."

"What word? You said you had received only this one postcard from him."

"Miguel sent a card to his mother, who is my sister, Rosita Barela. It said that he was working at a big . . . *lonja de productos* in Los Angeles."

"Produce exchange," I said to Dash and Ray. "It has to be the big downtown wholesale market."

Dash stood up. He handed María money, thanking her for her honesty and for the time she had spent talking to us. "It is much appreciated," he told her.

We were at the door when she stopped us.

"Are you going to find my son? Is that why you want to know about him?"

"We're going to try," I told her.

"If you find my Antonio, please tell him that I pray for him each day before the Baby Jesus, and that I want to know he is in good health and is content in your country." She hesitated. "Perhaps, if Antonio does not want to write to me, maybe *you* could write and tell me if he is safe and well. Would you do that for María?"

I nodded. "We'll do that," I said. "If we find him, I promise, we'll let you know."

She waved at us from the door of her room when we reached the stairs.

I waved back.

We walked in silence to the limo, each of us occupied with his own thoughts.

Inside the car, with Buddy making a wide U-turn across the road so he could drive north out of San Felipe, I said: "So now we have a strong suspect."

"Yeah . . . Antonio," Dash said. "He could have poisoned Amy and then knifed Thompson."

"How do you figure he's the one?" Chandler asked.

I counted the reasons on my fingers: "Consider what María told us: that Antonio is Thompson's son . . . that the kid knows what his father did to her . . . that he was plenty sore at Thompson's new wife . . . that he left for Los Angeles last year, soon after Amy showed up here . . . and that he didn't tell María why he was going."

"And that leads you to believe that he killed them both?" asked Chandler.

"Damn right it does," I said.

"I agree with Erle," Dash said. "A lot points to Antonio."

"After he got rid of Amy," I said, "he decided to work out his primary anger by knifing his daddy. Since I'd already been arrested for Amy's death, I became a perfect fall guy."

"So he plants the murder weapon in your camper," Dash added. "Everything fits."

Chandler was still dubious. "How do you expect to prove to the police that Antonio Sanchez is a double murderer?"

"We'll face that problem when we find him," I said. "Chances are he's still working at the produce market, so that's where we go first."

I seldom venture into the downtown section of Los Angeles. Too many people. Too much traffic. Too much noise. I do most of my shopping in Hollywood, where things are calmer, and I buy my groceries at the local A&P on Western.

But the A&P buyers *do* go downtown early each morning, to purchase their stock at the sprawling wholesale produce exchange. Every weekday, hours before dawn, the produce market is host to myriad rumbling vehicles loaded with fresh fruits, vegetables, grains, and nuts, most of them grown on California soil and trucked in from farms up and down the state.

Farmer to wholesale market, wholesale market to store—it's a vast, never-ending food chain that operates at peak efficiency all year round.

I was back in disguise—wig, mustache, and beard—the next morning when Buddy, exhausted from the nonstop drive back to L.A., parked the limo at the edge of the giant market. He stayed with the car to get some sleep while the three of us walked toward the multitude of produce booths and receiving platforms strung out along two city blocks.

Antonio Sanchez worked at one of those booths, or *had* worked here, according to María. We were going after a needle in a haystack, but there was no other way to find him.

At each booth we asked the same question: "Do you have a young man named Antonio Sanchez working for you—or have you employed him in the past?"

No.

No.

No.

No.

No.

We kept walking from booth to booth, sure that we'd strike pay dirt eventually. It just took patience. A lot of patience.

Finally, bingo! We'd reached a booth at the end of the first block. The manager there was wrestling a barrel of peaches onto a wheeled cart when Dash asked him our standard question. In his fifties, the fellow was as wide as the barrel he was handling, with a florid complexion and thick brown hair that kept falling across his eyes. He wore dirt-stained blue coveralls, faded from numerous washings and fraying at the buttonholes.

"This Sanchez kid you wanta know about," he said in a rasping voice. "Nineteen or so, would be?"

"That's his age," said Hammett.

"Good-lookin' kid, eh?"

"That's what we were told," said Dash.

He stared at us. "Who are you people, anyways? You plainclothes?"

"We're not the law," I said. "Just . . . family friends. We need to talk to him."

"Well, you can't do that," said the produce man. "That's one thing you sure can't do."

"Why not?" I asked. "Does he work here or doesn't he?"

"He did. Worked here, for me, right up to last Monday. Good kid. Full of energy. Strong. Wasn't afraid to put in long hours. Appreciated the job. Wish I could find more like him. I've hired and fired me a lotta lazy bums over the years, but Antonio, he was different."

"So why did he quit?" I asked.

"He didn't quit. He died."

Hammett's voice betrayed his shock. "Antonio Sanchez is *dead?*"

"Yep, sure is." The produce man sat down on the edge of the

wooden cart and swabbed at his neck with a red bandana. "Hot day," he said. "Summer can sure wear out a man."

"How did he die?" I asked.

"Happened real sudden. It was early, still dark. We'd just opened for the day and the farmers were coming in, delivering their goods. I was working out front, at the loading platform. Truck full of strawberries had just rolled up. Antonio was inside the building, alone in the back office."

"Doing what?" Dash asked.

"Some paperwork I gave him," said the manager. "I was having him add up how many extra wood crates we had around so's we could turn 'em in for credit. Every little bit of income adds up, y'know. Anyways, pretty soon I hear some funny noises from back there. Choking and gasping noises. It was Antonio. I found him facedown on the office floor. Wasn't breathing. By the time I got there, he was stone dead."

"Of what?" Chandler asked. "What killed him?"

The produce man shrugged. "Wish I could tell you. The cops filed it as an 'on-the-job fatality.' The doc who looked him over said it was probably a heart attack."

"Was his body examined for marks or bruises?" Hammett asked.

"Naw, it wasn't. I saw some red marks on his neck, but those coulda been anything."

Chandler wanted to know if an autopsy had been performed.

"On a kid like him? A produce worker? A *Mexican*? Heck, no. They just carted him away and next day stuck him in the ground at the pauper's cemetery over in Boyle Heights. East L.A., y'know?"

Chandler nodded. "I know where it is."

"Did you notify anyone of his death?" I asked.

"Like who?"

"Like his mother. She lives on the Gulf of California, in San Felipe."

He shrugged. "Didn't know the kid even *had* a mother. Never spoke of it to me, anyways. All I knew was he lived with some other Mexicans in a house over near Chinatown. The cops didn't find anything when they went there, and he didn't have the address of anybody on him when he died. For all I knew, he coulda been an orphan."

"Okay," said Hammett. "Thanks for telling us about this."

"Sure," said the beefy little man. He stood up, ready to tackle the barrel of peaches again. "Like I said, Antonio was a good kid. I'm sorry he's gone."

"Yeah," Dash told him. "We are too."

On the walk back to the limo, we discussed what we'd discovered.

"This is going to be tough on María," I said. "She really loved her son."

Chandler looked at me. "You seemed so sure that it was Antonio who killed Amy and Thompson."

"I had every reason to believe that," I said.

"What if you were right? asked Chandler. What if Antonio *did* kill both of them, then died of a heart attack?"

"I think he was murdered," I said firmly. "I think somebody strangled Antonio Sanchez."

"You mean those red marks on his neck?" Ray asked.

I nodded. "He was back there, alone, when the killer came into the office. Probably crept up behind him. Maybe used a cord to do the job. Looped it around his throat before Antonio could yell for help. Which was when he made the gasping, choking sounds. He could have been dead in seconds."

Ray was trying to make sense of what I was telling him. "So . . . if Antonio was murdered, then *why?* Does his death tie into Amy's death . . . or Thompson's?"

"Has to," put in Hammett. "I don't believe in coincidence—and it's a hell of a coincidence that Antonio Sanchez just happens to be killed right after Amy and Tink Thompson . . . and that he was

Thompson's son . . . and that he hated both his father and his father's second wife."

"Okay," said Chandler. "So it's not a coincidence. Where does that leave us? What would be the killer's motive in getting rid of young Sanchez?"

"I wish I could answer that one," I said. "I really wish I could."

TWENTY

Buddy dropped off Chandler in Santa Monica, three blocks short of his house in case of a stakeout, and was driving us back to the Palisades when a green '36 Dodge sedan roared up behind us, pulling even with our limo.

Two men were in the Dodge. Both the driver and the second man, who was in the backseat, wore dark hats and black face masks. Before Buddy could react, the man in the back of the Dodge poked the barrel of a big .45 automatic out of the open window and began firing at us.

Buddy hunched low over the wheel, and in the backseat Dash and I hit the floor, while bullets clanged and ripped through the car. A spray of shattered glass from the side window showered over us as the shooter kept pumping .45 rounds into the limo.

"Hit the brakes!" Dash yelled at Buddy. "Now!"

The limo lurched violently and the tires howled in protest as Buddy jammed his foot down hard on the brake pedal. The other driver was caught by surprise as the Dodge swerved ahead. Now we were behind him.

Dash grabbed his .38 from the holster on his calf and leaned out to begin firing at the green car.

That saved us. The two masked men obviously didn't like the idea of our shooting back at them; they swerved off down a side street. Gone.

Buddy pulled to a stop while we all took deep breaths, grateful to be alive. The right side of the limo was peppered with bullet holes.

"What the hell was *that* all about?" I gasped. "Who *were* those guys?"

"The Thompson boys," declared Hammett. "I remember seeing that green Dodge sedan parked behind the Texaco station in Santa Monica."

"Jeez!" I said. "They really want me dead!" I hesitated. "Didn't we agree that the two of them might be responsible for both of the murders?"

"Yeah, we did—but I don't believe that anymore. These guys are just a couple of violent hotheads who think you knifed their brother. But Thompson's killer wants the *cops* to deal with you. That's why he planted the knife in your camper. He's not out to gun you down."

"Are these two maniacs going to keep after me?"

"I'd say no," declared Hammett. "They've tried twice. Both times they faced my .38, and that's more than they can handle. They've made their point."

"Hope you're right," I said. "Guess my disguise didn't fool them."

"The problem is," Dash continued, "they know that you're with me in this car, and they'll tip the cops. We're going to have to ditch the limo. She's hot."

"Where do I get rid of her?" asked Buddy.

Dash told him to drive the car to M-G-M in Culver City. Three blocks away from the studio, Dash and I got out at a newsstand. We leafed through the magazines, trying to look inconspicuous. Dash had instructed Buddy to drive onto the studio lot, then park the limo in the vast outdoor area reserved for "picture cars"—vehicles that are used in films. "They won't even notice the limo is there," Dash had said.

When Buddy returned on foot, Dash phoned for a taxi to pick us up. Taxis are a fairly uncommon means of transportation in Los Angeles; calling for one usually means a long wait.

While the three of us were waiting, I stripped off my disguise and said: "I'm going to turn myself in to the police. That way, you'll be off the hook in terms of harboring a fugitive. I just have one more thing to do first."

"What's that?" Dash asked.

"I want to have a close look inside Thompson's house."

Dash frowned. "Why? The police have already checked it out."

"Sure. But they could have overlooked some evidence that I can use in court to help defend myself. Maybe nothing will turn up, but it's my last chance. I can't keep on running."

I looked at Buddy. "We can drop you off at Margaret's place while Dash and I tackle the Thompson house."

"Won't that compromise her?" he asked. "I drove you to San Felipe, and now I'll be going to Margaret's to hide out. Won't the police go after her?"

"Nobody but the Thompson brothers can prove we helped Erle," Dash told him. "And even though I'm sure they'll tip the cops to the fact that Erle was seen in the limo with us, their call will be anonymous. They won't testify against anybody."

"Why not?" asked Buddy.

"They don't want to have to defend themselves against the beatings and shootings we could charge them with," said Hammett. "So the cops won't have hard evidence against any of us. Anyway, all they really want is Erle."

I nodded. "So Margaret won't be taking a legal risk. And once I've turned myself in, you can go back to the Palisades."

"Okay," said Buddy. "You've convinced me."

When the taxi arrived, we gave the driver Margaret's address.

At the sound of the buzzer, Margaret Stetler stopped playing the piano and opened her apartment door. She obviously hadn't expected company and was wearing a flowery quilted-cotton house robe and fuzzy pink slippers. Her face was bare of makeup, but even without it, she was extremely attractive, her dark skin dominated by a pair of large, intelligent brown eyes. She stood in the open doorway, blinking at us.

"We're sorry to intrude this way," said Buddy, "but we need your help."

"You're always welcome, Buddy." She acknowledged me and Dash with a smile. "I'm sure you're all here for a good reason."

"I guess you've read about me in the newspapers," I said. "Gardner, the fugitive murderer. Another Dillinger on the loose."

"Yes," she said. "The police came here to ask me if I knew where you were." She gave me a penetrating, straight-on look. "You didn't kill those two people, did you?"

"No, of course not," I told her. "I've been framed. Dash and Buddy have been helping me, but we had to get rid of the limo, and—"

"Don't stand out in the hall," she said. "Come in. All of you, come in."

She gave Buddy a warm kiss on the cheek.

Dash and I planned to wait until after dark before we went to Thompson's house. In the meantime, Margaret brought out a tray with a pot of coffee and a large plate of home-baked gingersnaps. And then she settled down to listen to our story.

I did most of the talking, telling her about my relationship with Amy, beginning from the time she came to work for my law firm. I ended by telling her what Amy had revealed to me about her marriage to Thompson . . . all the sordid details, including the death of her son, Larry.

"That man was a real brute," Margaret said. "And he had the entire world fooled. Including me. I almost invited him to one of my concerts. I loved his songs . . . listened to him all the time on the radio. He seemed so *nice*."

"Thompson had his routine down pat," said Dash. "He was a great actor. His whole life was a performance."

Margaret and Buddy were sitting side by side on the sofa. He had his right arm around her; her left hand was casually resting on his thigh. They looked like high-school sweethearts. It did my heart good to see them together.

Later, when Margaret turned on the table lamp because the room was getting dark, I got up from my chair. "We'd best get started," I told Dash. I had to keep moving. If somehow the police were to get on my trail, I didn't want it to lead them to Margaret.

Buddy walked over to shake my hand. He told me he'd be glad to testify in my behalf as a character witness during the trial. I was touched. I told him I didn't think it would be necessary, but I appreciated the offer.

Just before leaving, I told Margaret: "You've got a good man here. Hang on to him."

She gave him a wry look. "I think he's the one who's going to have to hang on to *me*." We all laughed, and then she gave me a hug for luck.

I left her apartment with the uncomfortable feeling that the world was closing in on me. That if I didn't find a way out soon, I'd be lost forever.

It was what great authors call "the dark night of the soul."

When we got to Beverly Hills, we had the cabbie drop us off north of Sunset Boulevard, on Elm, close to the house of a film director Hammett knew. That way, if the cops cruised by and asked what we were doing, Hammett could say he was on the way to visit his friend. The B.H.P.D. does not appreciate unknown pedestrians on the residential streets of their town.

Our first priority was to see how well guarded the Thompson estate was. The presence of police in the vicinity would present us with problems we didn't want to deal with.

We walked a few blocks north until the streets began to gain altitude along the foothills of the Santa Monica mountains. Then we circled over so we were behind the Thompson estate, looking down onto the property. The area was lightless and deserted. No noise or movement anywhere. So far, so good.

We returned to the estate's ground level and peered through the spiked iron fence. The driveway was empty. No sign of the police.

We knew that a man would be posted at the main gate, and there was bound to be at least one security guard at the house. But we couldn't be sure of anything until we got there.

Hammett and I walked quietly along the fence line, keeping well back from the gated entrance. Dash was carrying a large brown-paper shopping bag with something bulky inside that he'd obtained from Margaret before we left her place. I was curious, but figured he would let me know what it was when he was ready.

"We go in over the fence," Dash said. "When I was with the Pinks, I had to penetrate a lot of joints like this. I'll go first, then you follow."

"Those spikes are sharp," I said, looking up at the high iron fence.

"That's why I brought this along," he said, taking a folded blanket out of the shopping bag.

"How's that going to help?"

"We drape it over the spikes so they don't stick us," he said. "A trick I learned from a burglar I arrested in Sioux City, Iowa. The guy had a cute little Scotty dog. Used to take the mutt with him on all his jobs."

"Did you arrest the dog, too?"

"Naw, we left it with his sister while he was in the slammer."

"I've heard of cat burglars," I said. "Guess you could call that guy a dog burglar."

This amused Hammett. "The blanket's a little thin," he said. "A strip of canvas is better, but this will do."

We began scaling the fence. It was much easier than I'd imagined, although I hadn't climbed a fence like this since I was a kid. At the top, Hammett's blanket took care of the spikes. Then we dropped down into deep grass; it covered the bottom of a small hill that led up to the main house.

Hammett stashed the blanket behind a large rock for our return use and then we moved uphill, through a thick screen of eucalyptus trees, toward the main house. It must have taken ten minutes to get there, and I was breathing heavily by the end of the climb.

There was a full moon imaged in pale silver on the windows of the house. We came in from the back, moving slowly. When a dry twig snapped under my foot, it seemed as loud as a gunshot.

"Watch where you're stepping," Dash cautioned.

"I'm trying to," I said, peering ahead as we edged closer to the mansion. "See anyone?"

"Not yet," said Dash, keeping his voice to a near whisper, "but there's got to be a guard on duty. We just have to spot him and check his rounds to see what his routine is."

Light danced and flickered from one of the ground-floor windows. A flash beam.

"That's him," declared Dash, "making his rounds inside. When he comes out, we go in."

"What if he doesn't come out?" I asked.

"If he's alone, he'll have to—in order to check the grounds."

"What if he's not alone? What if there are other guards?"

"You worry too much," Dash said. "My instinct tells me he's the only one, and when it comes to detective work, I've always trusted my instinct. Let's play it that way."

"Okay," I nodded. "You're the expert housebreaker. You call the action."

We waited silently in the dark, listening to the pulsing sound of hundreds of crickets around us. Five long minutes passed. Then the front door opened and the guard appeared. He was short and stocky; he wore a visored cap, had a belted revolver at his waist, and carried a silver flashlight in his right hand. Shutting the door firmly behind him, he made sure the lock had engaged, then began a slow walk along the drive toward the lower gate. He finally disappeared around the long curve.

"Lucky break for us," said Dash. "He's going down to have a chat with his buddy. Now's the time to do your looking inside."

Dash pried open a ground-floor window at the rear and we entered. I was immediately concerned that we might have activated a house alarm.

"Forget it," said Dash. "With the guard going in and out all night, they've shut it off. Where do you want to look first?"

"Thompson's study."

"Know where it is?" he asked.

"*Life* ran a feature story on the house last year," I said. "With photos of the main rooms. The study is at the end of the lower hall, next to the library."

"Then let's get moving," Dash said. "We don't know how much time we've got before the guard comes back."

The hallway was like a dim tunnel, interspersed with thin drifts of moonlight that emanated from the doorways of open rooms. Back in Margaret's apartment, I'd asked her about borrowing a flashlight, but Hammett had nixed the idea; a flash could be seen from the outer grounds.

We passed the library and entered Thompson's study. Luckily, the large window that faced the patio was undraped, allowing the natural light of the moon to provide enough illumination for me to conduct my investigation.

Everything looked normal: desk and leather wing chair, a long couch, two upholstered chairs, several lamps, and two filing cabinets. Framed photos covered the walls. Tink—always smiling—with Bob Hope, Clark Gable, Spencer Tracy, Jean Harlow, James Cagney, Bette Davis, Mickey Rooney, and a host of other luminaries, including the mayor of Los Angeles, the governor of California, and the president of the United States.

I began by rifling through the two filing cabinets, folder by folder. Contracts. Employment records. Royalty statements. Bills. Receipts. Canceled checks. Tax records. Repair lists. Nothing of value to me. Nothing to help my case. Same with the desk drawers. Nothing.

While I was sifting through Thompson's effects, becoming more and more frustrated, Hammett stood by the window, keeping a sharp eye out for the guard.

"All clear so far," he told me. "Find anything?"

I shook my head. "The police have already been through everything. Guess I was just dreaming when I thought I could—" I hesitated. "Wait a minute!" I pointed out an object on the desktop. "Look at that."

"Uh-huh," nodded Hammett.

I sat down in Thompson's desk chair and snapped on his machine, adjusting the headset. I began to listen intently.

Hammett was standing by one of the file cabinets, watching me. I concentrated totally on what I was hearing.

"What are you—" he asked.

I raised a hand. "Shhh! This is important. Let me—"

Which is when I was caught square in the beam of the guard's flash. He'd returned and was standing directly outside the study window, shining his light inside. Then he ducked away, running for the gate.

"He's going for the cops," Dash said. "We'd better get out of here."

"Not yet," I declared. "I need to hear the rest of this."

"The guard will phone from the gate. The law will be here in nothing flat."

"Quiet," I told him. "I've *got* to hear it all before they show up."

It seemed to take forever, but finally I was satisfied. I scooped my evidence into a manila envelope lying on the desktop as we heard a siren approaching, growing louder by the second. Then another siren, farther away, joined the wail of the first.

I handed the envelope to Dash. "The guard didn't see you," I said.

"It's me they want. I'll stall them at the front door. While they make their arrest, you go out the back window. Bring me this envelope in court, along with the marriage certificate. It's at my place. Ask Tomas for it. I gave him instructions to turn it over to you in case I was arrested."

"Maybe we can still both get out," he said.

I sighed wearily. "No. I'm tired of running. I was going to give myself up tonight anyway. So it happens here and now. You just go, Dash. And hang on to that envelope."

"Okay," he said. "If that's how you want it."

I walked toward the front of the house while Dash headed for the rear window. Directly outside, I heard a police patrol car skid to a stop in the graveled drive.

I looked out the window at the night sky—at the moon and stars. If I couldn't win in court, I'd never stand free under them again.

I turned to open the front door.

TWENTY-ONE

Two days later, at the spotless and sweet-smelling Beverly Hills jail, I was allowed to have my first visitor, who turned out to be Ray Chandler. Before they led me out to the visitors' area, they shackled me at the wrists and ankles, as befits a "desperate criminal." The truth is, I *was* desperate—to prove my innocence and get out of jail.

Chandler was pale and solemn when I sat down to face him in the visitors' room. A steel-mesh screen separated us at the table and a guard stood at each end of the featureless, institutional-gray room. They could overhear everything we said, although we kept our voices low.

"You look terrible," I said to Ray, trying to lighten the tension. "*I'm* the one who's supposed to look terrible."

"I haven't been getting much sleep," Chandler declared. "The papers are full of stories about your case, and that's all I seem to be hearing on the radio."

"Yeah. I'm hot news right now."

"Cissy's been very worried about you," Ray told me. "She wanted to come with me today, but I talked her out of the idea. She's just not up to it . . . with her getting over a cold and all. I'm always worried she might catch pneumonia. You know how delicate she is."

"I understand. Give her my best, and tell her how much I appreciate her concern."

"I'm just as worried as she is," admitted Ray. "You're in one hell of a mess here, Erle. I hope you've rounded up a first-rate lawyer."

"I have. *Me*."

He looked startled. "You plan to defend yourself?"

"Why not? I've handled hundreds of cases with far less personal interest in my clients. This time, I have a great deal of personal interest."

"I hope this won't prejudice a jury against you."

"Not with my prior background in the profession. I have every right to defend myself, and no one else can do it better."

He leaned forward, closer to the screen. "Have you talked to Dash?"

"Not since my arrest," I said.

"He phoned right after he left you . . . told me what happened that night."

I glanced at the guards, shaking my head. "Not here. Not now."

"Yeah . . . well . . . he's working hard. Up to his neck in that Charlie Chan job. They want the finished script this week, so he's under a lot of pressure."

"I can see how he would be."

"They had a tough time at the studio . . . trying to figure out where to send him next."

"You mean Dash is going to leave town?" I asked, a note of panic in my voice.

"Oh, no. I'm talking about their detective," said Ray. They've done *Charlie Chan at the Opera*, *Charlie Chan at the Circus*, *Charlie Chan at the Olympics*, *Charlie Chan in Egypt*, *Charlie Chan in London*, *Charlie Chan in Shanghai*, and *Charlie Chan on Broadway*. Reason I know is because Cissy is a real nut for this guy. That's about the only way I can get her out of the house—to see a Charlie Chan movie."

"So where is Dash sending him this time?"

"I think he said his title was *Charlie Chan in the Alps*. He's putting the guy on skis."

"I'd like to see that," I said. "Chan, the portly intellectual from Honolulu. He should be a real hoot on skis."

We laughed, and then there was a moment of silence between us.

"When is your trial?" he asked.

"There's an election coming up in November and the D.A. is worried," I said. "He's not all that popular, so he needs to win a big headline case in order to impress the voters. He's ordered a speedy trial."

"How speedy?"

"I expect to be in court within four weeks," I said. "The D.A. is confident of a quick conviction. Claims it's an open-and-shut case."

"Is he right?" asked Chandler.

"I hope not," I said.

A guard walked over to tell us our time was up.

"Thanks for coming, Ray."

"I'm with you, partner," he said. "All the way."

And the guards led me back to my cell.

Over the next three weeks, while the D.A.'s office was preparing its case against me, I was allowed one visitor per day.

Several people came by. Natalie. My daughter, Grace. Tomas, my houseboy, who needed instructions on how to handle some things that had come up at home. Barney Oldfield. Margaret Stetler. Buddy. Beth Winniger. And I was pleasantly surprised when Marisol came all the way from Montecito to lend her support.

Dash didn't show up, but that was okay so long as he made the trial. I was sure he'd be there.

The head guard at the jail, who happened to be a Perry Mason fan, arranged to have a typewriter installed in my cell when I promised to put his name in my next Mason novel.

So, to keep my mind occupied while I was awaiting trial, I wrote three long novelettes—one per week—about a new character I named "Jailbreak Billy Brisken." Billy was a brave, good-hearted housebreaker who was stealing just enough from the homes of ultra-rich Chicago socialites to pay the hospital bills for his little sister, Molly, who was on the verge of death from a rare jungle fever she'd contracted on a trip up the Amazon. Billy would get caught, break out of jail, and then go right back to housebreaking. In and out of jail in each story, which is how he earned his nickname.

Pulp editors eat up this sort of stuff and I had no doubt that I would find a solid market for the series (helped, no doubt, by the headline value of my present notoriety). At least I was working from an authentic background, the one advantage to being arrested and thrown into the slammer.

I wasn't thrilled with the news that old muttonchop whiskers himself, Zeb Carter, would serve as my trial judge. After I'd jumped bail and apparently committed a second murder, I was not under any illusion about Carter being predisposed in my favor. He would be tough on me, but I had no say in the matter.

Whether I liked it or not, Zebediah B. Carter would preside.

Jury selection went quickly. From behind the defense table, I faced eight women and four men who, as the trial began, refused to meet my gaze. When I glanced over at them, they turned their faces away—obviously prejudiced against me from the moment I entered the courtroom, wearing one of my best suits. I wondered how many of them had listened to Winchell's vitriolic radio attacks, or had read news accounts in the Hearst papers, which labeled me "the butcher." Trust ol' William Randolph to exploit the most jaundiced potential of yellow journalism.

Judge Carter, with some reluctance, had granted permission for me to act as my own counsel, although he had advised me to change my mind. He told me that he had never personally heard of a defendant winning a case in which he represented himself.

His words were depressing. I knew the odds were heavily against me and that it would take a miracle to win back my freedom. Right now, I thought, I could use the expert services of Perry Mason. Too bad he existed only on paper.

My opponent, seated confidently at the prosecution table with two of his assistants, was District Attorney Sheldon Flowers, who had made the stunning decision to conduct this particular trial himself. He must be pretty desperate for reelection, I thought. A D.A. just *doesn't* conduct criminal trials; as the top law officer of the entire County of Los Angeles, he's supposed to have far more important things to do. Evidently Sheldon Flowers didn't.

He was by no means a handsome man. His protuberant eyes, not unlike those of a frog, blinked behind thick-lensed glasses. A sparse misting of gray hair clung to his upper skull like lichen on a rock, and his domed forehead shone under the courtroom lights. His smartly tailored blue suit did little to conceal weak shoulders and a thrusting stomach.

Despite these unfortunate physical characteristics, his mind was sharp, clear, and calculating. This was the potent weapon that he would use so effectively against me.

The courtroom was packed. A sea of faces, many of them familiar. Natalie was seated next to Grace; Ray was with Cissy, who looked fragile and sylphlike. Beth Winniger was there; so was Barney Oldfield, walking normally again and giving me a thumbs-up. Margaret Stetler. And, as she had promised, Marisol had come down from Montecito.

But where was Dash? He'd show. I was certain he'd show.

On the other side of the room, Len and Freddie Thompson were on hand to cheer the prosecution. Their set, sullen faces radiated hatred as our eyes met. Tink Thompson's parents were also in the courtroom, to make sure I got what I deserved for murdering their son.

In his opening statement, delivered with the fire and passion of a Pentecostal preacher, Sheldon Flowers said that the people would prove, beyond the shadow of a doubt, that I had not only exploited Amy Thompson sexually, but had cold-bloodedly poisoned her in order to gain her estate. According to Flowers, I then went on to butcher her husband, one of the finest men to walk God's earth, in a fiendish and depraved manner worthy of Jack the Ripper.

"There *is* such a thing as evil, ladies and gentlemen," he told the jury. "That materialization of Satan now sits in this very room with us—in the person of a vicious, conscienceless double murderer—" he pointed dramatically at me "—Erle Stanley Gardner!"

I raised my chin to stare at him, refusing to hang my head like a criminal.

Flowers went on to declare that Lloyd Thompson had no doubt discovered that it was I who had poisoned his wife, and therefore Thompson had had to die. He enumerated the variety of stab wounds on the body of the deceased, pausing to draw in deep breaths when he described my "bestial acts," as if the horror of my crimes had left him so shaken that it was difficult for him to continue. But continue he did, pointing out that I had brazenly fled from the law as a fugitive—which was in itself proof of my guilt—and that I would still be at large, a menace to the community, had I not been captured in the act of burglarizing the very house of my two victims.

But fear not, he promised: I would be made to pay for my homicidal acts. He, Sheldon Flowers, with the help of this jury of tried-and-true citizens, would see to that. "And of course," he concluded, "the people of the sovereign state of California *will* seek the death penalty."

By the time he walked back to his chair, the jury seemed ready to lynch me. I saw anger and outrage etched into their tight-lipped faces. If looks could kill, I would have been dead on the spot.

My opening statement did little to ease the situation. Speaking for myself, as a lawyer, I told the jury that I'd had nothing to do with the two murders of which I was accused. I told them that I had loved and respected Amy Thompson, and that she had loved and respected me in return. I claimed that I'd had no knowledge of Amy Thompson's new will until *after* her death . . . and that, following the second murder, the real killer had planted the murder knife in my camper. I was absolutely *not* guilty, I told them, and would prove, in this trial, that this was the truth, the whole truth, and nothing but the truth.

I walked back to my table, crossing in front of the smugly confident D.A., without looking at the jury for a reaction. I didn't want to see what was in their eyes at that moment. I had done my best, but I was certain it had not been enough to sway them.

Flowers called his first witness to the stand. A pale little man, with nervous hands, who took the oath and was seated.

"Please state your name and occupation."

"Alvin P. Stanich. The 'P' is for Percival, but I don't like anybody to call me that. My mother used to call me 'Percy,' which was even worse."

Laughter rumbled through the courtroom.

"Occupation?" prompted Judge Carter.

"I am an attorney, specializing in estate matters."

Flowers leaned toward him. "Did you prepare a recent will for a certain Amy Latimer Thompson?"

"Yes, I did. At her request, just a few days before she was . . . before her death. She told me that her prior will was no longer satisfactory and she wanted a new one drafted."

"And you did this?"

"Yes. I followed her instructions precisely."

Flowers smiled at him, his voice calm and assured. "Who did Amy Thompson name as her sole beneficiary in this new will?"

"Mr. Erle Stanley Gardner. He was to get everything."

The eyes of the jury bored into me.

Flowers affected surprise. "*Nothing* was to go to anyone else?"

"No. Nothing."

"Thank you, Mr. Stanich. That will be all."

Judge Carter nodded toward me. "Your witness."

I approached Stanich. "Is it true that Amy Thompson had no direct heirs, that her parents were both deceased, as was her only child, and that she had no brothers or sisters?"

"Yes, that's true."

"Did she indicate to you that I had asked her to name me as beneficiary, or that I had in any way pressured her to do so?"

"No—but in my opinion, she didn't have to, since she came to me right after she spent the night with you."

"Objection," I snapped. "The witness was asked for an answer, not an opinion."

"Sustained," said Judge Carter.

I decided I was actually losing ground here and that I'd gain nothing by questioning Stanich further, so he was dismissed.

The second witness was Ida Favershim, of the Silver Gate Spa in Carmel. She testified that I had appeared at the spa unannounced, telling her I planned to use the Silver Gate as background material for a novel. She said that I had shown particular interest in Youth-O-Vim and had inquired about its taste and ingredients.

On my cross-examination, she admitted that I had declined the free bottle of Youth-O-Vim that she had offered me. Therefore, it was obvious I had no personal knowledge of its taste.

The third witness to take the stand was my Filipino houseboy, Tomas Lecayan. He looked nervous and upset, knowing that whatever he said might hurt my case.

Flowers began by asking him how long he had worked for me.

"Long time," said Tomas. "Many years."

"And are you aware of the growth around you employer's home?"

He was confused by the question. "Growth?"

"Trees . . . bushes . . . plants . . . flowers—that sort of thing."

"Oh, yes." Tomas nodded rapidly. "Many flowers. Like your name."

A giggle in the courtroom.

"What about oleander? Does oleander grow on Mr. Gardner's property?"

"Yes, yes." Again the rapid nod. "Much oleander."

"So . . . it would be a simple matter for Mr. Gardner to go into his yard at night, say, and cut away enough oleander to boil down into a toxic poison. Is that correct?"

I objected on the ground that the witness was not qualified to comment on toxic poisons; Judge Carter instructed Flowers to rephrase the question.

Flowers nodded. "If Mr. Gardner went into his own garden—during the night, let's say—and he cut away oleander leaves from his own bushes, would those leaves be missed? Would you, or any other employee of Mr. Gardner's, notice that Mr. Gardner had taken away some of his own oleander leaves?"

Tomas thought carefully. "No. No, sir. No one would notice." He looked miserable.

Flowers was satisfied and I was given permission to cross. I asked Tomas just one question: "Isn't it true that every yard in the neighborhood has oleander growing in it, not just my yard?"

"Yes. There is much oleander all over the neighborhood . . . all over Hollywood . . . all over southern California," he said.

He smiled at me, glad to have been of help. And Tomas was excused.

Flowers called his third witness, private investigator Mark Silver. He was a no-nonsense character in a pin-striped suit, and he looked like he'd earned his reputation as Hollywood's toughest, most respected private investigator.

"Mr. Silver, were you employed by the late Lloyd Thompson to follow his wife, Amy, and submit a report on her activities?"

"Right. I was hired to do that."

Flowers turned his back on Silver to face the jury box. "Would you please tell the ladies and gentlemen of this jury where Mrs. Amy Thompson spent the night of June second of this year?"

"With him," said Silver, pointing directly at me. "She spent that night with him."

"Let the record show that this witness has pointed out the defendant, Erle Stanley Gardner, as Amy Thompson's sexual playmate."

I leaped to my feet. "Objection, Your Honor! The term 'sexual playmate' is deliberately slanderous, partaking of overt character assassination."

Carter sustained my objection, instructing the jury to disregard the offending words and ordering that they be stricken from the record. The problem with objections that have been sustained is that the damage has already been done. The jury has already absorbed the words and there is no way to erase them. Every lawyer has indulged in this sort of thing to get a point across; I've done it myself on numerous occasions.

When it was time for my cross, I decided to add an element of uncertainty to Silver's testimony. There were only two people who knew what had really happened between Amy and me that night. She was dead, and I certainly had no intention of testifying as a witness. Therefore, I could not be forced to tell what *had* happened.

"Mr. Silver, when you said that Amy Thompson spent the night of June second at my home, did you mean to indicate by your statement that she and I had indulged in a sexual act during that time?"

He looked confused. "Uh . . . what *else* would you have been doing?"

The courtroom erupted in laughter, which I had expected. Now I could introduce at least the possibility of doubt.

"We could have been talking all night, Mr. Silver. We could have spent the entire night *talking*. From your surveillance, did you observe anything that would allow you to swear, on penalty of perjury, that Amy Thompson and I did anything *other* than talk on the night of June second?"

He shook his head. "No. I guess you *coulda* been talking." He shifted uncomfortably in the witness chair. I had the sudden insight that Mark Silver, private detective, had never before considered the possibility that a man and woman *could* talk all night long. Under other circumstances, I would have been amused.

Silver was excused from the stand.

Several members of the jury were glaring at me, making no attempt to hide their hostility. And the next witness would make things even darker for me.

"State your name and occupation, please."

"Irma Glassman," she said. "*Mrs.* Irma Glassman. I'm a housewife, and the mother of three. Two fine sons and a wonderful daughter."

"Did you attend the burial of Amy Thompson at Oak Hills Cemetery?"

"Yes, sir. I did."

"Why were you there, Mrs. Glassman?"

"Because of what Amy and Tink Thompson meant to me. I just plain loved them both. I read all the articles in the movie magazines about poor Amy—I even named my daughter Amy, after her. Amy Glassman, that's my daughter's name. And I went to all of Tink's pictures the first day they came out. Never missed a one. I saw *Song of Saint Margaret's* five times, and it always made me cry."

"And did you observe an angry exchange on the afternoon of Amy Thompson's burial between the defendant and Mr. Thompson?"

"Objection," I said. "Mr. Flowers is leading the witness."

Before Carter could respond, the D.A. withdrew the question, asking: "Would you please tell us exactly what you observed with your own eyes that afternoon, following the burial service?"

"Well, I wanted to get close to Tink—to Mr. Thompson—so I kind of stayed with him, hoping maybe I could get his autograph. But since he'd just buried his wife, I figured that maybe it wasn't such a good time to ask."

"Please," said Flowers with a touch of impatience, "just tell us what you personally observed."

"All right." She cleared her throat and sat up stiffly in the witness chair. "I saw Mr. Gardner and Mr. Thompson arguing. He—Mr. Thompson—told Mr. Gardner that he'd had a detective follow him, and then he said: 'You slept with my wife!' and he sounded real upset."

More hard glares from the jury.

"And then what happened?"

"Well, Mr. Gardner said that Amy had never loved Mr. Thompson—which I thought was an awful thing to say—"

"Just your observations, please, not your opinion," Flowers said before I could object.

"Mr. Thompson said that it was 'a damn lie'—about him not loving his wife—and he grabbed Mr. Gardner by the front of his shirt. Then it ended, because a lot of people were watching. But Mr. Gardner was very angry."

When I got the chance to cross-examine, I challenged her account: "Didn't Lloyd Thompson threaten *me*, not the other way around?"

"Uh . . . how do you mean?"

"Didn't he say to me: 'I'm going to fix you for this, you bastard'?"

"Objection," said Flowers. "He's leading the witness."

The judge looked down at her. "What actual words did you hear, Mrs. Glassman?"

"I . . . I don't recall exactly . . . but I guess they were both kind of mad at each other."

I knew that this was the best I could get out of her and told the judge I was finished with the witness.

"You are excused," Judge Carter told her.

I took my seat again, fully aware that Sheldon Flowers was winning this case hands down; any points I might have made with the jury were inconsequential.

And Dash Hammett, who was to bring me the one piece of evidence I'd managed to gather in my favor, had not shown up in court.

Worse yet, the most damaging testimony was still to come.

TWENTY-TWO

One by one, in rapid succession, Sheldon Flowers called four of Thompson's employees to the stand: Rene Clarfait, the French cook; Ellen Wheatley, the maid; Martha Ledding, the nanny; and Okiro Tanaka, Thompson's gardner.

Clarfait was loftily skeptical of Amy's health-food regimen, re-marking acidly on her "excessive vanity." Under my cross, he admit-ted that he was prejudiced against health food, and resented the fact that Amy often rejected his cream-rich French dishes. Clarfait was a vigorous supporter of Tink Thompson, testifying during my cross-examination that he had never heard Thompson pressure his wife re-garding her physical attractiveness.

Ellen Wheatley, the maid, talked in a tone of awe about the many expensive dresses that Thompson had bought for Amy, and what a "wonderfully generous" man he had been. Did she have any knowl-edge, I asked her, of Thompson's affairs with other women? She was shocked at my question, testifying that such accusations were no more than "lying gossip."

Miss Martha Louise Ledding, as she gave her name to the court, was the British nanny who had taken care of young Larry. She praised

Tink Thompson as an "ideal parent," who always brought home "wonderful toys" for his son.

I asked: "Is it not a fact that Larry was terrified of his father?"

Flowers stood up to object, but before he could speak, the nanny angrily replied: "That's absolute rot! From the way you have attacked Mr. Thompson in this courtroom, it is obvious that you are trying to blacken the memory of the man you so cruelly butchered!"

I protested this, and Judge Carter sustained my objection, directing that Miss Ledding's comment be excised from the record, but her damning words had struck home with the jury.

Okiro Tanaka testified in glowing terms about how dedicated his employer had been to the estate gardens, and how much Mr. Thompson appreciated the beauties of nature. In addition, Tanaka declared, every year Thompson would gift each of his employees with a handsome Christmas bonus.

"Very fine man, my boss," he nodded. "Very fine."

Again, more fulsome praise for America's favorite saint, Tink Thompson.

I declined to cross-examine.

The D.A.'s pièce de résistance was the final Thompson employee, the witness everyone in the courtroom had been waiting for: the handyman who had discovered Tink Thompson's corpse.

He was a slim-bodied, yet muscular young man, with a Pancho Villa mustache, a three-day's growth of beard, and a strong, aquiline nose that gave him the look of a hunting hawk. His dark hair was tangled and uncombed, and—obviously a poor man—he seemed ill at ease facing the immaculate, neatly tailored figure of Sheldon Flowers.

A court translator stood beside him at the witness stand since he spoke only Spanish. To avoid confusion in this account, I will report his dialogue in English.

He gave his full name as Carlos José Montoya y Muro, then

explained—via the translator—that in the United States, he was known simply as Carlos Montoya.

When asked his occupation, he said *"trabajador de hacienda,"* which literally translates as "landed-estate worker." It sounds much less grand in the English vernacular: handyman. However, as he explained his duties, maybe *trabajador de hacienda* was more appropriate. It appeared from Montoya's testimony that his responsibilities ranged far beyond miscellaneous odd jobs and included just about everything that actually kept the Thompson estate running smoothly. After establishing Montoya's various job responsibilities, the D.A. asked him to explain what had happened on the morning of Mr. Thompson's death.

Montoya nodded and tugged nervously at the collar of his starched shirt; obviously, he was more accustomed to wearing overalls. "I arrived at Mr. Thompson's at dawn and went to the main house."

"Tell us why."

"Mr. Thompson had asked me to fix a leak underneath the kitchen sink." He shifted nervously in the witness chair.

"Tell us what happened when you entered the main residence."

"None of the other employees had arrived for work, so the house was quiet. The sun was starting to come up, but most of the house was still dark. I went into the kitchen and looked under the sink, but I could not find the leak. Since the cook wasn't there to tell me where it was, I went to ask Mr. Thompson. I wanted to get it fixed before the cook had to make breakfast."

"Weren't you afraid that your employer was still sleeping?" Flowers asked.

"No. Mr. Thompson always arose before dawn. It was his habit."

"Could he speak Spanish?"

"Yes. Very well."

"Continue."

"I went upstairs to his bedroom and knocked, but he did not answer. I thought he was probably downstairs, working in his study—he did that sometimes—so I went there."

"What did you find?"

"The door to the study was half open, as if someone had run out fast and forgot to close it."

"Conjecture," I objected. "Not fact."

"Sustained," nodded Carter. "Just tell us what you saw, Mr. Montoya. The jury will draw its own conclusions."

The D.A. decided to make the point another way. "Was that particular door always kept closed?"

"Yes. Always."

"Yet it was not closed when you first saw it that morning?"

"No, sir, it was not."

"Please, go on with what you saw, Mr. Montoya."

"There was a ray of sunshine that ran across the desk to the floor in front of it. That's where he was."

"Mr. Thompson was on the floor?"

"Yes. On his back in front of the desk. He was very bloody. There was much blood around him. I could see that he was dead."

"How could you be sure he was dead without checking his body?"

"Because his throat had been cut."

A stifled gasp from the courtroom.

Sheldon Flowers looked up at Carter. "May I approach the witness, Your Honor?"

"You may."

The D.A. picked up several glossy photos of Thompson's body from the prosecution table and took them to Montoya. "Is this what you saw that morning, Mr. Montoya?"

"Yes. That is how he looked. I thought to myself, how could any person do such a terrible thing to this wonderful man?"

What he thought or did not think was not the issue, but I withheld my objection in the emotion of the moment.

Flowers gave the photos to the jury, who passed them from hand to hand. Each of them winced at the graphic impact of the pictures. One woman visibly shuddered; she seemed on the verge of fainting.

The D.A. resumed his questioning. "Did you see anyone else in the house at this time?"

"No, sir. There was no one else in the house. There was just me and poor Mr. Thompson."

"What did you do next?"

"I crossed myself, sir, and said a prayer to the Blessed Virgin Mary for Mr. Thompson's soul. Then I went to a phone in the hall and phoned for the police. I did not want to touch anything in the study. The police soon arrived. They asked me a lot of questions—like the ones you're asking."

"And what do you feel should be done to the man who committed such a heinous crime?"

"Objection," I declared. "The feelings of this witness are not pertinent."

"Withdrawn," said Flowers. But he smiled at me; he'd made his point to the jury.

"No more questions, Your Honor," he said as he returned to his seat.

"Your witness," Carter said to me.

I was uncertain of exactly how to proceed, but I knew that this was not the proper time to question Montoya. I asked that he be held for recall later in the trial.

"Very well," said Carter. To Flowers: "You may call your next witness."

A uniformed police officer took the stand, firing a look at me that was hot enough to melt my shoes. His name was Edward Hutten; he told the court that everyone called him "Big Ed." I could see why. He must have weighed two hundred fifty, and he had the height to carry it. Hutten looked strong enough to pick me up and toss me out the nearest window, and his expression told me he'd enjoy doing just that.

He testified that after the news of Thompson's murder had reached police headquarters, a search warrant had been obtained and that he and two other officers had been sent to my home in Hollywood to search the premises.

"Did you find anything relating to the murder at Mr. Gardner's house?"

"Yes."

"Tell us what happened, please."

"When we got there, we divided up. The other two officers searched Gardner's house, while I went out back. A camper was parked in the yard."

"Describe this 'camper' for the court."

"Well . . . it's sort of a big trailer, with a driver's compartment up front. There are all kinds of special equipment in it, like fishing gear and tents, an outdoor cook stove . . . stuff like that."

"Did you search this vehicle?"

"Yes."

"Tell us what you found."

"Nothing at first," said Big Ed. "Then I got me an idea. I decided to have a look under the driver's seat—and that's where I found it."

"Exactly what did you find?"

"A hunting knife. With blood all over it."

Flowers held up the murder weapon, and his voice rang through the courtroom: "*This* knife?"

Big Ed nodded. "That's the one. With a little notch in the handle. Had blood all over it."

"What did you do next?"

"I bagged the knife, took it back to headquarters, and turned it over to the lab in order to have the bloodstains checked."

"Was anything else found at the Gardner house?"

Hutten grinned. "Nope—but what else did we need? We had the knife that Gardner had used to cut Thompson's throat."

I leaped up with my objection. Naturally, it was sustained, but every word of Big Ed's had registered with the jury. Another triumph for the D.A.

My cross-examination was brief.

"Was the camper locked when you entered it?"

"No. I just opened the door and went in."

"Then *anyone* could have entered the vehicle and planted that knife under the seat—isn't that true?"

"I never for one second believed that it was planted," he said gruffly.

I bored in: "I'm not asking what you *believed,* Officer Hutten, I'm asking for a direct answer to my question. Isn't it true that *anyone* could have put that knife there—yes or no?"

"Yeah, I guess."

"So that's a yes?"

"It is." He glared. "Yes."

I was finished. Big Ed gave me another withering look as he left the stand.

I'd gotten a "yes" out of him, but what had it accomplished for me? Not damn much, I thought.

Flowers called his final witness, a wispy fellow named Henry Akers, who came across like a bank clerk but was actually head of the crime lab at Beverly Hills Homicide. He looked gaunt and undernourished, with sunken cheeks and a nose so thin his glasses kept slipping down throughout his testimony.

Flowers began by asking about Akers' background and medical qualifications. They were lengthy and impressive.

"Doctor Akers, were you asked to examine a certain hunting knife suspected to be the weapon used in the murder of Lloyd Thompson?"

"I was. Yes."

"Is this the knife you examined?" asked Flowers, holding it toward the witness.

"Yes. That is the same knife."

"And, as I understand it, you conducted a careful, scientific examination of this object, is that correct?"

"That's correct."

"What were your findings, Doctor?"

"There were no fingerprints on the blade or the handle, but the bloodstains were significant."

"Please explain to the jury what you mean by 'significant.' "

Akers adjusted his slipping glasses. "The blood type on the knife matched the blood type of the deceased," he stated. "An exact match, in fact."

"So would you be willing to state, as a qualified professional, that it was indeed Lloyd Thompson's blood on the knife found in Erle Stanley Gardner's camper?"

"Yes, I would say so. And I would add that to my mind, there is no question but that this is the weapon used in the perpetration of the crime."

I didn't try to object. This knife had done the job on Thompson. Why dispute the obvious? I also declined to cross-examine, since there was nothing to challenge in his testimony.

Akers was permitted to step down.

"Your Honor," said Sheldon Flowers, "the prosecution rests."

He had manipulated the jury with the skill of a veteran puppeteer. My chances looked very bleak. So far as I was able to determine, not a single juror believed in my innocence. Were they to retire at this juncture for a verdict, I would be found guilty on both counts of first-degree murder.

At the lunch recess, with two police guards at my elbow, I spent most of the hour trying to locate Hammett. He wasn't at home, or at the studio. I phoned a couple of his girlfriends, but they hadn't seen him. Chandler also had no idea of where he was.

"He could be having a drink somewhere," said Ray.

"Yeah," I sighed. "Dash gets off the booze and then he goes back to it again. Maybe he's dead drunk in the corner booth of some bar." I shook my head. "If he doesn't show up by the time court resumes . . ."

I let the sentence trail off. Dash had never failed me in the past, but that was then and now was now. He *was* unstable, with a checkered reputation in Hollywood. I remembered what director Hunt Stromberg had said when a news reporter asked him what it was like working with Hammett. He swore that he'd rather have Attila the Hun writing for him.

When court resumed, with Judge Carter seated in his chair at the bench, I scanned the room for a sign of Hammett—but he was not there.

Damn the man! My life was on the line.

"Are you ready to proceed, Mr. Gardner?" asked the judge.

"Yes, Your Honor. I wish to recall Carlos Montoya to the stand."

When Montoya was seated, with his translator standing beside him, I began my questioning: "Was the testimony you gave this morning rehearsed with the district attorney?"

Again, his replies were all in Spanish.

"Rehearsed?" he asked in a bewildered tone.

"Did he *coach* you as to your testimony?"

Flowers stood up to object, but he was overruled. "The witness may answer."

Montoya blinked at me. "We talked about what I was going to say today, but he didn't ask me to lie. I would never lie, sir! What I said was the truth."

There was a stir in the room; something was happening. My heart leaped as I saw the thin figure of Dashiell Hammett moving down the aisle toward the rail with a manila envelope in his hand.

I stepped over to him and took the envelope.

"Sorry," he whispered, "but I couldn't get here earlier."

"I just thank God you made it," I said.

The judge looked upset, and Flowers was on his feet, demanding to know what I was doing.

I returned to the witness stand, stuffing the envelope in my coat pocket. "I apologize to the court, and to counsel, for the interruption. It was unavoidable."

The crowd's murmur had increased and Carter was rapping his gavel for silence. Plainly vexed, he accepted my apology and permitted me to continue. Flowers sat down again, scowling.

I faced the witness. "Mr. Montoya, do you know—or *did* you know—a certain Antonio Sanchez?"

"No, sir."

"Do you know—or *did* you know—a man named Miguel Barela?"

"No. I do not know such a person."

I turned to face the jury. "Ladies and gentlemen, I have a story to tell you that bears directly on this case, and on the testimony of this witness."

They looked at me with dubious expressions—as if nothing I had to say would affect their negative opinion of me. Three of the men had their arms folded across their chests, and the women were frowning.

"Let me begin with Lloyd Thompson. In nineteen-seventeen, after his graduation from high school, Thompson took a motorcycle trip to the village of San Felipe, in Baja California. There he met a young woman named María Sanchez. One thing led to another and in a short while, Lloyd Hadley Thompson and María Teresa Sanchez were married in the village church. To my knowledge, that union was never dissolved. Until Mr. Thompson's death, the marriage was still valid."

I could hear a shocked murmur building in the courtroom as the implication of what I was saying became clear.

"Soon after their marriage, Lloyd Thompson abandoned his wife.

When he left San Felipe, he did not know that María Sanchez Thompson was pregnant. Therefore, he never knew of the birth of his son, Antonio, who grew up in San Felipe thinking that his father was an unimportant Anglo drifter. Thompson's wife was eventually forced to support herself and her son by becoming a prostitute.

"Many years later, Antonio Sanchez—as he was known—found a Mexican movie magazine containing an article about his father. The magazine said that Lloyd Thompson was now called 'Tink,' and that he was a rich and famous American film star. It also said that he had married again—and that his new wife, Amy Thompson, had given birth to a son.

"As you can imagine, Antonio became very angry. His father had not only abandoned him and his mother, forcing her to become a prostitute, but another woman—and another *son*—were enjoying what should have rightfully belonged to María and Antonio Sanchez.

"Then, late last year, having learned about Tink's first marriage from Thompson himself, Amy went to San Felipe to see María Sanchez. She offered María one thousand American dollars for the marriage certificate. She had determined to use it against Lloyd Thompson in her planned divorce proceeding, but no one knew that at the time. María, who needed money, sold Amy the document.

"Antonio already hated Lloyd Thompson, but his hatred now also became directed at Amy Thompson, whom he mistakenly believed had 'bought' his and his mother's rightful claim to a future inheritance."

Sheldon Flowers stood up in frustration. "Your Honor, I must protest. This fanciful—totally unproved—story is irrelevant to the case at hand. It's a waste of the court's valuable time and that of the jury."

"Not so, Your Honor," I countered. "I will prove what I am saying, and I will show that it relates *directly* to the murders of which I stand accused."

"I will allow you to continue, Mr. Gardner," said the judge in a disgruntled tone, "so long as what you are telling the jury can indeed be proved and tied into this case . . . but *do* get to your point."

"Thank you, Your Honor," I said, turning back to face the jury. At least I had engaged their interest.

"In late December of last year, Antonio Sanchez, accompanied by his cousin, Miguel Barela, left San Felipe and came to Los Angeles. I will get back to Miguel Barela later. For the moment, it would appear that Antonio Sanchez arrived in Los Angeles and subsequently obtained employment at the wholesale produce market downtown.

"Antonio had a plan: he wanted to obtain a sizable portion of the rightful money that had been denied him as Thompson's child. Amy and Lloyd Thompson's son, Larry, had recently died as the result of a tragic household accident—a matter that had been widely reported in the press. Antonio believed that with young Larry Thompson now dead, he had clear title as Thompson's one and only *legitimate* son.

"But he also believed that Amy Thompson was an impediment to his plans, so he poisoned her. His uncle, Luis Barela, was an expert on plant life. Therefore, Antonio would have had no trouble concocting a poisonous mixture of oleander. Afterward, he was shocked to learn that Amy had revised her will, naming me as sole beneficiary of her estate. This meant that instead of her estate going to Tink Thompson, as Antonio had assumed would happen automatically, it would go to me instead.

"Antonio brooded over this, then went to Thompson, revealed himself as his son, and demanded one hundred thousand dollars in cash. Thompson refused his demand, and was stabbed to death on the spot.

"Amy Thompson's new will had inadvertently made me a prime suspect for her murder. In fact, I had been officially charged for that crime. Therefore, I was the ideal person to frame for this second murder. Antonio took the bloodstained knife and planted it in my unlocked camper."

I paused to let all this sink in.

"And now, ladies and gentlemen, let me return to Antonio's cousin, Miguel Barela. Barela already had a minor criminal record in Los Angeles County, which wouldn't have been much of a problem, except that he also had an outstanding warrant that was issued after he had previously failed to appear in court on a burglary charge. Therefore, when he returned to Los Angeles from San Felipe with his cousin, he couldn't get a job under his own name. Antonio generously offered to let Barela use *his* name. Therefore, although employment records list "Antonio Sanchez" as an employee in the produce exchange, the person who was *actually* working under that name was Miguel Barela.

"Now known as 'Antonio Sanchez,' he must have become suspicious when he heard about the murders first of Amy Thompson, and then of Lloyd Thompson. His mother was María Sanchez's sister, so he had grown up knowing the story of how María had married a gringo named Lloyd Thompson, who had then abandoned her before he learned that she was pregnant.

"Suddenly, Miguel Barela was a threat to the real Antonio Sanchez, so Sanchez strangled his cousin to shut him up. The red marks on the boy's throat were proof that he had been strangled, but his death was officially termed a heart attack and was never investigated.

"Antonio was now in the clear. Once *I* had been convicted for the two murders, he could appear before the proper authorities and claim the Thompson fortune for himself and his mother as Thompson's legal heirs. Even though the actual marriage certificate was missing—since María had sold it to Amy Thompson—the marriage could be validated through church records and the village priest. In the unlikely event that anyone realized that 'Antonio Sanchez' had died in downtown Los Angeles, Antonio would freely admit that he had allowed his cousin to use his identity in order to help him obtain work. A worthy example of family loyalty."

The district attorney was again vigorously protesting: "This charade has gone far enough, Your Honor. Mr. Gardner, who is an expert in the manufacture of fictional stories, knows very well that he has no way to prove the validity of this lurid, unconvincing fairy tale he has concocted for the jury in an attempt to obscure his own obvious guilt."

"I am about to offer proof, Your Honor, if the court will indulge me for a few moments longer."

Judge Carter was frowning and looked as if he intended to cut me off when—from his seat in the back of the room—Chandler suddenly stood up: "Skippers, please . . . let him finish!"

Judge Carter glared at him. "Sit *down*, Boogles! Er . . . I mean, Mr. Chandler."

Ray sat down amid scattered giggles from the courtroom.

Carter, plainly embarrassed, nodded to me: "Continue, Mr. Gardner. But make it quick."

I returned to the jury box. "Ladies and gentlemen, as I have told you, Antonio Sanchez did *not* die at the produce market. He is, in fact, alive today and sitting in this very courtroom—with the blood of three people on his hands!"

A buzz of raised voices. I swung around to the witness stand and pointed directly at Montoya. "Here is your murderer!"

The accused jumped to his feet and yelled, without translation: "That's a damned lie!"

"Ah," I said, "so you *do* speak English!"

I turned back to the jury. "He got himself hired by Thompson as a handyman under the phony name of Carlos Montoya—but his real name is Antonio Sanchez."

"Proof!" shouted Antonio. "I defy you to prove that what you say is true!"

I pulled the manila envelope from my coat, ripped it open, and held up a black cylinder. "Here is the proof! From the Dictaphone in Lloyd Thompson's study. Thompson was dictating a letter when Antonio burst in, demanding the hundred thousand dollars. Antonio said that if he didn't get it, he would go to the press, telling them what Thompson had done to María, how she'd had to become a prostitute to survive, and how Thompson had ignored the marriage and had never contacted her after he left San Felipe. It would have destroyed his career.

"But if Thompson handed over the money, Antonio said, he would go back to Mexico and forget all about this. He boasted that he'd already killed Amy and Miguel, and he'd do the same to Thompson if he didn't produce the cash.

"They argued. Lloyd Thompson was furious, saying he would not be blackmailed. He went for a gun in his desk—and that's when Antonio used the hunting knife on him. It's all here on this Dictaphone cylinder. I listened to it in Thompson's study the night I was arrested.

"What Antonio Sanchez didn't know was that the machine had *stayed* on—recording every moment of what happened between them in that room!"

I had delivered a bombshell.

TWENTY-THREE

The court was in an uproar. Carter was pounding his gavel for order. Flowers was shouting in protest, claiming that he had never been shown this "so-called proof."

Taking sudden advantage of the chaos, Antonio Sanchez pulled a gun from his jacket—the same gun that had originally been in Thompson's desk—and leaped up to the bench, jamming the weapon against Carter's head. Two court bailiffs rushed forward.

"Stay back or I'll kill him!" warned Sanchez. His tone was high-pitched, frenzied. "I'll shoot this old bastard's brains out!"

The deputies stopped, hands hovering over their belted guns, as Antonio forced the judge ahead of him, down the aisle and out of the courtroom. People spilled away from him. A woman screamed. A man on the jury began to pray.

Holding the gun to Carter's head, Antonio moved along the outer hallway, down to the lobby, and out to a parked police car. I followed—and saw him smash the driver over the head with the gun barrel, then jerk the unfortunate officer out of the seat onto the pavement. Sanchez then forced Judge Carter into the car. With a squeal of smoking rubber, he gunned away from the court building.

I felt a firm hand on my shoulder. It was Oldfield. Pointing to his Stutz, he said: "C'mon. We're goin' after them."

We sprinted for Barney's car. Out of the corner of my eye I saw Dash and Buddy pile into Ray's Duesenberg. They were behind us when Barney powered the big white racing machine out of the lot.

"Which way?" I yelled.

"I figger they'll go for the coast," Barney said, his foot hard on the gas as we roared west on Wilshire Boulevard, headed toward the ocean.

"What if you're wrong?" I argued.

"Then they'll probably get away," he yelled back.

He wasn't wrong. Once we reached the coast highway along the Pacific, we were able to spot the patrol car a mile ahead. Sanchez had the siren blaring to clear his way and was moving at a very high rate of speed.

I twisted around to look back. A half mile behind, the big Duesenberg, with Chandler driving, was definitely losing ground. The Stutz was much faster and we were gaining steadily on the speeding patrol car. Several other police vehicles had joined the chase, but they were too far behind to threaten Sanchez.

The wind battered and fisted me in the exposed cockpit as the Stutz bucked and swayed over the highway like a horse at full gallop. The sound of the open exhaust was deafening.

To our left, the Pacific Ocean spread its glittering waters. A big steamer dotted the far horizon.

"We're comin' up on him," Barney shouted as he leaned forward, his hands gripping the big wood-spoked wheel. He wore his round racing goggles, and an unlit cigar was clenched between his teeth, his hair wild and wind-whipped. Oldfield was thoroughly enjoying himself in full-throttle pursuit of a fleeing killer. He was in his natural element, and I had total confidence in his ability to overtake Sanchez; what I worried about was what would happen when we did.

We were tracing the wide circle of Santa Monica Bay when Old-field yelled: "He's turnin' right, up Big Rock Canyon Road."

Barney downshifted and slammed the Stutz into a hard right turn. I was thrown against the side of the cockpit as we fishtailed into Big Rock Canyon, with Barney fighting to keep us upright.

The asphalt road looped ahead in a series of tight curves, and I saw a broad smile crease Oldfield's weathered face. "We got him," he told me, patting the wheel of the Stutz. "This baby was *made* for curves. On a road like this, we'll eat him up."

Barney was handling the big racing machine with all of his legendary skill, thundering around the curves on the ragged edge of traction and closing fast on Sanchez.

Within minutes, we were at the killer's rear bumper. I saw him look back at us in nervous panic as he increased his speed, sliding through the curves like a madman, struggling desperately to maintain a thin margin of control.

To our left, the brush-cloaked canyon wall towered up in a mass of tumbled boulders; to our right, the road dropped off into a shallow gorge laced with a sun-flashed ribbon of water along the bottom.

Now, with a fresh burst of speed as he rode the inside edge of asphalt, Barney brought the Stutz level with the Sanchez vehicle. I looked across to see a terrified Judge Carter hunched in the passenger seat, with Sanchez bent over the wheel, pushing the swaying police vehicle to its limit.

"Hang on!" yelled Barney. I gripped the cockpit as he banged the Stutz into the side of the other car. Again. And yet again.

"You'll force him off!" I warned.

Barney nodded vigorously. "Only way to stop him."

Sanchez took a hand off the wheel to point his weapon at us. I ducked—but before he could trigger the gun, he lost control. The speeding police car tipped over the edge of the road, sliding and bumping wildly along the side of the gorge. Halfway down, it slammed into a large boulder, which crumpled the car's hood like tissue paper. A geyser of white steam shot up from the ruptured radiator.

Barney skidded to a stop, jumped free of the cockpit, and began to make his way down the slope to the smashed vehicle. I was right behind him.

"Hope to hell I haven't killed the judge," he declared.

The windows of the police car were cracked and splintered; there was no movement from the two men inside.

"Gimme a hand with this," said Oldfield, tugging at the jammed passenger door.

On the upper road, Chandler arrived with Hammett and Buddy in the Duesenberg. By the time they'd climbed down to join us, we had the door open. Barney lifted Judge Carter carefully from the seat; he had blood on his face.

"Skippers!" moaned Chandler. "Are you all right?"

Carter looked up at his old friend with dazed eyes. "Boogles . . ." he said weakly, and then lapsed into unconsciousness.

Antonio Sanchez, slumped over the twisted steering wheel, remained motionless.

There's not much left to tell.

When they examined Judge Carter at the hospital, he was found to be injured far less seriously than we had feared. He had a bad cut over his right eye, along with a minor concussion, a sprained ankle, and some bruises. But he had a lot of very nice things to say about me and Barney.

Sanchez suffered a skull fracture and three broken ribs, but he recovered. Sheldon Flowers, ever-mindful of the upcoming November election, chose to schedule Antonio's trial immediately after he was pronounced fit by the doctors. The D.A. didn't manage to win a death sentence, but Antonio *was* convicted on three counts of murder: two in the first degree for his cousin, Miguel Barela, and Amy

Thompson; one in the second degree for Tink Thompson. Sanchez is now serving three consecutive life sentences in San Quentin.

The unsleeping shark had finally been netted.

Chandler went home to Cissy and wrote a new crime story for *Dime Detective*. One of these days, he's going to get around to that novel Dash and I keep nagging him about.

Hammett finished his script on *Charlie Chan in the Alps*, but the project was put on hold. So he got a job at Republic for a Western with Gene Autry, and now he's complaining about having to write lines for a singing cowboy.

Barney Oldfield went back to running his country club, telling us—and everyone else he can collar—that he hasn't had so much fun on the road since he won the Cactus Derby.

I wanted to get back to work, but first I had something far more important to do.

Before Antonio's trial, Buddy and I made one final trip to San Felipe to see María Sanchez.

I explained what had happened to her son, Antonio, and it broke my heart to see the sadness my words inflicted on her. Later, after many tears and prayers, she calmed down enough to listen as I explained the chief reason for my visit: as Lloyd Hadley Thompson's legal widow, she was now the principal beneficiary of his fortune.

It took less than fifteen minutes to pack her worldly goods. Ten minutes after that, with Buddy driving, María and I were on the road headed north, beginning the long journey to Beverly Hills. The rest of her life will undoubtedly have its share of problems—except for one.

María Teresa Sanchez Thompson is now, God bless her, a very wealthy woman.

AFTERWORD

Once again, as with my two previous Black Mask mysteries, this new novel is a mix of fact and fiction.

To my knowledge, Erle Stanley Gardner never went to jail, and he certainly never defended himself in court against a murder charge. However, all of his personal history from the opening chapters is true, including his early life with his parents, his schooling, and his experiences as a young lawyer in Oxnard and Ventura. Also true: his courtship and marriage to Natalie Gardner and their separation following the marriage of their daughter, Grace.

All of Gardner's thoughts on writing, his break into the pulps, and his relationship with Joe Shaw, are as factual as I could make them.

The fiction begins with Amy Latimer and her husband, Tink Thompson (not to be confused with Bing Crosby). Gardner's affair with her is my invention, as is Thompson's mistress in Montecito and his first wife in Mexico.

Barney Oldfield, who died in 1946, was a very real character, with the actual racing background I gave him, but to my knowledge, he never saved anyone from a flash flood, or drove to San Felipe, or chased a killer in his Stutz.[1]

The fishing village of San Felipe itself, however, is just as I have described it; I've driven down there twice from Calexico. And I've often been to Carmel-by-the-Sea, although I never visited a health spa there or met Mae West in a steam bath (or anywhere else). I do know, however, that Miss West believed that a clean bowel tract was the secret of her youthful appearance. Gloria Swanson *was* a devotee of healthy living; her husband, William Duffy, wrote an entire book on the evils of processed sugar.[2]

All of John Barrymore's background is true into 1937, but I doubt that he ever performed *Hamlet* in Palm Springs. Montecito's estates were carefully researched as a background for the character of Marisol Herrera-Quintano (of whom I grew quite fond). And Joe Shaw did become a literary agent when he was dismissed from *Black Mask*.

Despite the fact that Walter Winchell praised my biography of film director John Huston[3] in one of his columns, all evidence points to the fact that he was a ruthless gossip monger, just as portrayed in my novel.

Hammett *did* live for a time in the rented house in Pacific Palisades, but he had left there by 1937. I simply extended his lease for plot purposes, and added a secret room behind the real ice-cream parlor in the basement. In Hollywood, he functioned as what the industry calls a "script doctor," but I have no evidence that he ever worked on a Tarzan film or wrote about Charlie Chan. (But he *could* have!)

Edgar Rice Burroughs *was* upset at the "me-Tarzan-you-Jane" dialogue at M-G-M, but I don't know if Weissmuller's loincloth actually made his balls ache. Probably not.

So far as my title of this book, *Sharks Never Sleep*, is concerned, it may or may not be true, depending on how you interpret data. In recent years, marine research has shown that while sharks need to swim in order to facilitate breathing, they do (in a sense) "rest." They find a free-flowing current and face into it, allowing the water and oxygen they require to flow past their gills. While in this state, their metabolic rate decreases significantly and their heartbeat and breathing slow down; they become unresponsive to stimuli. So maybe, in a technical sense, sharks never sleep, but they certainly *do* doze.

However, in 1937, nobody knew any of this—so my title stands.

I suppose one could call these Black Mask mysteries of mine historical novels, but that label seems a bit pretentious for a series of colorful thrillers set in the 1930s. At any rate, whatever they are, I am having a grand time writing them.

A very necessary word about my wife, writer Cameron Nolan. Cam not only keyboarded each chapter into her computer, but functioned in the multiple capacities of remarkably gifted editor, critic, and co-researcher. She contributed so much to this book that it literally would not exist without her. She's the gem of my life, the brightest and best person I've ever known.

I can't thank her enough. Love you, baby!

William F. Nolan
West Hills, California
January 1998

NOTES

1. See William F. Nolan, *Barney Oldfield: The Life and Times of America's Legendary Speed King* (New York: G. P. Putnam's Sons, 1961).
2. See William Dufty, *Sugar Blues* (New York: Warner Books, 1986).
3. See William F. Nolan, *John Huston: King Rebel* (Los Angeles: Sherbourne Press, 1965).